HEARTBREAK AND HAPPINESS

A Selection of Recent Titles from Rosie Harris

LOVE AGAINST ALL ODDS
SING FOR YOUR SUPPER
WAITING FOR LOVE
LOVE CHANGES EVERYTHING
A DREAM OF LOVE
A LOVE LIKE OURS
THE QUALITY OF LOVE
WHISPERS OF LOVE
AMBITIOUS LOVE
THE PRICE OF LOVE
A BRIGHTER DAWN
HELL HATH NO FURY *
STOLEN MOMENTS *
LOVE OR DUTY *
MOVING ON *
THE MIXTURE AS BEFORE *
HEARTBREAK AND HAPPINESS *

* *available from Severn House*

HEARTBREAK AND HAPPINESS

Rosie Harris

This first world edition published 2016
in Great Britain and the USA by
SEVERN HOUSE PUBLISHERS LTD of
19 Cedar Road, Sutton, Surrey, England, SM2 5DA.
Trade paperback edition first published
in Great Britain and the USA 2016 by
SEVERN HOUSE PUBLISHERS LTD

British Library Cataloguing in Publication Data

Harris, Rosie, 1925- author.
Heartbreak and happiness.
1. Female friendship–Fiction. 2. Domestic fiction.
I. Title
823.9'14-dc23

ISBN-13: 978-0-7278-8585-2 (cased)
ISBN-13: 978-1-84751-631-2 (trade paper)
ISBN-13: 978-1-78010-748-6 (e-book)

All Severn House titles are printed on acid-free paper.

Severn House Publishers support the Forest Stewardship Council™ [FSC™],
the leading international forest certification organisation.
All our titles that are printed on FSC certified paper carry the FSC logo.

Typeset by Palimpsest Book Production Ltd.,
Falkirk, Stirlingshire, Scotland.
Printed and bound in Great Britain by
TJ International, Padstow, Cornwall.

For Simon and Susie, Luna and Ellis Randall

Acknowledgements

With many thanks to Kate Lyall Grant and her colleagues at Severn House, and to my agent Caroline Sheldon.

One

'That new supermarket that's opened up the road is definitely affecting our turnover, we'll have to try to do something about it.'

Bill Peterson was a tall, lean, handsome, dark-haired man in his forties. Usually he was very good-humoured, but at the moment his dark brows were drawn together in a heavy frown.

He held out the account book he had been poring over to his wife, Sandra, who was busy ironing.

'See for yourself. Look how much the takings were over the last three months, and then compare them with the same period last year.'

Three years younger than her husband, Sandra was an attractive blonde and although rather glamorous, she was far more practical than he was.

'All businesses have their ups and downs,' she murmured with an encouraging smile as she paused in her ironing and placed the iron on its stand before taking the ledger from him.

'We've got to do something. I don't intend letting that upstart at the new supermarket put me out of business,' Bill said with determination.

'You can't really blame him,' Sandra argued. 'He's only young. And anyway it's not his business, he's only the manager. I don't suppose for one minute that it was his decision to open in Shelston.'

'I know, I know. But he's the one in charge, he's the one running the place and ruining our business. Shelston is not really a town, only an overgrown village. We don't need a supermarket here.'

'Very true,' Sandra agreed as she passed the ledger back to him and resumed her ironing. 'And that's why you can't expect to do a roaring trade like you might be able to do in a large town. If that's what you want, then perhaps we should move. Find a shop in a town, or even in a city somewhere, so you can expand the business.'

'Leave Shelston? Not likely!' Bill said heatedly. 'I was born and bred here and so were you. We both went to the village school, it's our home and it was our parents' home before us, and it's where we'll stay until we die.'

Sandra carefully folded the shirt she'd ironed and placed it on the table, before reaching for another one from the crumpled pile in the laundry basket on the chair beside her.

'Can you imagine leaving here, one of the prettiest villages in the West Country, to go and live in some dirty, noisy town?' Bill persisted. 'Would you want to live all cramped up in one of those streets in a town, with houses on either side of you, when we can live here in a lovely old stone cottage surrounded by trees and a couple of acres of ground?'

'No, not really,' Sandra agreed. 'But if it was what you wanted, then of course I'd do it.'

'You wouldn't be able to have any hens running around to provide you with fresh eggs, and there would certainly be nowhere for a vegetable garden.'

'Then stop worrying about how much our shop takings are. We supply most of the people hereabouts with their meat and eggs. And from now on, since we've made that arrangement for the Masons to provide us with produce from their farm, we'll have butter and cheese as well.'

'Yes, I know that,' Bill agreed. 'In fact it's already proving to be very popular and we've only been doing it for a couple of months.'

'Precisely! So stop worrying.'

'What I'm saying is, what do we want with a supermarket? We've already got a baker's, a fruit-and-vegetable shop, a post office, and a newsagent's that does cards and fancy goods. So what do we want with another shop, and a supermarket at that?'

'It's progress, I suppose,' Sandra murmured.

'Progress! Load of codswallop that is. Who wants to buy their meat all cut to a standard size and wrapped in cling film so they can't tell whether it's going to be what they want until they get it home? Oven-ready they call it, or so they tell me down at the pub, but when it's all wrapped up like that you can't tell whether it's pork, beef or old mutton. The bacon's the same. And the mince is packed in little plastic trays, and when you open it up all the rubbish is at the bottom and the bright-red meat on top.'

'People think that having it packed like that is very hygienic, though,' Sandra pointed out. 'There's no problems with flies—'

'Even the pub trade is being affected because of that damned supermarket,' Bill interrupted. 'Only the other day, when I dropped in for a pint, Jack Smart at the Red Lion was complaining about them selling drinks and spirits at cut prices, as well as soft drinks. Give that supermarket another six months of trading and they'll have put all of us out of business.'

'Oh come on, Bill, things aren't that bad!' Sandra insisted. 'Your reputation as "Bill the Butcher" is far too well known in Shelston and for miles around for that to happen. Folk who shop with us have always liked to know where their meat and poultry comes from, and you just said yourself how delighted they all were when we started stocking butter, cream and cheese from the Masons' farm.'

'I'd like to think so,' he agreed. 'But I'm not so sure it's going to last. I've seen them coming out of that damned supermarket loaded down with plastic bags bulging with stuff they've bought in there.'

'Well, they do sell a wide variety of things, you know, not just meat and dairy products. Mavis Mason was telling me she goes in there for her soap powders and a good many other odds and ends she had to go into Gillingham or Yeovil or even Salisbury to buy before they opened.'

'You both managed well enough in the past, and you enjoyed the chance of going out for the day,' he said dismissively.

'True enough, but I had far more time then. I wasn't helping out in the shop so much, as we had Maggie Gray working for us.'

'Yes,' Bill snorted, 'that's another reason to hate that supermarket! Offered her better money and more hours than I could afford, but she puts on her coat and walks out after working for me ever since she left school.'

'Maggie's planning to get married next year,' Sandra reminded him. 'So she probably needs every penny she can get to save up for a deposit on a house.'

'That's as maybe, but I was the one who trained her and taught her all she knows about meat and such like.'

'It's the end of the school year, so I'm sure we can find another young girl to take her place.'

'No,' Bill said gloomily, 'we can't afford to take anyone else on, not even a school-leaver. At the moment we are barely covering our overheads, and if we are going to be able to afford to send our Becky to university then we're going to need more money, and no mistake.'

'Worrying about it isn't going to do any good, and Rebecca hasn't had the results of her exam yet,' Sandra said mildly.

'Maybe not, but she will be doing so any day now.'

'Yes, but she may not have good enough marks. Even if she does, she may not want to go to university. At one time she could talk of nothing else but coming to work here in the shop when she was old enough to do so. Remember how she used to dress up in one of your striped aprons and that cream straw hat and pretended to be taking over the business and changing the name to "Becky the Butcher"?'

'Don't talk rubbish! She was just a kid then and fooling around. Of course she will go on to university. And as for coming to work here, that's ridiculous. Whoever heard of a woman running a butcher's shop?'

Sandra bit down on her lower lip. She wanted to point out that she did almost as much work in the shop as he did, but she knew that wouldn't go down well with Bill.

'Of course Becky will pass her exams,' Bill repeated forcefully. 'She's as bright as a button, and she spends hours up in her bedroom night after night studying and working away on her computer.'

Sandra was about to argue with Bill, then she mentally shrugged her shoulders and let it pass. She was pretty sure that although Becky might be 'working away on her computer', as Bill put it, she wasn't always studying or doing anything connected with schoolwork. Telling Bill that would only start a full-scale row between him and Becky, and if that happened it would make Becky more argumentative than she already was.

Bill didn't know half of what went on, she thought resignedly as she folded yet another shirt, because his mind was so fully occupied with the shop and the figures it generated.

Ever since Rebecca had been a tiny tot, he'd put her on a pedestal and thought her incapable of doing anything wrong. It had been at his insistence that Rebecca had gone to a high school, even though it had meant they sometimes had to draw their horns in and spend less on themselves.

Sandra prayed that Rebecca would do well in her exams after all the sacrifices they'd made, but she was nowhere near as confident as Bill. She knew only too well that their daughter craved independence and even if she did pass her exams there was no guarantee she would agree to go to university.

Sandra suspected that Rebecca, like her closest friend, Cindy Mason, didn't always enjoy studying and longed to leave school. These days both girls seemed to regard Shelston as a dull backwater and longed for bright lights and excitement. Becky would probably have been pleased if the family moved to Salisbury or some other busy town where she could enjoy the nightlife.

She had tried to tell Bill this several times, but he always dismissed it as nonsense. 'It's just her age, she'll grow out of it. She's ambitious and once she gets to university she'll settle down and study. I want to see her become a doctor or lawyer or something like that.'

Sandra was pretty sure he was going to be bitterly disappointed. Rebecca was certainly ambitious, but not in the way Bill thought she was.

Sandra put the hot iron down on its stand and switched it off. 'This is supposed to be our half-day, Bill, so put those damned account books away and I'll go and make us both a cup of tea.'

'Becky will be needing a car soon. I thought we could give her one for her twenty-first birthday.'

'A car!' Sandra was conscious that her voice had risen. The idea of giving their daughter a car was outrageous.

'Becky can't even drive! And anyway what about me having a car before she does?' she exclaimed in a voice that was far more accusing than she intended it to be.

'You don't need a car. You use the van whenever you want to go anywhere, the same as I do. You know that.'

'The van, yes, that's what I have to use. A van with a grinning pig's head on the side! How do you think that makes me feel?'

Bill's eyes widened and he stared back at her in shocked surprise. He opened his mouth to say something, then closed it again and jumped up abandoning the ledgers and other papers.

'Don't bother with making tea for me. Finish the ironing or whatever it is you are doing,' he told her as he reached for his jacket, which he had hung on the back of his chair.

Grabbing Sandra's face between both his hands, he gave her a smacking big kiss on her forehead. 'You've given me an idea. I'm going for a walk to clear my head of those damn figures and devote some thought to a great new way of increasing our profits.'

Two

Giggling nervously, Cindy Mason and Rebecca Peterson stood on the pavement outside the village post office waiting for Paddy Atkins, the postman, to return from his rounds.

They were both tall and slim, but quite different in looks. Cindy had shoulder-length straight dark hair and dark-brown eyes. Rebecca had honey-coloured hair and grey eyes.

Both girls were casually dressed in jeans and T-shirts. Rebecca's was a pale leaf green, Cindy's a jazzy mix of red, green, purple, blue and black. It was mid-August and they were anxiously waiting for the results of their A-level exams.

Their apprehension increased as the mail van drew up alongside them.

'I hope he's remembered what we asked him to do,' Rebecca murmured.

'Of course he has,' Cindy said confidently as the postman leaned out of the van and with a broad smile handed each of them an official-looking envelope.

'There you are, girls, I hope the results are what you want them to be,' he grinned as they took the letters from him and thanked him profusely.

They smiled nervously. They both knew their futures depended on what was in the two envelopes. It was why they had arranged for him to keep the letters back when he delivered the post to their homes, so not only would they be the first to read them but they could do so away from their families.

Now they had the letters in their hands, they stared at each other uncertainly, afraid to slit open the envelopes for fear of what they would read.

'It's no good. I can't do it!' Cindy admitted ruefully.

'Neither can I,' Rebecca nodded in agreement.

They were lifelong friends, inseparable since the first day they went to school, when they were five years old. Now, as they stood there holding the brown envelopes and staring at each other, the affinity between them was patently obvious.

Almost simultaneously they both held their letter out towards the other and said, 'You open mine and I'll open yours.'

Solemnly they exchanged letters, their eyes wide, their lips clamped together, as they perused the information.

'You first,' Cindy ordered, looking at Rebecca.

Rebecca shook her head. 'No, you first.'

'OK.' Cindy paused dramatically, then grinned broadly. 'You've got an A or A* in everything,' she exclaimed excitedly. 'You'll definitely be accepted for the course we decided to go for.' Her eyes shone with delight. 'Oh, Rebecca, how wonderful! I'm so pleased, it's going to be the start of a whole new way of life.'

'Whew!' Rebecca let out a long sigh of relief.

'What about mine?' Cindy urged.

Rebecca's face clouded. 'You . . . You've not done too well, Cindy. B's and C's. I'm so sorry.'

'You're joking!' Cindy stretched out a hand. 'Let me see.'

She snatched the report from Rebecca's hand and her face fell as she perused it.

'Great! I never wanted to go to university. Now there's no chance, so perhaps they'll all stop going on about it!' Cindy declared, her chin jutting stubbornly.

'You can't give up that easily,' Rebecca protested. 'It may still be possible for you to take your exams again.'

'When I've only got B's and C's?'

'Yes, if you resit a couple of subjects and get really good marks.'

'Not a chance!'

'Well, then, maybe you should query your results in case they've made a mistake in the marking. It has been known to happen,' she said forcefully when Cindy didn't answer.

'Stop talking such rubbish!' Cindy said dismissively.

Rebecca bit her lip. She was overjoyed by her own results but didn't quite know what to say to Cindy. They had shared everything and done everything together all their lives, they had played the same games and even dressed alike at times.

Like their daughters, their mothers were good friends and complete opposites in appearance. Sandra Peterson was of medium height and build and blonde with grey eyes; Mavis Mason was short and plump with dark hair and eyes. Because the Masons ran a farm and the Petersons owned the butcher's shop they had a great many interests in common, and they enjoyed each other's company.

Rebecca and Cindy had pushed their dolls in identical prams side by side up and down the village. They'd joined the Brownies and then the Girl Guides together. They'd taken part in concerts and plays together at school. They'd both had red scooters and then identical bikes.

At eleven they'd both passed to go to high school, which meant a daily journey on the bus to the nearest town.

Rebecca could still remember their first day at the new school. Wearing identical dark-brown gymslips, white blouses and yellow blazers, they'd walked up the driveway holding hands, the same as they'd done on their first day at infant school.

As they grew older, they'd gone off together on their bicycles for journeys of exploration that had taken them to King Alfred's Tower at Stourton, to Castle Hill in Mere, to Wincanton, and even further afield if Cindy's brother Jake was with them to make sure they were safe and didn't get lost.

They were only allowed to go to the dances occasionally held in the village hall if Jake and his friends were going as well. They even had to promise their parents they would stay together and that, when they came home, Jake and Cindy would see Rebecca to her door.

They'd both been so confident that they would go to

university together that Rebecca found it difficult to accept she would now be going on her own.

She suspected that Cindy's mum and dad would also be bitterly disappointed, and would probably give Cindy a hard time when they heard her results.

She knew that in the past year Cindy hadn't really been keen on studying. She was far more interested in fashion and dreamed of one day becoming involved in fashion writing or becoming a model, or even going on the stage. Nevertheless, because they'd always done everything together, they had still anticipated that they would be going to university together.

For a moment they stood staring at each other, then they were hugging.

'Congrats, Rebecca, I'm so happy for you because I know it's what you wanted.'

'I also wanted you to be there with me,' Rebecca told her and hugged her again.

'We had to go our separate ways sometime,' Cindy said resignedly as they pulled free from each other.

'Not like this,' Rebecca said ruefully.

They stared at each other for a moment in silence and then giggled nervously.

'I suppose we'd better go home and face the music – triumphant in your case and doleful in mine,' Cindy grimaced

'See you later – that's if you are allowed out,' Rebecca joked.

Cindy flicked back her shoulder-length hair defiantly. 'I'll be in such disgrace I'll probably get kicked out for good,' she quipped. 'Can I borrow your tent? Jake's planning to use ours for a camping holiday with some of his mates this weekend.'

'Perhaps we should ask him to take us with him? It might be our last chance to do something together.'

'Go to a music festival? You must be joking! It always rains and we'd be up to our ankles in mud.'

'Is that where they're going? How exciting!'

'Believe me, it's not. You have to take a shower in a communal block and that's where the lavatories are as well. Even Jake complains about how they smell.'

'That shouldn't worry him too much, seeing as you live on a farm!'

'Half the time I don't think he bothers about showering,' Cindy went on, ignoring Rebecca's comment. 'It's the first thing Mum makes him do when he comes home. You should see his clothes and the state he's in when he gets home. It would make you heave.'

Both Sandra and Bill Peterson were overjoyed at Rebecca's results. But Sandra couldn't believe it when Rebecca told her that Cindy's grades weren't good enough to take her to university.

'Poor girl, her mother will be so disappointed! I wonder if I should phone Mavis?'

Before she could decide, the phone rang. It was Cindy's mother.

'You must be delighted by Rebecca's results, Sandra, I'm so pleased for her,' Mavis told her before she could say a word.

'Thank you, we are relieved. Extremely sorry to hear that Cindy didn't do quite so well.'

'Cindy failed,' Mavis stated exasperatedly. 'I knew she would, even though Tom was sure she'd do well. But I wasn't. Her heart hasn't been in it for months. When she should have been studying, most of the time she was up in her room emailing her friends or reading comments on Twitter or checking out Facebook.

'All she seemed to think about was getting a job and earning her own money. That and becoming something glamorous, like a model or an actress. I've just been telling her that's about as likely as going to university, so she can come down to earth and start doing her share of the work on the farm – like mucking out at six in the morning, the same as I have to.'

'You're being a bit hard on her, aren't you, Mavis?' Sandra said in a conciliatory tone. 'Maybe she was a bit off colour or it was the wrong time of the month when she did her exams. Perhaps she can sit them again?'

'I don't think Tom would agree to that. No, she's had her chance. Now she must accept the consequences of not applying herself diligently enough, and grow up and work for her living.'

'Don't be too hasty. Think about it, Mavis. You are probably surprised by her results. That is why you feel the way you do, but—'

'I'm very pleased for Rebecca,' Mavis cut in abruptly. 'Tell her so, will you? I must go, there's work to be done. See you soon. Bye!'

The receiver at Mavis's end went down with a clatter and Sandra sighed. 'Poor Mavis!' she murmured as she replaced her own receiver. 'She really was counting so much on Cindy going to university.'

'So was I,' Rebecca said sadly. 'We've always done everything together for as long as I can remember, and I dread the idea of having to face university on my own.'

'You'll have to get used to the idea. That's part of growing up,' Sandra told her.

'I know, Mum, but it's going to be so strange having no one to confide in. When there are two of you, you can face most things. Between us we've always managed to sort out all our problems. I'm not sure how I'll be able to do that on my own.'

'Well, don't start getting ideas about leaving school and starting work just because that's what Cindy will have to do,' her mother said sharply.

'I'm not. I want to go to university,' Rebecca stressed quickly.

'Your dad has always dreamed of you doing so and achieving great things in the future,' Sandra went on, ignoring what Rebecca had said. 'He's talked of nothing else for years, and now he knows what good results you've achieved he'll expect you to make the most of your opportunity.'

'I know and I intend to do so,' Rebecca assured her.

'Well, mind you do! Don't you ever forget what he expects of you, passing your exams for university is only the first step on the ladder.'

Three

Sandra had finished her ironing, put everything away, and made herself and Rebecca a cup of tea. Then they'd watched their favourite TV programme and still Bill had not returned.

Sandra was puzzled. After Rebecca went off to bed, she sat there trying to work out where he could be. She hoped she hadn't upset him by her outburst about not having a car and having to use the van whenever she went anywhere.

It was as much her choice as his, she reflected. Years ago when he had suggested they should get a car she'd pointed out that it was really an unnecessary expense – the van was very smart and extremely comfortable and easy to drive, and because of its distinctive picture and lettering it was always easy to find in a crowded car park.

He couldn't really be upset, she told herself, because he had kissed her and seemed to be in high spirits when he'd left the house.

She watched the ten o'clock news, then decided to go to bed and read her book. She was so tired that after a few pages she switched off the light and settled down to sleep.

She slept so soundly she didn't hear Bill come in. And when the alarm went off at seven o'clock next morning they were all so rushed she forgot all about what had taken place the previous night.

After Rebecca left for school, the two of them had to get to work. Then they were busy in the shop all day and there was no time to talk about their problems.

When they put the 'Closed' sign on the door at six o'clock, Bill said, 'I have to go somewhere. Keep my supper warm if I'm not home by seven.'

'Where are you going?' Sandra asked as she picked up her handbag and the bag of lamb chops she had put to one side for their supper.

'I'll tell you all about it when I get home,' he said cryptically as he jingled the keys to the van and, holding the shop door open, waited for her to leave.

Surprised by his behaviour, Sandra shrugged and said nothing. But as she walked home, she tried to puzzle out what Bill was up to. He had an unusually smug look about him, as if there was some secret he was bursting to disclose.

Sandra and Rebecca had almost finished their meal when Bill reached home. He washed his hands at the kitchen sink, kissed them both and, without a word to explain where he had been or why he was late, sat down to the plate of chops and mash and carrots that Sandra placed in front of him.

The moment their meal was over, Rebecca pushed her chair back and said she was going up to her room to read for an hour then was going up to the Masons' farm to see Cindy.

Once they were on their own, Sandra asked Bill what was going on.

'As soon as I've finished eating, I'll show you,' Bill promised.

Sandra collected up the dirty dishes and took them across to the sink.

'Leave those for the moment,' Bill told her. He took her by the arm and guided her outside and towards where he'd parked the van.

'Look!' he grinned as he unfastened the rear doors of the van and opened them as wide as he could.

Sandra stared at the roll of roofing material, lengths of wood, wire netting, wooden posts and galvanized sheets stacked inside, then turned with a puzzled frown to look at Bill.

'What's all this stuff? Why on earth do we want it?'

'To build a home for Molly—'

'Molly? Who on earth is Molly, for heaven's sake? What on earth are you talking about, Bill?'

'Molly is a white Landrace pig,' Bill explained. 'I'm going to build a pen and a run for her.'

Sandra looked so bewildered that Bill laughed. 'I'm collecting her the day after tomorrow. I had to go and get all this stuff tonight so I can start building the pen for her right away. You can help if you like.'

'What on earth do we want with a pig?' She shuddered. 'Dirty grunting beast, it will ruin the garden with its rooting.'

'Pigs aren't dirty. In fact they're very clean animals. They like to have a bed of fresh clean straw and they never ever foul it,'

'They roll in mud!'

'Only when they're hot. They're very sensitive to heat and can even suffer from sunburn. They like to paddle in water or roll in mud to cool down and to get rid of fleas and parasites. As for grunting, well, that's their way of communicating.

It means they are happy and contented. They give a sort of bark when they're hungry and a shrill shriek when they're frightened.'

'Really!' Sandra commented sarcastically. 'You seem to know a great deal about them. Is this how this Molly is going to behave?'

'Wait until you meet her and you'll love her. She's very docile and she's expecting a litter in about three weeks' time.'

'A litter! You do realize that pigs can have a litter of twelve piglets? We'll be overrun if she produces that many.'

'Yes, that's the idea. Think seven or eight months ahead when they are all full-grown and ready for market. We're going to be able to sell home-produced pork. How about that!'

Although Sandra understood that Bill thought it was a great way to increase their turnover, she was not enthusiastic. She would far sooner they continued to buy in carcasses of pork from the abattoir, as they had always done, rather than try to breed their own.

'It's going to cost a small fortune to feed them,' she pointed out.

'No, not a bit of it! Pigs eat practically anything and everything, from meat and vegetables to bread and milk. We'll be able to feed them on all the scraps we have from the shop as well as from our own kitchen. I've had a word with Tom Mason and he'll let us have milk or anything else he has left over or can't sell. The only thing we'll have to buy to supplement their diet is some wheat or barley, or some other grain.'

'Well, good luck! I can see you've done your homework and that your mind is set on it. All I can see is extra work,' Sandra said drily.

'You wait until you meet Molly, you'll love her.'

'If you say so! You'd better get started on that pen,' she added as she poked at one of the posts jutting out of the van. 'Where were you planning to build this mansion?'

'At the top of the garden. Then the garden fence on one side will serve as part of her run and she'll be as far away from the house as possible,'

'You mean where we've always grown potatoes?'

'Mm!' Bill frowned. 'I suppose we'll have to reorganize

things in the garden so we can grow them somewhere else. Perhaps in that plot where we have the sweet peas and dahlias?'

'You mean I'll have to sacrifice my flower garden!' Sandra murmured.

Bill grinned and he gave her a quick hug. 'Sorry, love, but look on the bright side. It will save you a whole lot of hard work tending them and watering them all through the summer.'

'Well, since I won't be using any energy doing that, I suppose I'd better give you a hand getting this lot into place.'

It took them almost an hour to carry all the planks and other materials to the top of the garden. Rebecca came out to see what they were doing.

Sandra left it to Bill to break the news to her about Molly.

Rebecca was far more enthusiastic than Sandra had been, especially when Bill told her that in a few weeks' time Molly would be giving birth to piglets.

'That's so cool. I've always wanted a pet. We've never had one, not even a cat. Mind you', she sighed. 'I always wanted a dog,'

'You know that's not practical,' her mother said sharply. 'Dogs need exercising, and with you at school and both your dad and me working in the shop that would be impossible.'

'I know, I'm just saying,' Rebecca replied sulkily. Then her face cleared and her smile returned.

'Wait until I tell Cindy and Jake!' she enthused. 'I wonder why the Masons don't have pigs? They've got almost every other animal on their farm.'

'Perhaps they don't like them because they are so smelly and they do so much damage with their rooting and they're so noisy with all their grunting,' Sandra muttered.

'I've been trying to explain to your mother, Becky, that pigs are not dirty animals. They're very sensitive and extremely clean in their habits. Grunting is their way of communicating.'

'Yes, they're supposed to be quite intelligent and soon get to know your voice and recognize you,' Rebecca said, smiling.

'Really? I didn't know that,' Bill admitted.

'What breed is Molly?' Rebecca asked.

'She's a Landrace,' her father told her.

'Oh how lovely! That's a breed that originated in Scandinavia.

In Denmark, as a matter of fact. The Americans imported them into the USA in the 1930s.'

'Really!' Bill looked even more impressed.

'Yes, they've got big floppy ears that hang down over their eyes – the largest ears of any breed of pigs.'

'How on earth do you know that?' Sandra said in surprise.

'We were told all about them when we were doing a lesson on the history of America. We started with the early settlers then covered all the changes and improvements they've made down the ages. They're very docile, by the way.'

'The pigs or the Americans?' Sandra asked facetiously.

'Mum!'

'Your mum's not too keen on the idea of us having a pig,' Bill explained.

'Oh you'll change your mind when Molly arrives,' Rebecca assured her. 'Landrace are lovely pigs and they're not only docile but very easy to manage. They are good mothers, too.'

'Well, it seems we'll see in a few weeks' time!' Sandra said quizzically.

To Sandra's surprise, Rebecca insisted on helping to build the sty and run for Molly. She manhandled the heavy posts and held them in place while her father hammered them into the ground. She held things for him, she passed tools to him, and all the time they chatted away happily as they worked.

Sandra felt she wasn't needed and went indoors to make a pot of tea. She left the two of them enthusing about what it was going to be like once Molly arrived and what would be entailed when it came to making her feel at home.

She still thought pigs were dirty, smelly creatures and wished Bill had discussed his idea of having one with her instead of going ahead like he'd done. It was too late now to do anything about it because he was committed to buying the creature and she'd have to live with it, but she was not at all sure that it was going to work out as well as he seemed to think it would.

When she called Bill and Rebecca in to have their tea they were still both enthusing about raising pigs and making plans about the future of the expected litter.

'Becky says she'll take her turn feeding Molly and will help look after the piglets when they arrive,' Bill said happily as he took his mug of tea from Sandra. 'I've never known her to be so keen about anything before,'

Sandra smiled but said nothing. She wondered if Rebecca would be quite so enthusiastic about helping once Molly was actually installed in her pen in the back garden.

Rebecca hated any kind of manual work and didn't even like getting her hands dirty. She usually changed into wellies when she went up to visit Cindy because she claimed their farmyard was always dirty underfoot, and yet Sandra knew for a fact that the Masons' farm was the cleanest for miles around.

Sandra didn't think Rebecca would be very happy when she was asked to carry buckets of smelly mash made from leftovers all the way up the garden to tip into Molly's trough. She certainly wouldn't want to do it when it was pouring with rain or when there was snow on the ground.

Four

Molly's arrival the next morning caused a mild furore in Shelston. Becky and her father were waiting in the narrow unmade side road that led from the High Street to their cottage, Woodside, to see if they could help in any way.

As the very large lorry backed up from the High Street towards their house, they could hear frightened squeals coming from the metal-sided crate loaded on the back.

When it came to a stop at the iron gate in front of their gravel drive Rebecca hurried forward eager to see Molly, but her father placed a restraining hand on her arm to hold her back.

'Wait until she's had a chance to settle down, Becky. She's probably upset by all that's happening and she may be vicious,' he cautioned.

A few of the villagers who had followed the lorry right into the Petersons' garden stood there patiently waiting to see the huge white pig unloaded.

The lorry driver took his time. After filling in some details on his clipboard he jumped down from his cab and looked around, frowning as if the place was not what he had expected it to be.

'Are you Bill Peterson?' he asked as Bill held out a hand to greet him.

'That's right.'

The driver frowned and looked at his clipboard again and then at the pretty stone cottage and the neatly laid out garden that disappeared into the distance. 'So where's your farm? I've got a pig on board for you.'

'Yes, I was expecting one, but I'm not a farmer,' Bill explained. 'I'm a butcher and I have a shop in the High Street.'

'Hmm!' The driver pushed back his cap and scratched his head.

'So where do you want her?' he asked, looking at Bill in a puzzled manner. 'You ain't thinking of taking her indoors are you?' He laughed loudly at his own joke.

'No, I've got a sty and run all ready and waiting at the top of the garden. Just unload her and I'll take her up there.'

'You and whose army?' The driver laughed loudly again. 'Once I let her out of that cage she'll go wild. She complained all the way here and she's so damn scared that it would take half a dozen of us to get her up that path.' He indicated with his head towards the neat gravel path that led from where they were standing to the far end of the garden.

'With the help of some of my friends here I'm sure we'll manage,' Bill said confidently as he looked enquiringly at the small crowd still watching avidly.

'Well, we can try, I suppose. I'm damned if I want to take her back with me. As I said, she squealed all the way here, so I'll be glad to see the back of her.'

He walked back to his lorry, climbed up on to the platform at the back, and began unfastening the straps that had kept the metal cage in position.

Half an hour later, hot, tired and dusty, they had got Molly into her run.

Before letting her out of the metal cage, they'd taken the precaution of putting a halter round her neck. Then, when she was safely on the ground, Bill had placed a bowl of water in front of her and waited for her to have a drink and calm down a little before walking her the length of the garden.

Rebecca went in front, tempting her along with titbits of food and encouraging noises, while the small crowd formed a barrier to stop her straying from the path.

Molly was so strong that when she once or twice took it into her head to try to wander off into the garden it took all Bill's strength to control her.

Persuading her to enter the run took even more cajoling. Even the fresh bowl of water and trough of food he placed inside the run failed to convince her that at last she was safe and that this was her new home.

Once she was inside the run they made no attempt to lure her into her sty, where there was a bed of clean straw waiting for her, but left her to make that discovery for herself.

Bill's hearty thanks, together with bottles of beer all round, rewarded the dishevelled helpers. After about an hour they had all left, still chattering about their experience. Bill reckoned it would be a topic of conversation at both the village pubs not only that evening but for many more to come.

Once they had all left, Rebecca went back up the garden to make sure Molly was settled in. She had stopped squealing and, as Rebecca approached the run, she could hear her grunting and assumed she was happy in her new surroundings.

Rebecca stood there for several minutes studying Molly. She was huge and her large floppy ears almost covered her eyes.

When Molly grunted and came towards the fence, Becky stretched out a hand in greeting and said her name very quietly over and over several times.

Molly looked up at her, grunted again, and then went over to her trough and began snuffling around in it as if picking out the tastiest morsels.

As Rebecca started to turn away, Molly came back to the fence and poked her snout through the mesh as if trying to be friendly.

Rebecca laughed, and reached over and rather tentatively scratched her between the ears. She was ready to jump back if Molly showed the slightest aggression, but the huge white pig stood there quite placidly and began to grunt softly as if enjoying the procedure.

Rebecca felt a thrill run through her. She was friends with Molly. She knew in that instant that she was going to enjoy looking after her and her piglets when they arrived.

It took Sandra almost a week before they could persuade her to walk up to the pigsty at the top of the garden and meet Molly.

She stared at the huge white pig for several minutes in complete silence then murmured, 'However can she see with those colossal ears hanging down over her eyes?'

Almost as if she had heard and understood, Molly lifted her head, leaving her eyes uncovered, as she stared at Sandra and gave a short grunt.

Sandra stepped back in alarm, a scared look on her face.

'She's trying to talk to you,' Rebecca told her, laughing, and handed her mother a piece of apple. 'Here, give her that and she will really be your friend.'

Sandra waved it away and drew back. 'She'd probably bite my hand off if I tried to do that,' she muttered.

'Nonsense, she'd be your friend for life.'

'I don't trust her,' Sandra said firmly, as she turned away and began walking back down the garden towards the house.

Bill had followed them up the path and now he shook his head sadly as his wife walked away. 'I've tried telling her that Landrace pigs are the most docile of all and what a beauty our Molly is, but she won't listen. Nothing more I can do about it,' he said with a deep sigh. 'Perhaps she'll feel differently about Molly when the piglets arrive.'

By the time Molly was ready to farrow, Rebecca was completely confident about being with her. Molly's eager grunts whenever she appeared with buckets of mash or the special grain mixture were music to her ears.

At first Molly had been so anxious to get at her food that she would push roughly against Rebecca as she tipped it into her trough. Gradually, when Rebecca spoke to her firmly, reassuring her that it was all for her, she learned to stand and watch as the buckets or bowls were emptied into the trough.

When Rebecca came back later to check that she had eaten everything and that her water bowl was full, Molly would sidle up to her and give small grunts of contentment as she scratched behind her ears or down her back.

Rebecca simply couldn't understand why her mother was so averse to Molly. She didn't even like it when they talked about the animal.

It was Bill and Rebecca who were with Molly when she gave birth to her litter of thirteen piglets. It was Rebecca who helped erect the crate they had ready for Molly to sleep in while the piglets were tiny, so she wouldn't overlay them. And it was Rebecca who made sure the infra-red lamp that kept the new-born piglets warm was safely placed.

Even after Molly produced her litter, Sandra didn't feel any differently about the pigs. 'They're so tiny and so many of them,' she said with a shudder when she first saw the little pigs. 'All huddled up together, they look a bit like young mice.'

'She's had a litter of thirteen,' Bill said in a highly pleased voice. 'Don't go too near them or try to pick them up, though. Molly's still a bit anxious about them.'

'Don't worry, I won't. I didn't even want to see them but Rebecca insisted.'

'For some reason she seems to think they're adorable,' she added as she turned away with another shudder.

Twelve of the piglets were in excellent shape, and fought and pushed and squealed to latch on to their designated teats. The other little pig was smaller and seemed to have a struggle to find a teat to feed on.

'There's often a runt in the litter,' Bill sighed. 'I suppose we ought to bottle-feed it for a couple of weeks to give it a chance to survive. As things are, it's going to get trampled in the mêlée that ensues at feeding time.'

'I'll do it, Dad,' Rebecca volunteered eagerly. 'Show me what to do and then leave it to me.'

'Well,' he hesitated. 'I was hoping that perhaps your mother would look after it.'

When he suggested it to Sandra, however, she shook her head violently. 'You were the one who wanted to keep a pig, so it's up to you to look after it and all its litters. I don't mind doing an extra stint in the shop, but I will not get involved with looking after the pigs.'

She was so adamant about it that Bill had no alternative but to ask Rebecca if she could help.

'I know you are already mixing up the mash and the grain for Molly and bringing them up to her—'

'That's all right, Dad, I told you I would help. After I've filled the trough I can pick up the piglet and bring him down and feed him, then take him back up later after the rest have filled their tummies.'

Rebecca found she thoroughly enjoyed acting as nursemaid to the little piglet. She called him Moses and was delighted when within a week he was almost as lively as the others and came running towards her whenever she appeared, as if he knew that she had adopted him and would feed him.

By the time the others were ready to be weaned, Moses was practically the same size as they were. He joined in with them and seemed to be well able to hold his own when they pushed and shoved at the trough.

Bill was delighted. 'You made a damn good job of him, Becky,' he told his daughter. 'You'll be a farmer's wife yet. I must let young Jake Mason know how proficient you are.'

Colour rushed to Rebecca's face. 'That will do, Dad,' she protested. 'Cindy Mason is my friend and Jake happens to be her brother, nothing more. So don't start getting ideas.'

Her father laughed and ruffled her hair. 'Only teasing you, my girl, because I'm hoping you will go off to university next year. Jake does seems to have been around here quite a bit recently, though,' he said affectionately.

'It's Molly he comes to see, not me,' Rebecca grinned. 'Both he and Cindy are fascinated by Molly.'

'I've never understood why Tom Mason hasn't got any pigs on his farm. He's got everything else.'

'I know. I said the same thing to Jake, and he said that for some reason his dad doesn't like them but he doesn't know why.'

'Perhaps when he's old enough and has a say in how things are run Jake will introduce them into the stock. That's if he takes over the running of the farm.'

'I don't think he will. He keeps saying he wants to specialize in rare breeds.'

'Oh, what sort of animals has he got in mind?'

'I'm not sure. He's rather vague about it, but I get the idea that he wants something special, not a general farm. Cindy certainly doesn't want to get involved with farming either. She's keen to become a model or something glamorous like that. She probably thinks I'm mad to have taken to Moses like I have, but she can't say much because she has that pet lamb, Snowy, that she thinks the world about.'

'Well, I don't think you're mad. Far from it. Without your help over the past few weeks I don't know how I would have managed. All I hope now is that this exercise pays off. In a few months' time these piglets will be old enough to go to market.'

'Not all of them, Dad!' Rebecca said in alarm. 'You can't send Moses for meat. He's mine! I bottle-fed him and brought him up.'

'It's no good being sentimental about them. I bought them to make money to help us fight that damned new supermarket by selling home-raised pork in the shop, and that's what I intend to do.'

Five

Molly was once again the talk of the village when it was discovered that she had given birth to thirteen piglets.

When a group of village women out doing their shopping had seen the huge lorry backing down the side road towards Woodside the morning Molly arrived, they'd decided that the driver had made a mistake and the pig he had on board should have been taken up to the Masons' farm.

'Driver must have missed the turning.'

'He should have known that an animal of that sort was for a farm, not a respectable dwelling house.'

'Dirty great creatures, pigs, wouldn't want them near me,' another commented.

'You don't mind a good knuckle of ham or some pork chops, Lizzie Smith. And where do you think they come from?'

Later that night, after their menfolk had been to the pub and heard the whole story of how the pig had been unloaded, they couldn't stop talking about it.

'So 'twas meant for the Petersons at Woodside after all!' they exclaimed in amazement.

Now, when the news reached them that the sow had given birth to a litter of thirteen piglets, they were agog with surprise.

'They're going to take some handling,' Lizzie Smith commented. 'I remember my old dad once kept a couple of pigs but not for long. They were all over the place, so it'll be interesting to see what sort of carry-on there'll be up at the Petersons. They'll ruin the garden in next to no time, you mark my words.'

Lizzie Smith took such an avid interest in the Petersons' pigs that she was the first to spread the news that the runt of the litter was being bottle-fed by Rebecca.

'She's calling it Moses, did you ever hear the like? Blasphemous, I calls it. She's besotted by it by all accounts. Takes it everywhere with her, tucked up under her arm like a doll or a baby. I don't know what the world's coming to, that I don't.'

She was even more shocked when she heard that Rebecca had been seen taking the pig for a walk on a lead with a dog collar round its neck.

'I'm surprised that Bill the butcher allows such a thing to happen,' she exclaimed. 'It's as if that girl of his has gone wrong in the head. Never heard of such a caper in my life.'

'You're forgetting about that Cindy Mason and her lamb,' chuckled one of the other women. 'You gawped the first time you saw her taking it for a walk.'

'True, and those two girls are as close as peas in a pod. All to do with going to the same school, I suppose.'

Rebecca's friends were highly amused. Cindy thought that Moses was sweet, although not as cuddly as her pet lamb, Snowy. Over the next few weeks it became commonplace to see Cindy and Snowy along with Rebecca and Moses taking a stroll together in the village.

Jake warned Rebecca that she shouldn't bring Moses up to their farm on a lead, in case one of their dogs attacked him.

Within a few weeks, Moses was so attached to Rebecca that he followed her everywhere, even if he wasn't on the lead. When she was going out, she had to make sure he was safely in the pen with the others. Or else by the time she reached the High Street she would find he was scurrying down the side road behind her, desperate to keep up with her.

Sometimes, even though she had made sure that Moses was safely penned, he would turn up at her side almost as if by magic. It made Rebecca smile, but she knew she ought to try to find out how he managed to escape.

Lizzie was also the first with the news that some of the other piglets had managed to escape from their run.

It seemed they had followed Moses, burrowing under the wire netting the same way he had done. Not only had they broken out, they had rooted up the vegetables in the Petersons' garden and at another cottage a short distance away.

'I did warn you both,' Sandra said, a note of triumph in her voice, when Rebecca rushed into the shop to tell her father what had happened.

'Can you hold the fort here while I go with Becky and sort things out?' Bill Peterson asked his wife as he whipped off his striped apron ready to go with Rebecca.

Tight-lipped, Sandra nodded in agreement.

When they reached Woodside, Bill stared at the devastation the pigs had wrecked on his garden, as if he couldn't believe his own eyes.

'Becky, run up to the Masons' farm and ask if anyone can come and help us round them up.'

'I'm sure Cindy will if she's at home,' Rebecca told him.

It was Jake who came to help and he brought two farmhands with him. Even so, it took them and Bill Peterson well over an hour to retrieve all the piglets and get them back inside the run.

'They'll be out again in next to no time unless you do something about that fencing,' the older of the farmhands warned.

'As far as I can see, there are no holes in the fence,' Bill said, a worried frown creasing his brow.

'The little varmints burrow underneath and squeeze through,' the farmhand told him. 'You have to bury the fencing three or four feet deep to stop them. They can squeeze through the smallest of holes and where one goes the others follow.'

'It'll be to the abattoir for the whole lot of them if they carry on like this,' Bill Peterson said angrily.

'Tidy while to go before 'tis worth doing that with 'em,' the farmhand laughed. 'No, best mend the fences and keep the little blighters in safe and sound. Give them something to play with like an old basket or bucket or summat. They love a toy or two, it keeps them amused for hours.'

'Take no notice of what he says,' Sandra intervened when Bill repeated their conversation over their evening meal. 'Get rid of them all right now. Their grunting and squealing is driving me mad and the garden's already ruined. Next thing they'll be escaping into the woods. And then how will you round them up and get them back?'

'We can't get rid of Moses! You will let me keep Moses, Dad?' Rebecca pleaded, her voice laced with concern.

'Well, Becky, if the others have to go then—'

'No, no, I won't let you kill him. Moses is mine. He stays, please!' Rebecca begged.

'So who do you think is going to look after him when you go off to university?' Sandra asked sharply.

Rebecca looked at her blankly for a moment or two before saying in a pleading voice, 'You will, won't you, Dad? You'll take care of Moses while I'm away?'

'Well, Becky, I'm not too sure about that,' Bill Peterson said hesitantly, looking across at his wife as he spoke.

'No! You should never have made that pig into a pet. It will have to go when the rest of them do,' Sandra said firmly.

'I'm not going to let you take Moses to the abattoir!' Rebecca's voice rose to a shout. 'If neither of you will take care of Moses, then . . . then I won't go to university. I'll do the same as Cindy is planning to do, only I'll get a job where I can come home every night and look after Moses.'

'Don't talk so silly, you sound like a spoilt child,' her mother told her angrily. 'Give up the opportunity of going to university for the sake of a pig! I've never heard such nonsense in all my life.'

'I mean it,' Rebecca said through clenched teeth.

Her mother sat tight-lipped, refusing to discuss the matter any further. Rebecca resolved to see if she could get her dad to change his mind as soon as she could get him on his own.

She realized that at the moment he was angry about the devastation the piglets had created in the gardens, but it had been his idea to have them. Although he had only decided to raise the pigs in an attempt to overcome the fall in their trade since the supermarket opened, Rebecca was sure that he had grown as fond of them as she had.

At the moment she knew he was looking for a quick solution because of what had happened, but she felt sure that once he had calmed down he would realize that in order to make money from the pigs he would have to wait until they were the right size and weight to be worth his while.

She was also well aware that he was grateful for all the help she had given him looking after Molly and her litter, and was sure he would reconsider his decision and let her keep Moses. She couldn't see him getting rid of Molly either, as she was already expecting another litter.

This made her wonder if there was any other way the animosity that existed between her parents and the supermarket could be resolved. She wondered if Cindy might have some ideas. It might be worth mentioning it to her when they met up later on.

She knew that both Cindy and her mother used the supermarket regularly. She would have liked to do the same, but her mother had forbidden it.

'Having a supermarket in Shelston is progress,' Cindy pointed out when they met up later that afternoon to take Moses and Snowy for their walk.

'Shelston can hardly be classed as a town, yet in some ways it's too big to be called a village. The High Street, which runs from the church down past the school to the Harpers' farm on the outskirts, is the main road between Wincanton and Mere and then it carries on right into Salisbury, so we are on the map.'

'Yes, and there are two pubs and both of them offer accommodation and we have six shops,' Rebecca argued. 'As well as our butcher's shop, there's a baker's, a greengrocer's, a post office, a newsagent that stocks cards, newspapers, magazines and stationery, and a haberdashery that sells everything from reels of cotton to wellington boots. So do we really need the new supermarket?'

'Well, it replaces the general grocery store that was run by old Mr Greenslade. It was his son who sold it, he didn't want anything to do with the business because he lives abroad somewhere.'

'Dad said that he put the property in the hands of an estate agent in Salisbury for disposal and that was when the supermarket moved in.'

'If someone had only taken over the existing shop and not extended it to three times its original size and not stocked so many lines that all the other shops in Shelston were affected, no one would have minded,' Rebecca said gloomily.

'I think your mum is making a fuss about nothing,' Cindy told her. 'We find it a boon, leastways my mum does. Now she doesn't have to drive all the way into Wincanton or Gillingham for things she can't buy in the village.'

'My mum still does, or else she goes to Salisbury to buy her groceries. When the supermarket arrived, she vowed she would never go in there and she has forbidden me to go in there as well,' Rebecca sighed.

'Well, most of the villagers think it's progress, especially those who don't own a car and had to take a bus to Mere or Wincanton.'

As Cindy went on singing the praises of the supermarket and the fact that it carried toiletries and make-up and also some small fashion accessories and CDs, Rebecca was curious to know more.

Up till now she had obeyed her mother and had not ventured across the threshold of the new supermarket. Now, though, she determined that before she left home for university she would see for herself if the supermarket was as great an opposition to their own shop as her parents seemed to think it was.

She turned the idea over in her mind for a couple of days. Twice she went as far as the door, hesitated, and then turned away. She felt nervous about going in there on her own, so in the end she decided to ask Cindy if she would go with her.

Six

At breakfast in the Petersons' house next morning, Rebecca's forthcoming departure for Cardiff University was the main topic of conversation, as if they were all determined not to mention the pigs.

'Our girl has done well, hasn't she!' Bill said proudly as his wife placed a bowl of porridge in front of him.

'Much better than I expected,' Sandra admitted grudgingly as she selected a piece of toast and began to butter it.

'I knew she would with all her studying.'

Rebecca frowned. 'I was hoping to be going to university with Cindy.' She pushed back her chair and stood up. 'I think I'll go up to the farm and see how she is, and see if I can find out what she's planning to do.'

'It will give that young Jake something to think about when you go off to university,' Bill Peterson chuckled. 'Make him realize what a young fool he was not to study harder when he had the chance.'

'He's only interested in the farm,' Sandra stated. 'Mavis says he couldn't wait to leave school. He loves working with animals and he wouldn't want to do anything else with his life.'

'I wondered if he had ideas of having a farm with our Becky when he saw how much she cared about that runt in Molly's litter,' Bill murmured thoughtfully.

'Don't talk nonsense! Rebecca will never end up on a farm and certainly not a pig farm.'

It sometimes seemed to Rebecca that apart from Cindy the only people who understood her interest in pigs, especially her devotion to Moses, were her father and Jake.

Her father was delighted not only because they were a useful business proposition but because there was no one else at home he could talk to about them. Sandra still didn't want to know what was going on and she couldn't wait for him to get rid of them.

Jake was the other person who seemed to understand, especially about Moses. He was very supportive, but then she reasoned he would approve of almost anything she did and would take an interest in it.

At the moment, though, his chief topic of conversation was about his sister. Jake knew that she intended to leave Shelston as soon as she had saved up enough money to do so and he thought it was very foolish of her.

'This idea of being a fashion model or becoming a television actress is silly,' he said worriedly to Rebecca. 'I've heard how young girls like Cindy go off to the city and end up ruining their lives. I really don't see why she can't settle down here.'

'I think she wants to spread her wings, and meet new people and see what life is like outside Shelston,' Rebecca told him.

'There's several friends of mine who are keen on her but she won't have anything to do with them. Calls them country bumpkins because they've never left Shelston. If she came down off her high horse and went out with one or other of them, she'd find out how wrong she is. I bet you anything you like she'd end up marrying one of them and starting her own family here in the village.'

'Perhaps if she finds a job locally that she enjoys then she'll change her mind about leaving Shelston,' Rebecca murmured.

She knew that at the moment Cindy was banking on the fact that once she was earning money she would be able to save up towards a new life somewhere else, but she didn't mention this to Jake.

What worried Rebecca was that if Cindy was working full time it wouldn't be quite as easy as she had hoped for her to take Moses for walks. Fortunately Jake had volunteered to take him out in the evenings and, to prove he meant it, had already started accompanying her when Cindy couldn't do so.

Rebecca wondered if this arrangement would last after she went to university. She suspected that he was only doing it because it gave him an opportunity to be on his own with her.

She enjoyed Jake's company and listened attentively as he told her everything he knew about raising pigs and farming in general. He had a great many ideas about the changes he would make when his father decided to retire and hand the running of the farm over to him.

'The trouble is that won't be for a long time,' he sighed.

'Why don't you get your own farm then?' Rebecca suggested. 'You'll be twenty-two next birthday. It's time you stood on your own feet,' she added teasingly.

Jake laughed. 'Do you have any idea how much it costs to set up in a business like farming?'

'It need only be a small farm to start with and you would only have to buy a few animals, so you could run it yourself,' Rebecca pointed out. 'My dad started with just one pig and look how many he has now,' she added with a laugh.

'Yes, that's true enough, but he's had you to help him look after them. And look at all the trouble they caused when they escaped. He would never have managed to get them back single-handed, now would he?'

'You know more about their habits than he did, and you would know about making sure they didn't burrow underneath the fence round their run.'

'Yes, that's true. So what you're saying is all I need is a big field and a pig and I would be in business as a farmer. Could I count on you to give me a hand?'

'No,' Rebecca shook her head. 'I'm off to university in a week's time and I won't be home again until Christmas.' She frowned. 'Can I really rely on you and Cindy to take Moses out for his walk every evening?'

Jake didn't answer immediately. 'It might be difficult,' he said at last. 'Talk to Cindy and see what she thinks.'

Cindy was reluctant to make a commitment at first. 'It might not be very easy when I find a job and start work. Soon the nights will be drawing in and it will probably be dark before I get home,' she pointed out.

'Please, Cindy. If you don't then my mum will probably persuade my dad to send Moses to market.'

'Oh no!' Cindy looked shocked. 'Tell you what, I won't promise to take him out in the evenings but I will go up to your place once a day and either take him for a walk or talk to him and make sure he is being well looked after.'

* * *

Rebecca looked round her bedroom to check if there was anything else she wanted to take with her when she left for Cardiff University next morning.

She had no idea what to expect, as she would be living in the hall of residence provided by the university for first year students. In her second year, she would be expected to find her own accommodation and she hoped that by then she might have made friends with some of the other students and be able to share a house or flat.

Satisfied that she had packed everything she would need, she went to collect Moses and go for a last walk with Cindy.

He gave small grunts of pleasure as she fastened the lead on to his collar and set off up the village street for the Masons' farm.

As soon as Cindy joined them she handed over the lead to Cindy and explained to Moses that this would be the last time she'd be taking him out until Christmas, and that in the meantime Cindy would be taking him for a walk each day.

Moses grunted as if he understood, then pulled on his lead as though eager to walk on.

'Are you sure you are going to be able to take him out regularly?' Rebecca asked anxiously.

'I promised that I would try, didn't I!'

'I know, but it will depend on what you are going to do. Are you going to be working on the farm all the time?'

'No, I must get a job, but I don't know what. I was counting on university,' she admitted. 'Now I suppose I will have to settle for something much further down the ladder. Well, as a start anyway, until I save up enough money to be able to live in London,' she added with a grin.

'There's nowhere around here remotely connected with the fashion trade. It will mean travelling into Wincanton or Gillingham if you want to work in a dress shop even, because we haven't got one in Shelston.'

'They're not the sort of places I have in mind,' Cindy said quickly. 'They're far too small for the sort of job I want,' she added dismissively. 'My aim is for one of the big fashion houses in London or else to work in television.'

'Surely you would need training of some kind before they would take you on?'

'I know and that costs money. My plan is to save hard now, so I have enough to live on when I leave home and go for training.'

'Where are you going to get money to save?' Rebecca asked. 'You'll have to get a job of some kind.'

'I know that and I was thinking I might take a job at the new supermarket.'

'What!' Rebecca's eyes widened. 'You can't do that, Cindy! People would never forgive you.'

'Don't be daft, someone's got to work there. They're advertising for staff at the moment.'

'But what would your family say?'

Cindy shrugged. 'I don't think it would worry them. They know I'm not interested in working on the farm, and I'm sure Mum would rather I was there than up in Salisbury or London.'

Rebecca shook her head. 'I don't see how that could be of any help if you want a career in fashion,' she said thoughtfully.

'It would mean that I'd had training in selling,' Cindy argued. 'I thought of asking for a job on their cosmetics counter.'

'Surely it's not big enough for them to have specialist staff? And anyway isn't it all self-service in supermarkets?'

'True, but people do need advice from time to time,' Cindy pointed out. 'You've still not been in there, have you?'

'No.' Rebecca shook her head.

'Come on, let's go and have a walk round the place now, then you can tell me if you think it's a good idea for me to work there or not.'

Rebecca hesitated for a brief second, wondering what her mother would say when she found out. She was bound to hear, because someone would tell her. Then she remembered that this time next week she would be miles away from Shelston and how much she had always wanted to go in there. She nodded. 'OK let's do that.'

'We'd better take Moses home first,' Cindy told her as she picked him up in her arms. 'I'm not sure they would let him in,' she added with a giggle.

Seven

Shelston supermarket was in the centre of the High Street. At one time many years ago it had been a hut used by the Women's Institute and the Brownies and Cubs for their weekly meetings. It had been a dark, gloomy place and in time came to be considered unsafe, so they'd moved into another building at the other end of the High Street.

After that, the building had more or less fallen into disrepair and had become such an eyesore that the parish council had jumped at the opportunity of selling it very cheaply to Mr Greenslade, who had run a grocery store there until he died.

From the outside it now looked quite modern, with a large plate-glass window decorated with colourful images of fruit and vegetables and a wine glass filled with golden liquid. This design completely obliterated what was inside the building, so Rebecca had no idea what she was going to see inside.

When they did go in, the interior took her breath away. She could hardly believe her eyes. Shelves ran the full length of the building and they were all packed with goods.

As they went in, Cindy picked up a wire basket from a stack just inside the door. 'We may as well look as though we are customers,' she said. 'I'm sure there is something I will buy either for Mum or for myself.'

The two girls wandered round the store, stopping every now and again to look at some special offer or other. Cindy bought some make-up and a new comb and they stood looking at all the other items available, discussing them with interest.

Rebecca was amazed not only by the size of the store and its long aisles of shelves but by the wide variety of items that were stocked. There seemed to be everything from washing powder to cream cakes, from drinks to socks, bags of firewood to crockery.

They were so engrossed that they didn't notice the tall dark-haired man in his early thirties dressed in a smart dark suit and crisp white shirt approach until he spoke to them.

'Well, ladies, have you found everything you need? If there's something you can't find or we don't stock, let us know and I will do my best to get it for you.' He held out a hand. 'I'm the manager, Bruno Lopez.'

'You seem to stock absolutely everything,' Cindy told him with a winning smile. 'There's no need to go outside the village for anything except things like clothes and shoes.'

He nodded and smiled. 'I'm glad you approve.' He studied the two girls with interest: Rebecca with her honey-coloured hair contrasting with Cindy's dark hair and flashing dark eyes. They were both wearing jeans and short sleeved T-shirts.

'You two young ladies live in the village?' Bruno asked as he ran an experienced eye over the purchases in the wire basket.

'Oh, yes,' Cindy told him. 'We do at the moment. We've just finished school for good. Rebecca is going on to university next week.'

'Really? And what are you planning to do?'

'As a matter of fact,' Cindy said quickly, 'I was wondering if you had any openings for an assistant here. I'm very keen on fashion and I know a lot about make-up and—'

'We do not have product advisors, I'm afraid,' Bruno Lopez interrupted. 'The whole idea of a supermarket is that customers select items themselves.'

'Surely there are times when they need help and advice, especially when it comes to hair and beauty products?' Cindy said, affecting surprise.

Bruno ignored her comment. 'I do have an opening for an assistant on the checkout. Perhaps something like that would appeal to you?'

Cindy hesitated for barely a second before saying with a smile, 'Possibly. I would like to try it out. When can I start?'

He laughed good-naturedly. 'You are very eager. Have you done that sort of work before? Do you have you any references to show me?'

'No.' Cindy shook her head. 'I only left high school a few weeks ago. This would be my first job, but I'm a quick learner.'

Bruno studied Cindy for a long moment before asking, 'How old are you?'

'I was eighteen in May,' Cindy stated, her cheeks flushing.

Bruno nodded thoughtfully. 'Perhaps if I give you a week's trial from next Monday. What do you say?'

'Great!' Cindy nodded enthusiastically.

'We open at eight. Be here ten minutes before that. Come to the side door, I'll be expecting you.'

The two girls said nothing about his offer until after Cindy had paid for her purchases and they were outside and on their way back to the farm. Then they both began discussing what had just happened.

'What on earth is your mum going to say when you tell her?' Rebecca asked.

'I'm not going to tell her. He might say I'm no good.'

'What if she comes into the supermarket and sees you working there?'

Cindy shrugged and flicked back her hair. 'That's a chance I'll have to take.'

'What are you going to say you are doing on Monday?'

'I shall tell her I'm going out for the day with you,' Cindy said firmly.

'You can't say that. I will have gone to university by then.'

'She won't remember which day you're going,' Cindy said confidently.

'What if Jake or someone else sees you in the village and you're not with me?' Rebecca persisted.'

'I'll have to take that chance. If I get the job then it won't matter, they'll all be too surprised to remember where I said I was going. If I don't get it, then I won't have to say anything unless someone sees me working at the till – and then I'll just have to make some excuse or other about how I happened to be there. Don't worry, I can handle it.'

'Do you really want to work there?' Rebecca mused. 'Sitting at a till all day ringing up what people have bought sounds pretty tedious.'

'It'll mean I'm earning money and because I will be living at home and have no fares to pay I'll be able to save almost every penny of my wages. In next to no time I'll have enough saved up to move out, and it will also give me time to find the sort of work I want to do.'

'You mean in the fashion trade?'

'Either that or modelling or acting, or something of that sort.'

'You'll have to train for that sort of work.'

'I know. But I'll get a chance to study magazines and stuff if I'm working at the supermarket. And who knows, Bruno may know of an opening or the best way of going about it?'

'Cindy! You can't ask him something like that. He's going to be your boss. If he tells you how to get another job, then you're going to leave after he's trained you and he won't want that to happen.'

'Trained me? There's no training to be done. Anyone can pass goods over a sensor and ring up the till and take the money. The tills in there even tell the assistant how much change to give. I can do it with my eyes shut.'

As they said goodbye to Rebecca that evening, knowing she was due to leave for university in the morning, both Jake and Cindy said they were sorry she was going away and that they would miss her.

'I'll be home in December,' she reminded them, 'and we'll all have plenty to talk about and I'll be able to tell you all about my new life.'

'Aren't we going to write to each other?' Cindy asked in surprise.

'We'll probably be so busy sorting ourselves out we won't have time,' Rebecca laughed.

'I thought you would be anxious to have a regular report on Moses to make sure I was looking after him,' Cindy told her after Jake had taken his leave as he was meeting up with friends.

'Well, it would be nice, but will you have the time?' Rebecca asked, raising her eyebrows questioningly.

'I'll make time, or else I'll get Jake to email you. He'll be happy to do so,' she assured Rebecca. 'One of us will drop you a line each week, and we hope you'll find the time to email us as well.'

* * *

Rebecca did find time to email Cindy and Jake. As well as enquiring after Moses, she had so much to tell them about her new life that sometimes she had to make herself stop in case they didn't have time to read it all.

Cardiff was a busy, bustling place, especially the university, which had a universal reputation for excellence. There were students there from all over the world, people of every colour and race. It was quite the largest city she had ever been in.

She also found that Cardiff was architecturally stunning and she spent a lot of time describing the wonderful civic buildings, including the City Hall and the museum, all built in gleaming Portland stone, grouped together near Cathays Park, almost opposite the university building.

'A short way down the road,' she wrote in one email to Cindy, 'is Cardiff Castle. The keep of the old Norman castle stands on a mound and in front of it are buildings that have been added down the ages since the thirteenth century. Many of the ones in the newer part were built in the eighteenth century, and the lavish décor of the numerous chambers bears evidence of the gradual development of the great castle.

'You must come and see Cardiff for yourself,' she urged. 'You really would love it, especially the maze of arcades that run from St Mary Street to Queen Street. They're full of small shops stocking everything imaginable.

'There are also some big department stores with fashion departments, where the clothes are wonderful. From time to time they have fashion shows, with live models parading on a catwalk displaying the clothes. It's the sort of job you dream about, Cindy, and I know you would love to see these shows.

'I love it here and feel really settled. I'm longing to showing you my room. It has a bed, a chair, a desk, a wardrobe, and some extra storage space. I even have my own bathroom – well, a shower with a washbasin and lavatory and plenty of shelves for toiletries. A lot better than Jake has when he goes camping!' she added as an afterthought.

'I share a kitchen with three other students, but it has worked out fine because one of the boys loves cooking and he's very good at it. We let him cook whenever he wants to and the rest of us set the table and clear away and wash up afterwards.

'So far I've not made any special friends, but I have been out with a couple of the girls. We went into town to look around the shops and we had coffee in a lovely little café in one of the arcades.

'It's all so very different from Shelston or anywhere we've ever visited. You must come and see it all for yourself. I'm really looking forward to you doing so, because I do miss you and keep wondering how you are getting on at the supermarket. Love, Rebecca.'

Eight

The group of women huddled together chattering volubly on the pavement outside the post office stopped talking as Rebecca approached and stared at her almost guiltily.

Embarrassed, she wondered if they had been talking about her and if so what they'd been saying. They were probably saying that it was high time she got a job now she'd turned eighteen, or else commenting on the way she dressed or how she wore her hair.

As she made to pass them, the oldest woman in the group – a thin, stooped, round-shouldered old woman with iron-grey hair pulled back from her wizened face in a tight bun – spoke to her.

'Things round here have changed since you've been away at university, Rebecca Peterson. You should be careful about going round with a slut like Cindy Mason since you're a decent girl. It's as if you're encouraging her in her bad ways.'

Rebecca froze. She stared in bewilderment at the old woman, whom she now recognized as Lizzie Smith.

'Don't put on that innocent butter-wouldn't-melt-in-your-mouth look with me,' the old woman sneered. 'You and that pig of yours going for walks with her all cosied up together.'

'Yes, old Lizzie's right,' one of the other women agreed, moving her heavy shopping bag from one arm to the other. 'I'd have thought you could have got that Cindy Mason to mend her ways if anyone could.'

'Cindy? What are you talking about? What's Cindy Mason done to upset you?' Rebecca asked nonplussed.

'You mean you haven't heard!' the woman with the heavy shopping exclaimed incredulously.

'With you being away from home for months at a time, I suppose it is possible that you haven't heard,' another woman commented.

'Surely your mother has said something to you about the way Cindy Mason has been carrying on?'

'Hasn't Cindy told you herself? You two have always been as thick as thieves, whispering and giggling together from the first day you both started at school here.'

'I'd say that you still are. I've seen the pair of you out walking that great pig of yours in the evenings whenever you are back here,' another woman intervened.

The babble of comments buzzed around Rebecca's head like a swarm of bees. She tried to listen to what they were saying, but they were all talking over each other so she couldn't make sense of any of it.

'Perhaps one of us ought to tell you what's going on,' one of the women declared. 'In my opinion it is only right that you should know.'

'Yes, I agree with that,' said a plump middle-aged woman Rebecca recognized as Mary Roberts, who at one time had been their cleaner at Woodside. 'After all, 'tis only right you should know the sort of company you're going around with these days.'

'Yes, I think that might be a good idea, as I certainly don't know what you're all going on about,' Rebecca told them sharply.

'Go on, Lizzie, you tell her,' several of the women said in unison. 'You know more about it than most of us.'

The old woman clamped her lips together tightly as if to indicate that she was reluctant to disclose the gossip. As she took a deep breath and then began to speak, Rebecca noticed there was a note of relish in the old woman's voice.

'Cindy Mason is no better than she should be,' Lizzie Smith stated firmly. 'She's carrying on with a married man, a respectable local man at that, and doing it behind his wife's back.'

'I don't agree with you, his wife must have an inkling of what's going on,' a voice interrupted. 'I know I'd want to know where my old man was off to if he dressed up and went out every night and didn't tell me where he was going.'

'Well, if she does know that he's cheating on her, then she seems to be turning a blind eye to the state of affairs,' added another.

'Whether she does or doesn't know, it's all going to end in tears, you mark my words. That sort of carrying on always does.'

'Yes, and it won't only be tears for Cindy Mason herself either. There's her family to think about as well as his,' Lizzie said ominously.

There were murmurs of agreement from the other women at Lizzie's words.

'So who is this man?' Rebecca asked, looking around the group.

No one spoke, but Rebecca noticed how they exchanged looks with each other, some of them raising their eyebrows. But none of them seemed to be prepared to speak out.

'Come on, Lizzie, you know so much I'm sure you know who he is,' Rebecca persisted impatiently.

'Oh, I do and so do most of us standing here. But 'tis not for us to say, is it? That Cindy knows, the bloke knows, and it's my betting so does his wife.'

'It's a crying shame to entice a strong upstanding middle-aged man like that off the straight and narrow,' Mary Roberts commented.

'If he's as good a character as you claim he is, then he is as much in the wrong as Cindy,' Rebecca declared, flying to the defence of her friend.

She tried to think who the man might be, but from the limited description given by Lizzie and her cronies he could be any one of a dozen living in Shelston. It could be anyone, from the parson or schoolteacher to the postman or the retired major living in the big house on the hill outside the village. Obviously, whoever he was, they were afraid to mention his name.

'Perhaps you could have a word with that Cindy Mason and tell her how wrong it is to break up a family like she's doing,' one of the women appealed to Rebecca.

Rebecca shook her head. 'I couldn't do that, not on the little you've told me, could I? I'm not even sure there's any truth in your gossip, anyway,' she said defensively.

'Oh, there is and in my opinion you are the one person who could stop it. She takes notice of you because you've been friends all the days of your life,' Mary Roberts said firmly.

'Mm, but I wouldn't remain her friend for long if I accused her of something like that,' Rebecca said grimly.

Long after she'd left the group of women and walked on, Rebecca was still thinking about what had been said. The matter troubled her. Could there be a glimmer of truth in what they were saying about Cindy? she wondered.

Cindy had certainly altered since the last time she'd been at home. She now dressed quite smartly and her make-up was different and more sophisticated. The really noticeable difference, however, was that she seemed to have no time for their usual interests or chatter.

When they'd met up over Christmas, most of the time she seemed to be talking about her job and what went on at the supermarket and how much she was looking forward to being promoted. She had all sorts of ideas for improvements, both in the way things were organized and the way the goods were displayed.

What she did outside working hours Rebecca had no idea, but she was well aware that Cindy didn't seem to have time to go out with her very often these days like they'd done in the past.

Apart from her interest in the supermarket, she seemed to be preoccupied. But whatever it was on her mind, she certainly hadn't confided in her about it like she would once have done.

Whatever her other commitments were, though, Cindy had kept her promise to look after Moses and exercise him each day, Rebecca thought gratefully.

Now, though, she wondered if part of the reason why Cindy had so little time to go out with her was because she was seeing someone. If that was the case, then she must resent having to come up to Woodside after work each night to attend to Moses and take him for a walk.

'I promised you that I'd do it and I'm not in the habit of

breaking promises,' was all Cindy would say whenever Rebecca brought the matter up.

Now, going over it all again in her mind after hearing what the village women were saying, Rebecca decided that Moses would definitely have to go. It wasn't fair on Cindy to have such a burden, and deep down Rebecca knew that Moses had lost his appeal for her. Now he was no longer a cuddly pet but just a pig.

'Leave it all with me until you come home at Easter,' her father said when she brought the matter up that evening. 'He's no trouble really and Cindy comes up every night—'

'That's the whole point,' Rebecca said quickly. 'Cindy has been wonderful, but I think it is putting a strain on her to be so committed. Her own life and interests have changed since she went to work at the supermarket, and I'm sure she's only looking after Moses because she promised me she would.'

She waited to see if he would give any clue that he had heard the rumours about Cindy that were going round the village. But all he said was, 'I'm quite sure she comes up to see to Moses because she wants to. I've told her time and time again not to bother about him if she has other things she wants to do.'

'Mum still doesn't like Moses, though, does she?' Rebecca mused. 'I'm sure she'd like to be rid of him.'

'Well, she's not keen on us having him around, that's true enough. Then she's never taken to him because she doesn't like pigs very much. She's certainly relieved that I don't intend to breed them anymore.'

'You're not?' Rebecca looked at him in surprise. 'Why are you stopping, Dad? I thought they were a money-spinner for you.'

'They were at first, but people soon got tired of paying more for their pork chops or bacon joint than they thought they needed to do. Buying from the supermarket was so much cheaper, and most of them have to be careful about what they spend.

'Furthermore, because the gammon joints at the supermarket are all wrapped up in cling film they can pick them up, turn them over, and decide better what size and quality they want.'

He sighed resignedly. 'Gradually more and more people started to go there instead of coming to me, so that in the end I had to sell stuff for less than it cost me to rear them in order to clear my shelves. Butchering is not what it was,' he added sadly.

Rebecca felt sorry for him, realizing that his life's work and dreams were slowly disappearing no matter how hard he tried to bolster them up. Because of the long chats she'd had with Cindy, she also understood why this was happening and that there was no turning the clock back. Like it or not, the sleepy village of Shelston was being dragged into modern times.

Nine

Before returning to Cardiff, Rebecca made one further effort to find out why there was so much bad feeling in the village about Cindy.

'Mum, have you any idea how all these horrible rumours about Cindy started?' she asked as she lifted her suitcase up on to the bed and opened it so that her mother could put the pile of freshly laundered clothes into it.

'You must have heard them,' she persisted when her mother ignored her comment and said nothing.

'Gossip, nothing more,' her mother retorted quickly as she carefully arranged the clean clothes in the suitcase so they wouldn't become creased.

'Maybe, but you always used to say there's no smoke without fire.'

'Another old wives' adage,' her mother sighed as she straightened up. 'Even Cindy's mother has asked me if I know anything.'

'Well, do you?' Rebecca stared straight at her mother, forcing Sandra to meet her eyes.

'I only know what everybody is saying, that she's having an affair with a married man,' her mother replied evasively.

'You don't have any idea who this man might be?'

'You know I never take any notice of village gossip. We

can't afford to, because it's usually one of our customers that is being maligned.'

'I know, but I thought you might have overheard people talking while they were waiting to be served.'

'I never encourage gossip in the shop and most of our regulars know that,' her mother told her sharply.

'But you can't stop people from talking to each other, and if I know anything about this village it's the fact that people like to talk about their neighbours. If there's any scandal linked to Cindy's name, then you're bound to hear it.'

'Why don't you ask her yourself if you're so keen to find out? You've always confided in each other, so she'll probably tell you and then you can set all our minds at rest.'

'Old Lizzie Smith and Mary Roberts both told me I ought to have a word with her and tell her to mend her ways,' Rebecca said thoughtfully.

Sandra regarded her daughter in silence for a moment. 'I hope you told them to mind their own business. As I said to Mavis, stop worrying about it. I'm sure it's just gossip, and the gossip will die a natural death when they find something else to talk about.'

'You really don't even know who the man is?' Rebecca persisted.

Her mother was not to be drawn on the subject. 'You're going back to university tomorrow, haven't we more important things to talk about? Now finish your packing, then you'd better decide which train you're going to catch.'

'I'm ready to go. All I've got left to do is go up to the farm and say goodbye to Jake and Cindy.'

'Well, take my advice and don't say anything about the rumours to Cindy or her mother. Give it time and it will all be forgotten.'

'So you don't think there's any basis for these rumours, then?' Rebecca asked quickly.

Her mother ignored her question. 'Run along and don't stay there too long. I'll have a meal waiting for you when you come home. My last chance to feed you up before you go back to university,' she added with a smile.

* * *

The minute Rebecca went out of the door, Sandra Peterson picked up the phone and dialled a local number.

'Come on! Come on, pick up!' she muttered as she waited impatiently for it to be answered.

'Is that you, Mavis? Good! Rebecca is on her way to say goodbye to you before she goes back to university. She's been asking questions about things she's heard about Cindy. I've told her she shouldn't listen to rumours and not to mention anything about it to Cindy.'

'Thank you, Sandra,'

Mavis's voice sounded tired and irritable. 'I'm not sure if Cindy knows what's being said about her or not. She certainly hasn't mentioned it.'

'Stop worrying about it. As I keep telling you, all this gossip will settle down and it will all be over and forgotten in a matter of weeks. By the time Rebecca comes home again in the summer, everyone will be talking about something else.'

'Tom's heard the rumours and he's very upset about them. He says that one of us should speak to Cindy and find out if there are any grounds for them before the whole thing gets out of hand and people get hurt.'

'Then why doesn't Tom do it? Why doesn't he have a talk with her?'

Mavis gave a short laugh. 'He wouldn't know where to start.'

'Perhaps Jake could reason with her. She'd probably listen to him because he's her own age group.'

'I don't think so. In fact, I think the only person she would probably talk to about her problems, that's if she has any, would be Rebecca.'

'Yes, those two have been as close as birds in a nest ever since they were toddlers. It's a crying shame your Cindy didn't pass for university like Rebecca.'

'I agree,' Mavis sighed. 'There were never any problems or gossip when the two of them were together.'

'Except about them taking Moses and Snowy for walks. And there was certainly no harm in them doing that,' Sandra added with a laugh.

Suddenly Mavis rang off. Sandra stood for a moment still holding the receiver in her hand, wondering why she had cut off so abruptly, but assuming that it was because Rebecca had arrived.

On the train travelling back to Cardiff, Rebecca found herself pondering over the mysterious rumours about Cindy. She had certainly changed. She was no longer the tomboy she had once been and no longer so flamboyant. She'd restyled her hair, wore discreet make-up, even dressed differently, in the sort of styles and colours she would once have shunned. What really worried Rebecca, though, was that Cindy seemed to be in a world of her own most of the time.

Was she lovesick, Rebecca wondered? It must be that, she decided. She was sure it wasn't the day-to-day activities at the supermarket that were keeping her so preoccupied. Even Jake became impatient with her, because she didn't seem to be listening to what they said.

As Jake walked back to Woodside with her, Rebecca had been tempted to ask him what he knew, or what he thought about the rumours circulating in the village, but she kept remembering her mother's insistence that she should say nothing.

It was so unlike her mother to even listen to gossip that she had been surprised she knew so much about what was being said.

As the train left Temple Meads station and headed through the Severn Tunnel to Cardiff, she suddenly had a rather disturbing thought.

Had the gossip started because Cindy was visiting their place every night to help with the pigs and take Moses for a walk? Could the 'upright family man' that Cindy was supposed to be seeing be her own father?

No, it couldn't be! She must not let herself think like that. And yet . . . Her thoughts went back to her father saying he was getting rid of the pigs and wouldn't be breeding any more. He had said it was because the village preferred to shop for their joints of pork at the supermarket, but was that the truth? Or was it to stop Cindy coming up there every night and to help scotch all the distasteful rumours?

Initially, when her mother had tried to get him to give up his plans to breed pigs he had firmly stood his ground. So why was he giving in now?

Rebecca still hadn't clarified things in her mind when the train pulled in at Cardiff Central and she had to change to the local line to Cathays.

None of it made sense, she told herself as she unloaded her cases from the train and struggled to carry them to another platform.

Perhaps, she decided, if she telephoned her mother she might find out more. Sometimes it was easier to talk on the phone than face to face. It would be difficult to broach the subject, though, so perhaps it was better to say nothing. If she blurted out her suspicions about her father's decision to get rid of the pigs, her mother would be shocked. Unless they were true, and her mother had come to the same conclusion too.

Arriving back at the hall of residence, being greeted by her friends and catching up with their stories of what they'd done over the holidays put the scandal about Cindy into perspective. By the time she was on her own, she had decided that probably it was simply malicious gossip.

There wasn't usually that much going on in a small village like Shelston and they had to have something to talk about. As her father had once said when he overheard someone's lifestyle being discussed, 'While they're talking about her, they're not talking about anyone else.' And he hadn't seemed to consider it a serious matter.

Rebecca finished unpacking and decided to forget the whole thing. It was Cindy's life and really nothing at all to do with her.

Having studied the agenda for the coming term and noted down all the classes she would have to attend and the activities she wanted to take part in, she knew she was going to be exceptionally busy.

Life at university was going to be very demanding over the next three months and she was determined not to let herself be distracted.

If the gossip about Cindy was still rife when she went home in the summer, then she would definitely get rid of Moses, just in case he was the source of the problem.

Ten

Rebecca found returning to Cardiff rather like entering a new world. After the quiet of Shelston, the hustle and bustle not only of the university campus but of the city itself excited her.

People with whom she had shared classes or meals were eager to tell her about their wonderful holidays and various achievements.

Edna Wise had visited the Rockies and her description of how she had ridden on a mule right down into the Grand Canyon, a gruelling five-hour ride, was so full of drama that Rebecca felt quite envious.

Alan Jarvis had gone barracuda fishing with his father and regaled them with arm-stretching details of his catch. Peter Johnson, who had taken gliding lessons and almost managed to go solo, couldn't wait for the next vacation so he would have a chance to do so.

Most of the others had enjoyed exotic holidays in the Caribbean or the Canaries, and several of them had gone skiing.

All their holidays sounded so glamorous that Rebecca didn't bother to tell anyone how she had spent her vacation. Somehow, taking Moses for a walk didn't measure up to Edna's exploits or those of most of the others. Nor did a description of Shelston compare with anything as exotic as a trip to the Bahamas.

After greeting her special friends and hearing in great detail how they had spent their time since she'd last seen them, Rebecca went off into the city. She found it every bit as absorbing as she remembered.

The noise of cars and the bustle of the streets were so different from the quiet of the Dorset countryside that it filled her with an inner excitement she couldn't really understand.

As she walked down St Mary Street towards The Hayes, she revelled in studying the huge shop windows and felt as if she was in a completely different world.

The colourful, tasteful fashion displays filled her with longing, though she knew she could never afford such clothes no matter how much she would have liked to buy them.

Before walking back towards the Civic Centre and the university buildings, she spent a long time in The Hayes, which though lined with Edwardian and Victorian buildings was home to designer shops and boutique stores filled with well-known brand names.

She dawdled in Howells and the shopping arcades. Howells, Cardiff's oldest department store but now part of the House of Fraser group, dated back to 1865. Rebecca was intrigued by the way that, although it had been modernized, it still managed to retain some of its Victorian charm.

From there, Rebecca made her way to Cardiff's newest shopping centre, in Queen Street, and the nearby arcade that ran parallel to it.

As she moved from window to window soaking up the atmosphere, she couldn't help thinking how Cindy would enjoy being there and being able to view all the latest styles and fashions.

On impulse, she decided to email her and invite her to come for a weekend, so that she could show her how exciting living in Cardiff was.

It would help to take Cindy's mind off the gossip in Shelston. And once she was away from the village, she might open up and tell her how the rumours had started.

Back in Shelston, there was widespread commotion because the latest litter of piglets had broken out of their pen. Now nearly three months old, they had not only ravaged the garden at Woodside but also managed to get into neighbouring gardens and do considerable damage.

Two of them had run out into the High Street, causing cars and other traffic to sound their horns as drivers were forced to swerve or brake suddenly.

Bill Peterson tried his best to sort out the situation, but as fast as he chased them one way they turned, squealing, and dodged off in another direction. In desperation, he had to leave Sandra to take care of the customers in his shop.

As he tore off his striped apron before dashing out of the

shop, he paused and asked her to phone the Masons' farm and see if Jake or Tom, or better still both of them, could come and help.

'I'm sure they have much better things to do than chase pigs up and down the road,' Sandra sniffed as she turned and smiled at Mrs Beech, a middle-aged woman sombrely dressed in a dark-grey skirt and grey-tweed jacket over a silver-grey jumper, who was standing by the counter waiting to be served.

'Please, Sandra, see if they can come and help,' Bill begged as he pulled open the door to leave.

'Now, what can I get for you, Mrs Beech?' Sandra enquired, completely ignoring Bill's request.

'I think as how you should call them two from the farm before you serves me,' Mrs Beech told her. 'I'm not in no hurry and by the sound of things the sooner your husband has someone to give him a hand the better. I'm surprised you didn't want to shut the shop and go and see if you could help.'

'Me!' Sandra patted her perfectly set blonde hair. 'I hate pigs.'

'They're good for food, though, and I bet you enjoy a pork chop or two like the rest of us. Myself, I love roast pork and I always make sure I get some of the crackling.'

Sandra didn't answer but smiled enquiringly, waiting for the woman to place her order.

'Go on, Mrs Peterson, phone the Masons. I don't mind waiting, I'm not in any hurry,' Mrs Beech insisted.

Reluctantly Sandra reached for the phone, and when Mavis answered explained what had happened and asked if either Jake or Tom or someone could come and give Bill a hand.

'I'd give him a hand myself if I was a year or two younger,' Mrs Beech assured her after she had finished the call. 'It's my rheumatics. I can't run these days, not to save my life, and from what I've seen of those little devils they're like quicksilver. You dash one way and they dash the other.'

'Yes, that's true,' Sandra agreed.

'Where's your girl then? Now she would be able to catch them. Has a way with pigs has your Becky, look at how she takes that Moses for walks. Treats him like she would a pet dog.'

'Rebecca has gone back to university, she went off yesterday,' Sandra said primly.

'What! She's still at school then? That friend of hers, Cindy Mason, has been working for almost a year now. Down at the new supermarket I'm told, though I've not been in there yet.'

'Quite right! I haven't been in there either,' Sandra murmured.

'Really?' Mrs Beech looked surprised. 'I keeps telling myself that it's silly not to. All that convenience right here on our own doorstep, why take the bus to Gillingham or Wincanton?'

'Quite so, Mrs Beech. Now, what was it you wanted?'

'Couple of slices of cooked ham and a pound of mince,' Mrs Beech said, consulting a list she'd taken out of her shopping bag.

'Perhaps it's a good thing your Becky is still at school. At least you knows where she is, and she isn't getting herself into mischief like that Cindy seems to be doing.'

Sandra said nothing and concentrated on weighing the mince.

'Very nasty all these rumours going round the village about her. Some folks even think they know who the married man is, but I says I don't think they've got the right one.'

The woman looked at her expectantly, but Sandra tightened her lips as she whipped the meat off the scales and set it down on the counter alongside the slices of ham she'd already wrapped up.

'Thank you, Mrs Beech. Will that be all?'

'Yes, I'll pay you for those and then be on my way. I want to make sure none of them piglets get into my garden, they can certainly do some damage. I suppose this will be the talk of the village for the next few weeks,' she added as she made for the door. 'Still, it might stop the tongues wagging about Cindy Mason.

'Well, talk of the devil! Here she is!' she exclaimed as Cindy, clad in tight jeans and a dark-blue sweater, pulled up on her bicycle, which she parked against the kerb before coming into the shop.

'You come to round up them piglets then, Cindy?' she greeted her.

'That's right, Mrs Beech.' Cindy smiled then looked across at Sandra. 'Where are they? Dad and Jake couldn't come right away as they're unloading the tractor, so I thought I would come on down and see if I could do anything to help.'

'You'll do a fine job, Cindy, far better than your dad or young Jake, because them piglets know you so well,' Mrs Beech chimed in before Sandra could speak.

'After all,' she added as she made her way towards the shop door, 'you spends most evenings up there along with them, so they must think of you as one of the family.'

When neither Sandra nor Cindy made any reply, Mrs Beech opened the door ready to leave then stopped with a gasp. 'Look!' She waved her hand holding her shopping basket towards the road. 'Them piglets is right here. They've come to meet you, Cindy.'

Both Cindy and Sandra ran towards the door and Cindy squeezed past Mrs Beech, who was still holding the door open, jumped over the step, landing in the middle of the pavement, and grabbed the two piglets before they could run away.

Sandra watched from the doorway as her husband came out of the side road from their house. He looked very dishevelled and panted for breath as he paused, looking up and down the road for the piglets.

'They're here, Bill,' Cindy yelled as she tried desperately to hold the two squirming bodies struggling in her arms. 'Can you take one before I drop both of them?'

As Sandra and Mrs Beech watched from the doorway, Bill Peterson grabbed hold of one of the squealing piglets while Cindy held on to the other one.

'I need more help, there's another eight of these little terrors to find,' Bill told Sandra as he waited for Cindy to collect her bicycle from where she had parked it by the kerb.

'I phoned the farm, but Cindy said Jake and Tom couldn't come until they'd finished unloading the tractor.'

'Well, she's probably more use than either of them,' Bill said with a wide grin as Cindy came towards them holding the other piglet under one arm and pushing her bike with her free hand.

'We'll take these two little rascals back up to the pen and then we'll see how many of the others we can find,' Bill said to Cindy.

Sandra bit her lip and hastily withdrew into the shop before Mrs Beech could make any comment, as she saw Bill place an arm around Cindy's shoulders as they turned into the narrow road leading up to Woodside.

Eleven

Rebecca reread her mother's letter twice, then went to make herself a cup of strong instant coffee before sitting down to read it through again.

She simply couldn't believe what her mother had written. She knew her mother hadn't liked the pigs from the very day they arrived. She also knew that Tom Mason didn't care too much for them either. Although she had no idea why this was, she knew he wouldn't even consider rearing them on his farm.

For her mother and Mavis to fall out about them was beyond belief, though, and Rebecca simply couldn't believe it had happened, having been close friends all their lives, the same as she and Cindy.

'I never thought I'd live to see the day when Mavis would say things like she has,' her mother had written. 'I know there's been a lot of gossip in the village about Cindy and talk that she is seeing a married man behind his wife's back, but to accuse your father of being the man involved and say that he was using the pigs to entice Cindy to come up to our place every night is beyond belief.

'I know that when Cindy comes up each evening to collect Moses, she sometimes stops and chats to your dad and gives him a hand with the pigs. What she really comes up for, though, is to take Moses for a walk, like she promised you. But that's all there is to it. The minute she's done helping to feed them and clean them out and settle them, she takes Moses out. Where she goes with him I have no idea, but she is never away for more than an hour. When she brings him back, she puts him in his special little sty and shuts him in. Then she comes to the back door and shouts out goodnight to us, and then she's off. She won't even stop to chat or have a drink with us because she says she has things to do, and as far as I know she goes straight home.

'All this gossip has upset Cindy and although she still comes up and takes Moses for a walk as she promised, she says she can't go on doing it for much longer. The gossip really is making her very unhappy and causing her problems at home.

'Mavis and Tom are upset as well. Like her, they both say there are no grounds for people saying the things they are saying about her and your dad, and I believe them and her.

'Anyway, your dad has agreed that he will give up keeping pigs altogether and hopes that will put an end to all this scandalous talk. He's planning to take the pigs to the very next cattle market, even though they're not quite the weight they ought to be for him to get the top price for them.

'I know he's said all this before, but this time he really means it. He says things can't go on like they are. It's not right to have Lizzie Smith and the other old gossips in the village all talking about him and Cindy like they're doing. It's ruining her reputation, and it isn't doing his any good either and in time it will start to affect our business.

'I know he is serious because he is even prepared to sell Molly. If he can't find a buyer for her at the market, then he's going to send her straight to the abattoir.

'The reason I'm telling you all this is because we need to know what you want to do about Moses.

'I know both you and Cindy think of him as a pet, and I'm sure that if Tom Mason had been willing to let Cindy keep him on their farm you'd have agreed to that. But since he won't, what do you want us to do about Moses?

'It's a hard decision for you and it'll probably be hard for Cindy as well, but we simply can't have her coming up here every evening to take him for a walk.

'Making a clean break with the pigs is the only way we know to stop all the rumours and gossip.

'I've tried to explain all this to Mavis, but she simply won't listen. Perhaps you can get Cindy to talk to her mother? It's heart-breaking for me because I've been friends with Mavis since we first went to school, the same as you and Cindy.'

Rebecca put down the letter and finished her coffee. It was a tough decision but she reckoned it was one that had to be made. As far as she could see, the only thing they could do was get rid of Moses, but she thought it was only fair to ring Cindy and see what she felt about it.

When she dialled Cindy's number, there was no response. Wondering if she had misdialled, she tried again but the line was completely dead. Mystified, she tried Jake's mobile.

'I'm trying to get hold of Cindy but her phone seems to be dead,'

'It will be,' Jake cut in. 'She's switched it off and she's locked herself in her bedroom and won't come out or speak to anyone, not even to me.'

'Why? What's happened?'

'I thought you would have heard about all the gossip that's going around about her,' he said in an angry voice.

'I've just had a letter from my mother detailing everything. I don't know if you have heard or not, but my dad is getting rid of the pigs – all of them, including Molly.'

'Good!' Jake retorted. 'Not before time.'

'I wanted to have a word with Cindy, to see what she thinks we ought to do about Moses.'

'In my opinion the sooner you get rid of him the better,' Jake said. 'Crazy the way you two petted and pampered him. He's an animal for goodness sake, he was never suitable as a pet.'

'Well, yes, I'm sure you're right but we were both very fond of him and I wanted to know if Cindy agrees he should go. If she does, then how do we dispose of him?'

'Send him to market, the same as your dad's doing with all the others.'

'No, we couldn't do that to Moses,' Rebecca protested. 'He wouldn't settle into a herd, not after being so tame and being treated like a pet.'

'Then there's only one answer, isn't there?' Jake said quietly.

'What do you mean?'

'The abattoir. He'll be all right for the butchery trade, they won't care if he's been a pet or not.'

Rebecca shuddered and bit down hard on her lower lip to stop herself crying.

'Hello? Hello? Are you still there, Becky?'

'Yes, I . . . I was thinking,' Rebecca said in a shaky voice. 'It seems so hard on Moses but I suppose you're right.'

'Of course I am, it's the only way. It's always a mistake to get overfond of any animal you raise,' he said. 'Give them a name and suddenly you find yourself treating them differently.'

'You give all your cows names.'

'That's different. Cows have got to feel you are kindly towards them or else they won't let down their milk for you. You give them a name and treat them as individuals, but you must never get overfond of them.'

'Whatever you say, Jake,' Rebecca sniffled. 'That still hasn't solved the problem about Moses.'

'I've already told you, he will have to go to the abattoir.'

'I can't send him there without talking to Cindy first. She's had enough to put up with over the past few months and I wouldn't want to distress her any more.'

'Cindy's a farmer's daughter, she's been brought up to treat animals as they should be treated, the same as I have, so she'll understand,' Jake said firmly.

'I'd still like to talk to her about it,' Rebecca insisted. 'Will you ask her to phone me, please?'

Although he promised he would do so if Cindy ever came out of her room again, Rebecca waited in vain for the call. Finally, when none came she phoned through to her mother and asked her if she would tell her father that she thought the best thing to do about Moses was to send him to the abattoir.

'Your father has already done that,' her mother told her. 'That wretched animal was kicking up such a commotion because Cindy wasn't here to take him for a walk in the evenings that we couldn't cope with him any longer. Twice he broke out of his sty, and it took your father and a couple of other men over an hour to catch him. When they did, he turned on them and bit one of the men on the leg. Ruined his trousers, but fortunately his teeth didn't get through to the man's flesh. Your father had to give the man money for a new pair of trousers, though.'

'Oh, Mum! I'm so sorry. You'll definitely have to get rid of him.'

'I've already told you, your dad has done so. He sent him

and the old sow Molly off two days ago. The rest of the pigs are being taken to market next week.'

Rebecca felt too upset to even cry. She couldn't believe that Moses and Molly were now merely carcasses. Lumps of juicy pink pork chops, spare ribs, hamburgers and sausages on display in a butcher's shop window.

She would never be able to eat meat again. Well, certainly not pork, in case it was either Molly or, worse still, Moses.

She felt she needed fresh air. It was still light, so she went for a walk around Cathays Park.

After walking aimlessly for almost an hour, she stopped and studied the names on the impressive cream Portland stone War Memorial and wondered if she ought to erect a plaque in their garden at home to the memory of Moses.

She didn't have a body to bury, she reminded herself. Then, she thought sadly, nor had the wives and mothers and children of the men who had died in the war, but they had still erected a monument to their memory.

The late-February evening had suddenly turned cold and Rebecca shivered. She hadn't even thought to pick up a cardigan before coming out and now she felt really cold. Folding her arms across her chest, she hugged herself and hurried home.

Before she went to bed that night, Rebecca emailed Cindy inviting her to come to Cardiff either the following weekend or the weekend after that.

'Try and get the Saturday off, so you can travel down after you finish work on Friday night. Then we will have all day Saturday and Sunday together. I'll check out the time of the last train home for you on Sunday and you can ask Jake to collect you from the station.

'I have so much to tell you and so many questions to ask. And it will be great to be able to show you round Cardiff. I'm sure you'll love it.

'Let me know which weekend you decide to come and the time of the train you'll be on, and I'll be waiting for you at Cardiff Central when you get here.'

Rebecca read the email over twice and then rewrote it leaving out 'and so many questions to ask you'. Satisfied with the result, she pressed 'Send'.

Twelve

Rebecca started to think of all the things she wanted to discuss with Cindy. It was several months since she had left Shelston and she was sure she would get sidetracked once they began talking and forget something she meant to tell her or ask her.

The most important thing of all was to clear up this rumour about her father being involved with Cindy. It was all rubbish, of course, and had only arisen because Cindy went up to Woodside every evening to help him with the pigs.

It seemed ridiculous that Cindy couldn't do a good turn to help a friend without being maligned by people. She wondered when the rumour had started and who had started it. She suspected that Lizzie Smith was probably the culprit since she was such a well-known gossip.

She had so many questions to ask Cindy she decided to make a list in case she forgot some of them. She found a sheet of lined notepaper and started with the most important question of all. Did the rumours start because Cindy had been secretly meeting someone after taking Moses out?

There were so many things she wanted to find out that the page was completely filled before she had listed them all.

Whew! As she ran her eye down the page, she thought 'Poor Cindy! If I'm not careful, there isn't going to be time to talk about anything else.'

She looked through the list again, wondering if she could cut out some of the questions. Then she realized she had to ask Cindy which of the boys they had grown up with in Shelston she was seeing. Was it serious? And was she planning to get engaged?

If there was someone special in Cindy's life, then it was obvious that was the person she was seeing. That would immediately make all reference to her father or some other older man ludicrous.

If that was the case, why hadn't Cindy told her parents? Or told Rebecca's mum and dad or written to her, so the rumours could be scotched?

Shaking her head, Rebecca tucked the list away in a drawer. She'd look through it again once she'd heard from Cindy and knew when she was coming to Cardiff. In the meantime she'd get on with her studies and try to get well advanced with them, so she could devote the entire weekend to going out and enjoying herself with Cindy without having a guilty conscience about getting behind with her work.

Cindy's reply came three days later, saying she had chosen the second weekend Rebecca had suggested.

Delighted, Rebecca phoned her mother to tell her the good news.

'The last weekend in February? Oh dear, that's the weekend your father has arranged for the pigs to go to market. I think he was relying on Cindy to help him load them on to the lorry and be at the market with him.'

'Well, she couldn't do that because she'd be at work,' Rebecca pointed out.

'Yes, I suppose she would. Oh well, not to worry, I'm sure he can make other arrangements now you've let us know she's coming to visit you.'

They chatted on about various things and then said goodnight to each other. After she'd switched off her phone, she thought again about what her mother had said.

Why on earth had her mother thought Cindy would help get the pigs to market? Surely it was the very last thing Cindy would want to do, knowing that only a couple of weeks earlier her father had disposed of poor Moses? She thought about it for a while then, shrugged her shoulders and gave up.

In the ten days before Cindy was due to arrive, Rebecca concentrated on her studies to the exclusion of everything else. She turned down so many invitations from fellow students that they began to tease her that she was becoming a recluse. When she tried to explain why she was working so hard, they looked at her in either amusement or amazement. 'Live for today!' most of them advised.

After she had seen her tutor on the Friday when Cindy was

due to arrive, Rebecca spent the rest of the day cleaning her room and borrowed a camp bed.

She had intended it for Cindy, but then she thought it would be better if she slept on the camp bed in the living room and let Cindy have her bedroom.

That way she would be able to get up and prepare breakfast then wake Cindy up with a cup of tea without disturbing her too early.

She had no idea what Cindy liked for breakfast, so she bought a variety pack of cereals so that Cindy could choose whichever she preferred. Or even have two if she was very hungry.

When she collected her post, she found there was a letter from her mother enclosing two £20 notes and instructions to make sure they enjoyed themselves and had a sensible meal each day. She also said she didn't want to worry her, but her grandmother had had a slight stroke. 'Your dad is going to visit her after he has sold the pigs on Saturday, so I'll be in touch next week to let you know how she is.'

Rebecca sighed as she slipped the two crisp notes into her handbag. Granny Peterson was in a nursing home some twenty miles from Shelston. She was very frail and had been there for over five years, ever since Grandad Peterson had died.

At one time they had visited her every week but she now suffered from Alzheimer's and didn't know them, so they had decided there was no point in all of them going to see her so often. Her father went once a month and, since he was listed as next of kin, he was notified whenever she had a bad turn.

A stroke sounded quite serious to Rebecca and she wondered if she ought to pencil in the weekend after Cindy's visit to go home and see Granny Peterson. She'd leave making up her mind until after her father had been to visit her gran and see what he suggested.

For the moment, she could think only about all the things she planned to do when Cindy arrived. There were so many places in Cardiff she wanted to take her to see, including the museum and the castle as well as all the shops and the arcades. It was going to be a busy weekend, she thought excitedly as she completed last-minute arrangements.

Rebecca phoned Cindy early on Friday morning to check that the visit was still on.

'Of course it is!' Cindy's voice was eager and full of laughter. 'It's ages since we met and I have heaps to tell you.'

'I can't wait!' Rebecca laughed. 'I'll be at Cardiff Central to meet you.'

'Good! By the way, I'll be wearing my new red-leather jacket, so you can't possibly miss me.'

After that, Rebecca found it hard to concentrate on her studies for thinking of all the things they would do that weekend. She kept looking at her watch and working out how long it would be before she would see Cindy.

She arrived at the station in Wood Street ten minutes before Cindy's train was due in and bought a platform ticket so she would be able to meet Cindy as she stepped off the train.

As it pulled in, she looked along the full length of the train, hoping that Cindy would be peering out of the window. Then it came to a stop and the carriage doors all along the train opened and people streamed out. Not wanting to miss her in the crowd, Rebecca stood by the exit from the platform anxiously scanning the crowd as three abreast they surged towards her. But there was no sign of Cindy, or anyone in a red jacket.

As the platform cleared, Rebecca stood there bemused. She couldn't possibly have missed her. There was only one way Cindy could leave the platform and she had been standing right there, so she couldn't have walked past her. So where was she?

Rebecca ran down the stairs to the main exit, just in case they had missed each other. If so, then surely Cindy would wait for her by the main exit because she wouldn't know which way to go?

Again, there was no sign of Cindy or of anyone in a red-leather jacket and Rebecca began to panic. What had happened? Had she got out of the train at a previous stop? Or caught the wrong train? Or had she decided for some reason not to come?

Surely if that was so then she would have phoned her, Rebecca reasoned as she pulled out her mobile and dialled Cindy's number. It rang for quite a while and then it went dead. She tried again and the same thing happened.

Rebecca felt at a complete loss. She didn't want to ring Cindy's home and worry the Masons unnecessarily, nor did she want to ring her own home for the same reason. In the end she rang Jake.

'I took her to the station at Frome,' he told her.

'Well, she hasn't arrived. Do you think she got on the wrong train?'

'I shouldn't think so. She had about ten minutes to spare. I simply dropped her and her case off outside the station, because it's so difficult to find a parking space and anyway she said she didn't need me to come on to the platform with her. Then I turned round and came home. Dad was a bit peeved because I was taking time out when we were so busy, so I wanted to get back home as quickly as possible. Try phoning her again.'

'OK, I will. Don't mention anything to your mum, I don't want to worry her. I'll phone you as soon as I locate Cindy.'

Even more puzzled by the strange turn of events, Rebecca phoned home. Her mother answered the phone.

'Not arrived? Well, she probably caught the wrong train or missed the one she should have been on.'

'No, I phoned Jake and he told me he drove her to Frome station and she had ten minutes to spare before her train left.'

'Did she have to change at Temple Meads?'

'I don't know. Jake never said so and I never thought to ask him.'

'Well, there you are then. She probably did and caught the wrong train from there. Try phoning her again. Her train might have been going through the Severn Tunnel, and that would be why she didn't answer because there would be no reception.'

'OK, Mum, I'll try again.'

'Right. I must go, I want to keep the line open.'

'Why? Is something wrong?'

'Yes, your Granny is worse. They sent for Dad again today and he was going straight to the nursing home after finishing at the market. We both thought that would be a good idea because it's only five miles from there. He said he would phone and let me know how she is and what time he would be coming home.'

Thirteen

Rebecca hung around the railway station all evening, meeting every train that arrived from Temple Meads station. She felt sure that Cindy must have missed her connection. And possibly gone for a snack and then missed the next train as well.

After she'd been there for over two hours, the station staff became suspicious of her motives. She knew they were watching her and was not surprised when one of the railway police came up to her and asked her why she was hanging around.

He was a tall, broad man in his early forties with a hard-looking face and thin mouth. She felt intimidated.

'I'm waiting for a friend,' she told him and smiled nervously.

'A friend?' He sounded dubious. 'A boyfriend?'

Rebecca shook her head. 'No, a girlfriend.'

'Were you meeting for an evening out?'

'No, she was coming to stay with me for the weekend,' Rebecca told him.

'Where's she coming from?'

'She was catching a train from Frome, but she would probably have had to change at Temple Meads. I think she must have missed her connection.'

He frowned. 'Surely she would have been on the next train to leave there? There have been three trains since then that have stopped at Temple Meads, so she could have caught any of them.'

'I know. That's why I've been dashing from platform to platform,' Rebecca sighed. 'She said she'd be wearing a red-leather jacket, so I can't possibly have missed her. Anyway, I've phoned her mobile three or four times and there's no answer.'

The policeman pursed his lips and shook his head almost as though he didn't quite believe Rebecca's story.

'Perhaps you should give up and go home in case she has already arrived and is waiting for you there. It's almost ten o'clock, you know.'

'Yes, I do know, I've been checking the station clock and I'm worried sick about what can have happened to her,' Rebecca said in an irritated tone.

'Well, like I said, she may already be at your home waiting for you.'

'Then why doesn't she answer her mobile? I've phoned her countless times. Or else phoned me to let me know where she is?'

The policeman gave an imperceptible shrug. 'Who knows, perhaps the battery is flat.'

'I doubt it,' Rebecca said defensively. 'She would have made sure it was fully charged before she left home. I've never known her to have a flat battery.'

'Well, you can't hang around here all night. Go home. I'll keep an eye out for her, and if she arrives later this evening I'll tell her to phone you.' He pulled out a notebook from his pocket. 'I'll need your name and address and your mobile phone number. You'd better give me hers as well,' he added.

Rebecca hesitated. She didn't mind giving him hers. But if she gave him Cindy's address, would he ring her home and cause a fuss? She supposed it was a risk she'd have to take. As soon as she could, she would phone Jake again and let him know what had happened.

By the time Rebecca left the railway station it was so late that the pubs were turning out. The streets seemed to be full of slightly inebriated groups, all singing and chanting and pushing one another around, so she caught a bus home.

Cindy was not standing on the doorstep, so she tried ringing her again but she was still not answering so she phoned Jake. His phone was switched off, which meant he was probably already in bed or else driving home after an evening out with some of the village lads.

She thought of phoning her own mother, but remembering that she was already worried because Granny Peterson was so ill she decided it was better not to. It wasn't as if her mother could help, and even if she asked her to phone Cindy's mother most likely she would refuse and say that Mavis was probably in bed and asleep so she couldn't disturb her at this time of night.

Still puzzled by Cindy's absence but quite sure there had to be some logical explanation, she made herself a hot drink and got ready for bed.

She couldn't decide whether to sleep in her own bed or on the camp bed she had made up in the living room so Cindy could have her bedroom to herself. In the end she decided to sleep in her own bed and sort things out when Cindy arrived.

She slept fitfully, tossing and turning and waking up at the slightest noise in case it was Cindy trying to rouse her.

When she did sleep she had some fearful dreams, all involving Cindy.

She gave up in the end, and was up and dressed as soon as it was light. She made some toast and tea, and the minute she had swallowed them she set off back to the railway station in case Cindy had arrived very late and had spent the night in the waiting room there rather than disturb her.

It was a dull morning with misty rain falling and she felt cold and miserable by the time she reached Wood Street, even though she was wearing a fleece under her thin raincoat.

The staff on duty at the station were all different from the ones who'd been there the evening before. She was about to buy a platform ticket so she could make sure Cindy wasn't there, then hesitated. Would they have let Cindy stay in the waiting room all night? Perhaps it would be better if she spoke to one of the staff and explained the situation.

'No one has been here overnight, indeed no. Everybody who arrived on late trains scooted home the moment they could get through the ticket barriers,' the genial middle-aged porter told her.

Bewildered, Rebecca walked slowly home again. As she went along St Mary Street, the stores were just opening their doors and the thought of all the wonderful plans she had made for her weekend with Cindy flooded her mind.

Where on earth could Cindy be? That was what worried her.

Back in her room, she phoned her mother and explained the situation. Her mother didn't sound very interested or concerned. 'Perhaps she changed her mind? Have you tried her phone this morning?'

'Of course I have and it's completely dead,' Rebecca told her crossly.

'Then try it again,' her mother said irritably. 'Why ring me? What can I do about it? I've got enough worries as it is.'

'You mean about Grandma Peterson?' Rebecca said contritely, conscious that she hadn't even asked if there was any fresh news about her.

'Yes, she's so ill that your father stayed all night at the nursing home.'

'Oh dear, that does sound serious.'

'Yes, they are talking about moving your grandmother into hospital and he thought he ought to be there when they do and make sure she is settled and find out what the doctor's latest prognosis is.'

'And then he's coming home?'

'I certainly hope so. I don't like running the shop on my own. He needs to be here to cut up the joints and chops and so on. I can't face that sort of work. I don't mind serving the customers but I do draw the line at actual butchery,' her mother said grimly.

'Sorry I troubled you, Mum,' Rebecca murmured apologetically. 'Let me know how Granny is as soon as you hear from Dad.'

There was only one thing for it, she decided, she would have to ring Jake. If she couldn't get hold of him, then as a last resort she would phone Cindy's mother.

Jake was as bewildered as she was. He insisted that he had left Cindy at Frome station in plenty of time to catch her train.

'She really was excited about coming to Cardiff to see you and about all the things the two of you were planning to do over the weekend.'

'Then where is she? Why didn't she turn up? I couldn't possibly have missed her. I stayed at the railway station until after ten o'clock. In fact the railway police became suspicious and wanted to know what I was doing there. I went back there this morning in case she had spent the night sleeping in the waiting room for some reason, but there was no trace of her. I spoke to a member of staff and he assured me she hadn't been there.'

'Well, it's a mystery, that's all I can say,' Jake agreed.

'So will you tell your parents, or do you want me to phone your mother?'

There was a long pause before Jake spoke. 'I suppose I'd better be the one to do it,' he said rather reluctantly. 'Mum is going to be terribly upset.'

'I'm sure she will be, but she ought to know what's happened. And she might even be able to throw some light on what's going on.'

'I don't think that's very likely. As far as I know, she thought the same as the rest of us – that Cindy was coming to you for the weekend.'

'Well, don't forget to let me know as soon as there's any news. I'm terribly worried about her, Jake.'

As soon as Jake ended the call, Rebecca phoned her own mother to let her know what had happened.

'Poor Mavis, she'll be so upset and very worried.'

'I know, Mum, but I felt it was only right she should know Cindy isn't here in Cardiff with me.'

'Quite right, dear, but where on earth can Cindy be?'

'I don't know, none of us seem to know. Jake has promised he will phone me if there is any news.'

'I'll try and get up to see Mavis when I close the shop,' her mother promised. 'I can't really do anything until then.'

'I understand, Mum. How are you coping? I take it that Dad is still at the hospital with Granny Peterson.'

'Yes, I'm afraid so. They don't think she has very long to live and I think he will stay with her till the end.'

'Oh dear, it's all so sad. Everything seems to be happening at once. How on earth are you managing to run the shop?'

'Ah . . .' Her mother's voice lightened. 'Everything here is more or less satisfactory. I still have to be in the shop all day, of course, but your dad has arranged for a young man to come and help out. This young chap has completed his training as a butcher and can deal with the butchery side of things, but he hasn't had very much retail experience. Still that doesn't matter as long as I am at the shop to deal with that side of things.'

'Really! Well, that sounds fantastic. A load off your shoulders, Mum,' Rebecca said with a laugh.

'That's very true. He's a very nice young man, his name is Nick Blakemore. You ought to try to get home next weekend and meet him. I'm sure you'd like him.'

Fourteen

Sunday dragged by slowly. Rebecca tried to study, but although she read each paragraph over several times the words didn't sink into her brain. In fact sometimes they didn't even make any sense. She wanted to phone Cindy's mother, but she wasn't sure if Jake would have told her yet that Cindy was missing.

Or was she? Rebecca knew that Cindy was quite good at telling white lies. She remembered the days when she'd planned to start work at the supermarket in Shelston. Cindy hadn't wanted her mother to know anything about it until she was sure she had been accepted for the job, so she'd told her mother that they were going out together, even though Cindy knew it was the day when Rebecca would be starting at university.

There were countless other occasions when Cindy had skirted round the truth and got away with it. Was coming to Cardiff for the weekend a blind for something else she planned to do? Was Cindy really missing? Or had she used the proposed trip to Cardiff to indulge in a weekend away with her boyfriend?

But she would have known that Rebecca would be very worried when she didn't turn up, so surely she would have told her the truth and warned her not to expect her?

It didn't make sense. They'd shared so many secrets in the past that Cindy knew she could be trusted and that she wouldn't say anything to her family.

She looked at her watch. Had it stopped? No, it was simply that time was dragging. She'd wait until twelve o'clock and then she would ring Jake and find out if he had told his mother about Cindy and what she'd had to say. If he hadn't, then it would jog his memory and he'd have a chance to do so when they stopped for their midday meal.

When finally she phoned Jake, the news wasn't good. Cindy wasn't back home and no one had any idea where she was.

'Mum and Dad are very worried,' Jake told her. 'I wish I had said nothing, but I knew you were right and they ought to know what is happening. What's even more worrying is that the married man she was rumoured to be seeing is also missing from his home.'

'Really!' Rebecca felt stunned. 'Who is he?'

There was a long silence then Jake said, 'It's only a rumour, so I'll say no more.'

'You can't leave me with half a tale,' Rebecca said sharply. 'Come on, Jake, tell me his name. Is it someone I know?'

'I've got to go,' Jake said, evading the issue. 'Look, Becky, don't worry. I promise I'll phone you if Cindy turns up or if there is any fresh news about her. Take care. Bye.'

Before she had a chance to say anything more the line went dead.

Rebecca thought of ringing him back, but she wasn't sure he would answer. He so obviously didn't want to go into more details.

'Cindy could have let me know what she was planning to do, instead of leaving me to worry about her like this,' Rebecca muttered aloud resentfully.

As she opened up her books again, she found herself wondering which of the village men Cindy could possibly have gone away with, but was at a complete loss. Most of the married men in Shelston were rather staid and middle-aged and were either paunchy or going bald. There were no dashing young husbands.

Unable to make any sense of the situation, she pushed the matter from her mind and tried once more to concentrate on studying.

She'd go home next weekend, she told herself, and find out how her grandmother was – and meet this new assistant who was helping out in the shop and see if he was as dishy as her mother said he was.

The following Friday, although she studied until almost midnight, Rebecca still hadn't managed to catch up with all she had set herself to do. Nevertheless, next morning she was up in time to catch an early train home.

She hadn't told her mother in advance that she was coming home, because she hadn't been sure what train she would be on and didn't want to raise her hopes in case she couldn't make it.

She had phoned her a couple of times during the week to see if there was any fresh news about her grandmother, only to be told that she was still holding her own and her dad was still at her bedside.

She checked with her mother if there was any more news about Cindy, but apart from lots of gossip which her mother refused to pass on there was none.

No one had seen her or heard from her, and both her parents were very worried.

It was mid-morning by the time Rebecca reached Shelston. As she stepped down from the bus that had brought her from the railway station, the very first person she met was Lizzie Smith.

'Well, well, whoever would have thought of seeing you here, Rebecca Peterson,' she commented. 'Not looking for your friend Cindy Mason, are you? You won't find her here. Her mother's so worried about her she won't show her face in the village, either. And that man's poor wife! Well, I don't need to tell you how she is feeling, do I?' she cackled maliciously. 'Much too near to home for you not to know now, ain't it!'

'I'm afraid I have no idea what you are talking about, Mrs Smith,' Rebecca told her frostily as she made to walk past.

'Not in such a hurry, young lady,' Lizzie said as she grabbed Rebecca's arm. 'You won't find her at home, so it's no use you trudging up to the Masons' farm. Your friend Cindy Mason has gone off with her fancy man and you know well enough who he is! Old enough to be her dad,' she leered. 'That's the sort of little hussy your precious friend has become. She don't mind breaking up families, not even yours.'

Rebecca stared at the wrinkled old woman in disbelief. Was she simply making all this up? Or was there a grain of truth in what she was saying?

Lizzie seemed to know about most things that went on in Shelston, and although very few people liked her they usually listened to what she said because they were well aware that not very much missed her shrewd eyes or her ever-listening ears.

'You'd better hurry yourself home, Rebecca Peterson,' Lizzie went on. 'Be in time to comfort your mother and meet that young fancy man she's moved in with her. Didn't take her long to fill your dad's shoes, now did it!'

As Lizzie's words sank in and she realized what she was implying, tears of anger blurred Rebecca's vision. Too distressed to answer the old woman, she turned on her heel and began walking away.

'Going to share him with her, the same as your friend Cindy Mason shares your dad?' Lizzie called after her.

Rebecca felt sick as she hurried past their butcher's shop and made her way up the side road to seek solace at Woodside.

She couldn't bring herself to go into the shop. At this moment she didn't want to talk to her mother and she certainly didn't want to meet Nick Blakemore.

She fumbled in her purse for her door key, all she wanted was the seclusion of her own bedroom and a chance to sort out all the malicious things Lizzie Smith had said and try to make sense of them.

The thoughts tumbling round in her head were so ugly that they shocked her. They simply couldn't be true. She certainly didn't want them to be. It was too bizarre to even think they might be.

She went into the kitchen and made herself a cup of instant coffee, and took it up to her bedroom.

She curled up in the armchair and tried to reason things out and to recall what her mother had said when they last spoke on the phone.

With a sense of relief she remembered that her dad was staying at her granny's bedside.

Of course, that was the answer. That was where he was. Lizzie Smith wouldn't know about Granny Peterson being ill, and because her dad and Cindy were missing at the same time she had linked their names together in her evil mind.

But why had she thought such a thing in the first place? The rumours about Cindy and a married man had been circulating for quite some time.

Rebecca thought hard about it, trying to reason it all out and remembering that her mother had touched on the subject when she'd been talking about her dad disposing of the pigs.

She felt pretty sure it was because Cindy had been coming up to Woodside every night to help with the pigs and take Moses for a walk that all this gossip had started.

As for her mum's fancy man, it had been her dad who had arranged for Nick Blakemore to come and help out at the shop!

Old Lizzie had implied that Nick Blakemore was living with her mother. Well, maybe he was. If he came from a distance, it made sense since there was plenty of room at Woodside. She had been worrying about nothing.

Although she still didn't know where Cindy was, she was sure there was no connection between Cindy being missing and her own father's absence.

Feeling calmer, she finished her coffee and decided she would go to the shop and let her mother know she was home.

Maybe by now her mother had spoken to Mavis Mason and there was some fresh news about Cindy. And at the same time she could meet Nick Blakemore.

With a feeling of relief, she smiled at her own reflection in the mirror as she combed her hair and touched up her lipstick. What an idiot she had been to take any notice of Lizzie Smith and get so upset by her silly gossip!

Fifteen

Rebecca paused for a moment on the doorstep of their butcher's shop. Her dad was always very particular about keeping everything spotlessly clean, and even today it looked as though it had been scrubbed from top to bottom and everything from the outside of the window to the top of the marble counter had been cleaned to a very high standard.

Her mother, wearing a crisp long white-cotton overall over her dark dress, was standing by the door of the small office built into a corner at the end of the long counter that ran the full width of the shop. She was holding a ledger in one hand and talking to a tall young man in his mid-twenties. He was wearing a long white overall-coat over striped cotton trousers and had a cream straw boater on his head.

For a moment Rebecca wondered who he was, and looked back over her shoulder to see if there was a delivery van parked anywhere. Then she realized that he must be the temporary assistant.

So this was Nick Blakemore, the young man that Lizzie had described as her mother's 'fancy man'. She pushed open the door and walked into the shop.

Her mother looked up as the shop bell jangled and for a moment stared at her blankly.

'Rebecca! You never said you were coming home this weekend. What a wonderful surprise!' she exclaimed as she came rushing forward, her arms held out to greet her daughter.

'Nick,' she called to the young man who was still standing in the doorway of the office, 'come and meet my daughter Rebecca.'

He came over to where they were standing, holding out his hand in greeting, and Rebecca found herself looking into a pair of vivid blue eyes set wide apart in a very handsome face that had a firm chin, straight nose and engaging smile, revealing even white teeth.

'Rebecca, I'm so pleased to meet you,' he said as they shook hands. 'I've heard a great deal about you.'

His handshake was firm and warm, and the look he directed at her was so welcoming that Rebecca found herself responding despite her intention to be aloof and on her guard against his charm.

'Mum told me that Dad had arranged for you to come and help out while he was away,' she murmured. 'I hope you like it here.'

'It's my first experience of retail work, but your mother is an excellent teacher,' he said, smiling at Sandra as he spoke.

Rebecca noted a spot of colour burn high on her mother's

cheeks. Immediately she recalled Lizzie's implication and steeled herself to resist being taken in by Nick Blakemore's charm and smooth tongue.

'Village life is also new to me,' Nick Blakemore went on. 'So very different from living in a busy town.'

'We like it here,' Rebecca said defensively. 'It's wonderful for walking and there's quite a lot to see and plenty going on.'

'Really?' His eyebrows went up. 'Perhaps you can find time to show me some of these places.'

'I'd love to, but I'm afraid I'm only here for the weekend,' Rebecca replied brusquely.

'We're not terribly busy on a Saturday afternoon, so why don't you take Nick on a guided tour of the village and the local beauty spots?' her mother suggested.

'Wouldn't it be better if you and I went to see Granny Peterson?' Rebecca said quickly.

'We can do that tomorrow. No, you take Nick on a guided tour this afternoon.' She smiled at the young man. 'It's almost lunchtime. Can you hold the fort while I go and have a snack with Rebecca and catch up on family news? Then I'll come back and take over so you two can go out together.'

'That sounds like a splendid idea,' Nick agreed enthusiastically.

Sandra discarded her overall and took down the short grey jacket that was hanging on a peg in the office and put it on. 'Come on then, Rebecca,' she said as she picked up her handbag. 'Let's go.'

They said very little on the short walk home, but as soon as they were indoors Rebecca said crossly, 'Why did you do that, Mum?'

'Do what?' Her mother looked bemused.

'Suggest I show Nick Blakemore around. There's enough gossip about him in the village as it is.'

'Gossip?' Sandra looked taken aback. 'What do you mean? Who've you been talking to?'

'Old Lizzie Smith stopped me as I came off the bus and regaled me with some vicious gossip about Dad and also about you.'

'Really! What did she say?'

Rebecca hesitated, biting down on her lower lip and

wondering if she ought to tell her mother what Lizzie had said or whether it would be better to keep quiet and say nothing.

'Come on, tell me,' Sandra said impatiently as she took a plate of sliced ham out of the fridge and began making up sandwiches for both of them.

'She said Dad had gone off with Cindy.'

'What!' Sandra stopped buttering the bread she'd taken out and stared at Rebecca in disbelief.

'She also said you had moved a young fancy man in and were going to share him with me.'

Sandra's eyes were blazing with anger as she stared at her daughter. 'I hope you didn't take any notice of what that stupid old crone said. If this was a hundred years ago, that vicious old woman would be put in the stocks for maligning people and the rest of us would be throwing rotten eggs at her.'

'So there's no truth in any of it then,' Rebecca said, her voice registering relief.

'No, of course there isn't, but it's hard to convince people,' Sandra said wearily. 'Even Mavis thought that perhaps there was something going on between your dad and Cindy because she came up here every night to help him with those damn pigs.'

'They're all gone now?' Rebecca questioned.

'Yes and you have no idea how pleased I am about that. I never want to see another pig here ever again.'

'Moses as well?'

'I'm sorry about your Moses, but he had grown so big and become so dangerous it was a relief to see the back of him, I can tell you.'

'Oh, Mum! You're exaggerating!' Rebecca laughed.

'No, I mean it. He had started biting and I was scared stiff that he would attack someone and we'd have a court case on our hands.'

'Really? He was always so friendly.'

'Even your dad was frightened of him at times,' her mother went on. 'He could bite very hard and he caught him once or twice.'

'Well, he's gone now,' Rebecca said resignedly.

'Yes, so let's forget all about the pigs and get on with living.

You take Nick for a walk this afternoon and show him what there is to see around Shelston, then we'll go and see Granny Peterson tomorrow.'

Rebecca found herself enjoying her afternoon walk with Nick Blakemore. After telling him the history of each and every one of the shops and pubs, as well as the people who ran them, she took him to see the duck pond and the ruins of what had once been a thriving factory.

'It started out in the 1800s as an iron foundry and has housed a number of businesses since then. It ended up as a milk factory, but about five years ago they moved to larger premises in a nearby town and since then the building has fallen into ruins.'

She also showed him the local beauty spots, and around the Norman church and its well-kept graveyard with its weather-worn headstones.

Finally, she took him home through the woods that adjoined their house.

'These woods border our garden,' she told him. 'It's one of my favourite spots. I loved to come here with Cindy after school.'

'I've been for a walk here before,' he said, looking round as they began strolling along a footpath that wound its way in and out of the trees. 'I had no idea it was close to Woodside, although I suppose I should have worked that out from the name of your house.'

Rebecca smiled but said nothing.

'There are some very old trees here,' Nick observed as he paused to look at some of the giant oaks and then at a very tall fir that was higher still.

'Have you seen the one that is hollowed out?' Rebecca asked. 'We used to hide in it when we played here, or else pretend that it was our house and sit inside it and eat our picnic. A bit of a squash for two of us, but it was good fun – especially when someone walked by and didn't see us. We also used to use it as our very own private post office and leave messages for each other hidden in it.'

'No, I haven't seen that one.'

'Come on, I'll show you.'

Rebecca walked ahead, pushing back the brambles that were

growing out over the footpath in places. 'Here it is,' she said, stopping in front of a giant gnarled tree trunk hollowed out almost like a cave. 'Isn't it terrific?'

'I'll say and it's big enough to get right inside, just as you said.'

As he spoke, Nick went nearer to the old tree and poked his head into the dark hollow.

'Someone's been using it as a changing room,' he grinned as he straightened up.

'As a changing room? What do you mean?'

'There's a bundle of clothes and some rubber boots in there. Come and look.'

Nick moved back to give Rebecca room to peer inside the tree trunk. When she did so, she let out a gasp and the colour drained from her face.

'What's up?'

'Those are Cindy's clothes and her boots,' she said in a tight voice. 'Oh, no, they can't be! What does it mean?'

Nick looked puzzled. 'You said you used to climb in and picnic. It looks as though your friend has left some of her clothes in there—'

'But when did she leave them there? She's been missing for more than a week.'

'Missing?'

Rebecca took a deep breath and then, in a rather stilted manner, outlined how Cindy had been planning to spend the previous weekend with her in Cardiff but hadn't turned up.

Nick let out a long, low whistle. 'You mean none of you have heard from her since and you don't know where she's gone?'

Rebecca nodded. 'The village is full of gossip about it.'

She thought of adding 'And they are linking her disappearance with the fact that my dad is not here either', but felt it was more prudent not to mention this in case it gave Nick Blakemore the wrong idea.

Instead, she reached in and pulled the clothes out and held up the blue boiler suit. 'This is what Cindy always wore when she came to help Dad with the pigs. She put it on over her day clothes to protect them while she was dishing out the feed or mucking out their sty.'

'And the rubber boots?'

'She wore those instead of her shoes because it was often mucky in the pigs' pen, especially if it had been a hot day and Dad had filled up the big old sink he kept in there with water so they could slosh around and cool off. As you probably know, pigs don't like getting too hot and they can easily get sunburned when it's a very hot day.'

'Heavens! You seem to know a great deal about pigs,' he said admiringly. 'All I know about them is how to butcher them.'

'I had a very special little pig called Moses,' Rebecca told him. 'He was the runt of Molly's first litter and I raised him and he became a pet.'

'Really!' Nick gave an amused smile.

'Cindy had a pet lamb called Snowy and we used to take the two of them for walks. After I went to university, either Cindy or her brother Jake came up each evening after finishing work and took Moses for a walk.'

Nick looked grave. 'I think we ought to take these clothes back to her family, don't you?' He paused and frowned. 'Unless the police have been told she is missing. In which case we ought to leave them here and inform the police, so they can search the area and inside the bole of that tree to see if there are any other clues.'

Sixteen

Sandra Peterson couldn't believe her eyes when she saw the bundle of clothes that Rebecca brought into the shop and placed on the small desk in the office.

'You say you found them in a hollow tree trunk and they belong to Cindy?' she said with a frown.

'That's right, Mum. That old hollow oak up in the woods, the one where Cindy and I used to hide when we played hide-and-seek.'

'I know the one you mean, but why would Cindy leave clothes hidden in there? Are you quite sure they're hers?'

'Of course they are, they're the ones she changed into when she came to help with the pigs.'

Sandra Peterson stared at them more closely. 'I think you're right,' she agreed. 'What are you going to do with them?'

'I'm not too sure. I thought I'd better take them up to the farm and give them to Mrs Mason.'

'I suppose so.' Her mother sighed heavily. 'I think this will raise all sorts of questions from Tom and Mavis, though. Do you want me to come with you?'

'Would you, Mum? I'd feel happier if you did in case she gets all upset. I wouldn't know what to say.'

Sandra hesitated for a moment then she said, 'Very well, we'll do it as soon as I close up tonight, before we go home.'

'I'll lock up for you, Mrs Peterson, if you want to go up there right away,' Nick offered.

'Would you, Nick? That would be very helpful. Enjoy your weekend at home and I'll see you again next week.

'By the way,' she added, 'I haven't asked you if you enjoyed your tour of the neighbourhood?'

'I most certainly did. Rebecca made it extremely interesting. There's far more to see in and around Shelston than I'd imagined.'

Sandra smiled. 'Good. Well, if you will put the blind down and lock up I'll see you bright and early on Monday morning.'

'No problem.' He turned and held out a hand to Rebecca. 'Thank you, Rebecca, for a very interesting afternoon. I hope we'll see each other again some time.'

As they walked up to the Masons' farm, Sandra carrying a carrier bag containing the clothes that Rebecca had found in the tree, she commented, 'Nick Blakemore's a nice young man, isn't he?'

'Yes, very nice,' Rebecca agreed. 'How long is he planning to work for you?'

'As far as I know, it will only be until your dad gets home again. Nick has certainly been a great help but I don't think we could afford to hire him permanently, even if we wanted to. Anyway, I imagine he wants to find himself a better job than we are able to offer him.'

When they reached the farm, they met Mavis crossing the

yard. She greeted them coolly. 'I can't stand here talking, I'm just off to help with the milking,' she announced.

'We won't keep you a moment, but we thought we ought to bring you these,' Sandra said as she held the carrier bag out to her.

Mavis took the bag and her face creased into a frown as she looked inside it. Then she let out a strangled gasp. The colour drained from her face and she asked in an accusing tone, 'Where did you get these?'

'Rebecca was out for a walk this afternoon and she found them in the old hollow tree in the woods by us. She recognized them as belonging to Cindy.'

'Of course they're Cindy's. They're what she always wore when she came to help your Bill with those damn pigs.'

'That's what we both thought,' Sandra agreed.

'You say you found them in the woods?' she asked, looking directly at Rebecca.

'That's right. Rolled up and stowed away inside the old hollow tree. You know the one I mean, Mrs Mason. There's a huge hole in the bole and when Cindy and I were small we used to hide inside it.'

'Oh, I know which one you mean. But how did our Cindy's clothes get in there?'

'We've no idea,' Sandra said, shaking her head.

'Haven't you?' Mavis Mason placed her hands on her hips. Her stocky figure looked as if it was braced for a fight. 'Are you quite sure you don't know the answer?'

'We haven't any idea,' Sandra repeated.

'I don't believe you! So you'd better explain, because my Cindy certainly isn't here to answer, as you well know.'

Her voice quivered and her shoulders shook, and she looked as if she was going to collapse.

Sandra stepped forward to put an arm around Mavis's shoulder, but she pushed her away roughly.

'Don't you dare touch me!' she screamed. 'You know what's happened to my girl and I want the truth, and I want it right now.'

The sound of her raised voice carried across the farmyard and Tom Mason appeared from the milking shed to see what all the commotion was about.

'Hello, Sandra. Hello, Rebecca,' he said quietly. Then looking at his wife and seeing how distraught she was, he asked 'What's going on, why the raised voices?'

Choking with anger, Mavis held out the bag of clothes towards him. 'Look for yourself!'

For a moment he peered into the bag as if uncertain about what he was expected to find. Then with a quick intake of breath he pulled out the blue boiler suit.

'That's our Cindy's!' he exclaimed in astonishment. 'Did she leave it somewhere up at your place?' he asked, looking from Sandra to Rebecca with a puzzled look on his face.

'No! Rebecca found it, together with her boots, hidden in a hollow tree in the woods.' Mavis said quickly. 'How did they get there? That's what I want to know.' She looked directly at Sandra. 'She knows more than she's saying. I reckon she's got a guilty conscience, that's why she's brought them back up here.'

'Hold on, Mavis, I wasn't the one who found them!'

'No? I bet you know how they got there, though.'

Mavis's voice was strident and accusing, and her lips were pulled back in a sneer that made her normally placid round face look menacing.

'What on earth do you mean?' Sandra asked sharply.

'Collusion, that's what I mean. Collusion between you and your daughter. And probably that fancy man you've moved in with you as well, for all I know. You should be ashamed of yourselves, the lot of you. I think we should go to the police and tell them what we suspect, Tom,' she said, turning to her husband.

'Exactly what do you suspect?' Sandra asked without raising her voice.

'That you and your lot have done away with our daughter. Murdered her in cold blood and then fed her body to the pigs that your Bill sold at market.'

'You're off your head!' Sandra protested.

'Then why has your husband scarpered?' Mavis asked in a shaking voice as the tears coursed down her cheeks.

'Come, come,' Tom put an arm round his wife's shoulders. 'Don't take on so, my love. We've no proof and you shouldn't be saying such things.'

'Then where is our Cindy and where is Bill Peterson?' Mavis sobbed. 'Both of them vanished without a trace. Has she gone away with him as well?' Her face contorted with anguish, Mavis pointed an accusing finger at Sandra.

'My dad hasn't vanished, Mrs Mason!' Rebecca exclaimed. 'Tell them, Mum. He's with granny, because she's dying.'

'What?' Tom and Mavis both spoke together.

'Bill is at his mother's bedside. He's been there for over a week now because she is so ill and not likely to recover. He's always been very fond of his mother and he wants to spend what time she has left with her.'

'Oh, Sandra, I am very sorry to hear that,' Tom Mason said contritely. 'We had no idea.'

'No, and so you not only imagined all sorts of evil things about Bill but spread malicious gossip about me as well. I thought you were our friends!'

'We are, but this business over Cindy going missing has thrown us out of kilter over everything.'

'To straighten out another misconception on your part,' Sandra went on, 'Nick Blakemore isn't my fancy man, as you put it. He's someone Bill arranged to come and work for us so Bill could be at the hospital with his mother. We needed someone to deal with the butchery side of things because I can't manage it on my own.'

'So where is our Cindy in all this?' Mavis demanded. Her face was red and her eyes puffy, but she was still not mollified by Sandra's explanation.

'We don't know any more than you do.'

'All this talk and lies about her going to spend the weekend in Cardiff with your Rebecca.'

'That was quite true. I was expecting her to come to Cardiff last weekend—'

'But she didn't, did she?' Mavis butted in.

'No she didn't and I was very worried. I'd planned all sorts of things for us to do and I wanted to show her what a wonderful place Cardiff is.'

'You say she never arrived. That's all we know too,' Tom said glumly. 'Our Jake keeps telling us he left her outside the station in time for her train.'

'I know, and I met every train that came in from Temple Meads until after ten o'clock and went back again first thing on Sunday morning. What's more, I phoned Jake several times to ask what could possibly have happened and all he could tell me was that he'd taken her to the station in Frome in time for the train she'd said she would be on. And he was sure she went straight on to the platform.'

'No, there must be more to it than that,' Mavis asserted, shaking her head in a disbelieving way.

'Then tell the police and let them look into things. We have nothing whatsoever to do with her disappearance.' Sandra said firmly. 'Come on, we've nothing more to tell them,' she said, taking hold of Rebecca's arm. 'Let's go home.'

'This isn't the end of it by any means,' Mavis told her stubbornly. 'I'm going to the police. It's something we should have done days ago.'

'Mavis, let's give this some more thought. There must be some explanation,' Tom begged.

'I mean it, and you can bet your boots the police will be asking you Petersons some questions. The very first one will be to see if you are telling the truth about your missing husband.'

'Mavis, stop it. Sandra has told us where he is and Rebecca has told us all she knows.'

'Maybe. I still think the Peterson family are involved and they know more than they're saying. I'll get to the bottom of it, though. We're still going to the police,' Mavis asserted. 'And I don't care who gets hurt.'

Seventeen

The police treated Cindy's disappearance as a 'missing person' case and wasted no time in commencing their enquiries. They were avid for details. As well as the local policeman, a Sergeant Weathers came to Shelston to conduct interviews with the Petersons and the Masons.

He was a tall, thin man in his early fifties, with a hooked nose and a thin-lipped mouth. He barked out his questions rather like an army sergeant-major and made no comment in response to the answers, simply writing them down in his notebook.

When he interviewed the Masons, he listened without comment to Mavis's theory that Cindy had been killed and fed to the pigs by the Peterson family. Not even a muscle in his face or a change of voice registered his reaction to such a theory.

Even so, he was extremely thorough. He cross-questioned everything they said and warned them that everything in their statements would be checked after he went back to the station.

When he came to interview the Petersons, he asked to be taken to see the hollow tree where Cindy's clothes had been found and recorded exactly how they had been discovered, including the time of day.

He also noted down Rebecca's address in Cardiff and mentioned that the Cardiff police might pay her a visit if they needed confirmation of her statement or any further information.

Sergeant Weathers also asked for details of Bill Peterson's movements and his mother's address, even though Sandra told him that Granny Peterson was in hospital and that he had been spending all his time at her bedside because she was dying.

He then asked for the name and address of the hospital where old Mrs Peterson was, even though Sandra assured him that she knew nothing about Cindy and was too ill to answer any questions. He promised this would be noted, but cautioned her that a fellow officer would be contacting Bill at the hospital for confirmation of what she had said.

Nick Blakemore was questioned in detail about his movements, although he explained that he had only been in Shelston for a very short time and had never met Cindy Mason.

On Sunday afternoon, when Rebecca and her mother went to visit Granny Peterson they found Bill looking tense and drawn and both angry and confused.

The police had already visited him quite early that morning at his mother's home, where he was staying, and he'd been nonplussed by the things they said and the questions they asked.

'Mavis is accusing us of killing Cindy and feeding her body to the pigs,' Sandra told him.

'Well, I rather gathered that and she also implied that I'd run away from home and am hiding because I'm the guilty one,' Bill retorted.

'The police have even interviewed Nick Blakemore. Although how he could have had anything to do with it heaven alone knows. He's never met Cindy and he hadn't even met us when Cindy disappeared.'

'I wonder just what has happened to her, though?' Bill looked from his wife to his daughter and back again. He looked upset and haggard as he ran a hand through his hair. 'We have enough problems as it is without this as well,' he added wearily.

'We came to see Granny Peterson. How is she?' Rebecca asked.

'Very low, I'm afraid. I'm going back to the hospital now. Are you two coming with me? They say she has only a matter of hours now. Do you really want to come to the hospital to see her? She's lying there with her eyes closed and I don't think she can hear my voice when I speak to her.'

'Well, since we've come here to do that, I think we should. Though we can't stay long because Rebecca has to get back to Cardiff tonight in time for university tomorrow.'

Rebecca was shocked as they approached her grandmother's bedside to see her looking so thin and gaunt and weak. One blue-veined hand lay on top of the covers and Rebecca picked it up and held it gently between her own. The old lady barely stirred when she kissed her on the forehead and her skin felt damp and clammy.

Rebecca sat for a while holding the old lady's frail hand in hers, but it lay there completely lifeless. When a nurse came in and gently moved their hands apart, she didn't attempt to resist. Blinded by tears, she escaped into the corridor and when her mother joined her a few minutes later she agreed they should leave.

Rebecca returned to Cardiff feeling despondent. Her weekend had turned out to be very different from what she had anticipated.

She knew she would never see her grandmother again and she remembered all the lovely times they had spent together when she was small. Granny Peterson had lived in Shelston then, and had only moved away when Rebecca was in her teens.

Although she had been in her seventies, her grandmother had gone to look after her older sister who lived some twenty miles away and she had stayed on in the tiny cottage after her sister died.

When they pressed her to come back to Shelston, she had pointed out that she had given up her own cottage and it was unlikely she would find another place to rent. That would mean living with them, and she didn't want to do that because she valued her independence. But even that had been taken away from her when she became too old to look after herself and had to go into a nursing home, Rebecca thought sadly.

Rebecca was also more worried than ever about Cindy's whereabouts. She could imagine how concerned the Masons must be, but couldn't understand why they hadn't reported that she was missing to the police long before this.

Even so, she still felt stunned and angry that Mavis Mason had levelled such outrageous accusations against her family.

She and Cindy had been lifelong friends, almost like sisters. They had shared friends, toys, lessons and hobbies. They'd gone freely in and out of each other's homes and Jake had been as close to her as any brother.

She had no idea how Cindy's boiler suit and rubber boots had come to be in the hollow of the tree and now almost wished she had said nothing at all about finding them. Taking them up to the Masons had started what was turning out to be a nightmare.

She tried to concentrate, but her brain seemed woolly and she could do nothing but think of Cindy and wonder where on earth she could be.

Her concern about Cindy had even pushed the fact that Granny Peterson was dying to the back of her mind, so when a phone call came first thing on Monday morning to tell her that her grandmother had died she accepted it quite calmly.

'Now, don't get upset, she was in her eighties and she's had a good life,' her mother said consolingly. 'I'll let you know when we've arranged the date for her funeral.'

'Have you had any more visits from the police about Cindy?' Rebecca asked before the call ended.

'No, dear. The police have probably gone over all the information we gave them and come to the conclusion that Mavis's story is ridiculous. No doubt they'll be following things up by trying to find out what happened after Cindy boarded the train at Frome. That's if she did. Perhaps she simply waited until Jake had driven off and then went off somewhere else.'

'Why on earth would she do that?' Rebecca asked. 'We had a wonderful time planned, and we were both looking forward to her visit so much.'

'I don't know, dear, and I think you should stop worrying your head about it. If she did change her mind about coming to stay with you, then she should have let you know. But since she didn't, forget all about it and get on with your studies. Your exams are not all that far away, you know.'

After her mother rang off, Rebecca recalled the dreams Cindy had expressed about going to London and becoming a fashion model or a TV star or something glamorous like that.

Surely if she had changed her plans and had done that, Rebecca reasoned, then she would have let me know?

She suddenly wondered if Jake or any of the Masons had gone along to the supermarket to see if anyone there knew where Cindy had gone. In fact, she scolded herself, I should have done it on Saturday afternoon.

She started to dial her home phone number to ask her mother if she would go and ask the manager or someone else there if they had any news of Cindy's whereabouts. Then she put the phone down, knowing that she couldn't ask her mother to do that as her mother had always declared she would never set foot in the supermarket and she didn't think she would consider doing so even to set their minds at rest.

Anyway, she told herself, the police were so thorough that, knowing Cindy had worked at the supermarket, they were bound to go there and ask questions.

Still, she felt guilty about not thinking of doing so herself when she'd been in Shelston, instead of going for a walk with Nick Blakemore.

Eighteen

A team of detectives and fingerprint experts searched Bill Peterson's butcher's shop from top to bottom. They even inspected every carcass of meat he had hanging up in the cold room, as well as all the joints of meat that were in the freezers in the room at the back of the shop and in the shop itself.

They also searched every room at Woodside, including the attics and the two garden sheds.

Sandra was furious when they started opening drawers and examining the contents and demanded to know what they thought they were doing.

'You aren't going to find her tucked away in there,' she told them sarcastically.

'No, Ma'am, but we might find some clues that will help us in our search.'

'Really? What sort of clues?'

They didn't answer but completed their meticulous scrutiny of absolutely everything in the house before they left.

Outside, they scoured the bushes and chopped down clumps of long grass and they checked out the ditch that ran between the garden of Woodside and the woods beyond.

They spent a long time examining the pigsties, especially the one that had been Moses' special sty. When one of them found an old shoe lying in a corner, he held it up triumphantly.

Tension grew when further investigations revealed that it had belonged to Cindy Mason, and the investigating team asked Bill Peterson countless questions about how it had come to be there.

'She probably gave it to him as a toy, something to play with,' Bill explained. 'Cindy was very fond of Moses. She used to come up here every evening to take him for a walk.'

'A toy?' They looked dubious.

'Yes, a toy,' Bill repeated. 'Pigs get bored and they like to have playthings. We used to give him a tennis ball or an old box to play with sometimes, but best of all he loved old shoes or wellies.'

They didn't ask any further questions about Cindy's shoe, but carefully placed it in a protective bag to take back to the laboratory for testing. From the looks they exchanged with each other, Bill Peterson didn't think they believed him.

The Masons' farm was also thoroughly searched from top to bottom. Indoors, they went over every inch of the old farmhouse from the cellars to the attics.

Outside, the barns and all of the outhouses and even the chicken run were searched. Even the log pile in the yard by the back door was taken apart.

Extra attention was paid to Cindy's bedroom. Clothes were emptied out of the chest of drawers and the wardrobe, and every corner was investigated.

Cindy's laptop was taken away to see if there was anything on it that might provide clues as to why she had left home.

Apart from the emails between Cindy and Rebecca Peterson confirming their arrangements for the weekend they planned to spend together in Cardiff, there wasn't a shred of information that was of any help.

Before they left, the police dragged the farm's duck pond. The result was exactly the same. There was no trace of the missing girl.

Reports in the local South-Western News brought Shelston to the attention of the whole area and there followed a number of sightings. Cindy had been seen in Salisbury; she'd been seen with two men at a football match in Yeovil; she'd been seen at the races in Wincanton. The police investigations that followed proved them all to be wrong.

Gossip abounded in the village. Lizzie Smith was in her element, although few people took her malicious stories seriously. Nonetheless, there was plenty of incriminatory gossip and a great deal of speculation, even amongst the men when they met up in the village pub for a drink.

Rebecca was shocked to see there were even police present

at Granny Peterson's funeral the following week, her body having been brought back to Shelston to be interred in the family grave.

There were two plain-clothes detectives soberly dressed in long black coats standing at the back of the church. They followed the family and other mourners at a discreet distance when they moved out into the cemetery for the internment.

Before the coffin was lowered into the grave, which had been dug a few days previously by the local gravedigger, old Jack Smart, they inspected it closely.

Villagers nudged each other, exchanging knowing looks about what was going on.

'Is that some sort of new-fangled safety precaution?' one murmured.

Another shook his head. 'Evidence,' he muttered. 'They're looking for evidence. Young Cindy Mason has never been found. There's not even a hint of her whereabouts or even whether she is still alive or not.'

The detectives accompanied the mourners returning to Woodside to partake of the hospitality that the Petersons were offering, but after mingling for a few minutes they silently vanished.

Everybody in Shelston seemed to be looking at each other sideways, with doubt and suspicion. It was as though they were conscious someone was withholding information that might be useful in uncovering the mystery of what had happened to Cindy or about where she had gone.

There was a palpable tension between the Petersons and the Masons whenever they met or were even in the same place at the same time.

Rebecca returned to Cardiff feeling as though she had escaped from a bad dream. Once or twice during the journey, she suspected that she was being followed. She hoped she was wrong and the police were satisfied she had told them everything she knew and wouldn't come asking questions when she returned to college.

She had one regret: she had intended going to the supermarket in Shelston to ask if anyone there knew what had happened to Cindy. Because of Granny Peterson's funeral, she hadn't had time to do so. She assumed that the police had done so anyway and had not been told anything that was helpful.

Trying to concentrate on her work was impossible. She couldn't put Cindy out of her mind. Where on earth could she be? And why hadn't she contacted her? She had tried Cindy's mobile countless times but the connection was dead. Did that mean that Cindy was dead too?

She kept going over and over the arrangements they had made and wondering if she had somehow misunderstood their plans for Cindy to come to Cardiff that particular weekend.

Jake had known the details and had taken Cindy to the station, so she couldn't be wrong.

At night she dreamed about Cindy and the things they had done together. Sometimes the dreams became nightmares, with frightening events she couldn't put out of her mind the next day even though she knew them to be figments of her imagination.

Even so, she was fully resolved that if Cindy hadn't contacted her by half-term and there was no fresh news, then the first thing she would do when she got back to Shelston would be to go to the supermarket and see what they could tell her.

Nineteen

The lifelong friendship between the Petersons and the Masons was being sorely tested. Both families were so upset by all the police enquiries and the rumours circulating in Shelston that there were times when they could barely be civil to each other.

Their social get-togethers were abandoned and when they met in the village they barely acknowledged each other. When they were in the same company, the atmosphere was strained.

Tom Mason still sent produce down to the butcher's shop but it was usually Jake who delivered it. No word was spoken about Cindy, and Jake didn't ask for news of Rebecca as he had done in the past. All talk was kept strictly on a business level.

Tom Mason rendered his monthly bills for the produce he supplied and either Sandra or Bill signed a cheque for the amount due and either handed it to Jake or sent it by post.

This frostiness between the two families gave rise to even more rumours, and the villagers began to take sides.

When Bill returned home after his mother died, there had been two schools of thought in Shelston about his absence and plenty of gossip.

Some people believed he really had been spending the time at his mother's bedside. Others, like Lizzie Smith and her cronies, were convinced he had gone into hiding after Cindy disappeared because he knew what had happened to her; and now he was putting a bold face on things and had returned to Shelston so that people wouldn't think he had anything to do with Cindy's disappearance.

When the police found no evidence of any violence towards Cindy and no trace of her anywhere, except for the old shoe found in one of the deserted pigsties, the rumours and interest began to wane.

Many thought she had simply run away from home because she wanted something more exciting. Young girls often did that sort of thing and Cindy had always been rather wilful.

They knew she hadn't gone off with any of the local boys because they were all accounted for, and most of the villagers were gradually accepting the fact that the married man they'd linked her name with had not been guilty of any indiscretion.

Gradually life in Shelston returned to its mundane pattern, almost as if Cindy had been forgotten or never existed.

Occasionally someone would ask one of the Masons if they had any fresh news about their missing daughter. But the answer was always the same; there was no news.

Easter came and as usual Bill the Butcher's shop was exceptionally busy. It was well stocked with poultry of all kinds, and when customers learned that it came from the Masons' farm, as usual, they assumed the feud between the two families was in abeyance.

Rebecca had been home for the holiday, but she didn't go up to the Masons' farm as she had done in the past. She did, however, go into the supermarket to see if anyone there had any news of Cindy.

When she asked for the manager, she was startled to find it wasn't Bruno Lopez.

'I'm afraid Bruno left some time ago,' the fair-haired young man who came out of the inner office informed her.

'Oh, I didn't know that. Has he moved to one of your other branches?' Rebecca asked.

'No, he's left the company and I have no idea where he's gone. He hasn't kept in touch with anyone here.'

Rebecca felt at a loss. The Masons were the only other people she knew well enough to ask for further details, but she was afraid to ask Mavis because of the antagonism between the two families.

That year none of the Petersons participated in any of the public festivities held in Shelston over Easter.

It was noticeable that they kept themselves very much to themselves, the same as the Masons, and this gave rise to some malicious observations from Lizzie Smith and one or two other older inhabitants.

In the past, both families had joined in most things from services at the parish church to attending the concert given by the local schoolchildren in the village hall and the Easter play that was always part of Shelston's celebrations.

It was rumoured in the village that Tom and Mavis Mason were constantly bickering and openly blamed each other for Cindy's disappearance.

It was whispered by some of the women who worked at the farmhouse that Tom had been heard accusing Mavis of not taking enough notice of what Cindy had been doing and not noticing if she was unhappy or restless.

Mavis retaliated by saying she hadn't got the time for molly-coddling either of her children now they were adults. She had far too much to do on the farm. If he expected her to spend time sitting talking with Jake and Cindy and entertaining their friends or going on shopping sprees with Cindy, then he should have provided more help and not expected her to run a home and a dairy at the same time.

They were heard quarrelling in public over other things as

well, and Jake was heard to declare that he was looking forward to getting away from the farm as soon as he possibly could.

Whenever Sandra overheard customers gossiping about the Masons, she tried to turn a deaf ear. She wanted to tell them to shut up, but she knew it was more than she dared do for fear of losing their custom.

And it made her concerned about Rebecca, because she knew her daughter was looking far from happy these days. She tried asking her if everything was all right at university, but Rebecca insisted that she enjoyed every moment of it there and she not only loved living in Cardiff but had plenty of friends there. Sandra assumed that it must be because she was missing Cindy so much when she was at home. But the more she tried to talk to Rebecca about Cindy the more tight-lipped Rebecca became, so in the end she avoided the subject.

Sandra couldn't understand why Cindy hadn't confided her plans to Rebecca. They'd always been so close and always shared everything and told each other all their secrets.

Several times she tried to talk things over with Rebecca, but never with success. Rebecca remained monosyllabic and tight-lipped.

Apart from solitary walks, Rebecca spent her time indoors studying. She was due to sit her final exams in the coming term and she was determined to do well in them.

Jake no longer spent any time with Rebecca at all. He had found a new girlfriend, who lived in the next village, and there were rumours that they had recently become engaged and would be getting married the following June.

Rebecca had mixed feelings when she heard the news. Then she gave a mental shrug and dismissed the matter from her mind. He hadn't really been her boyfriend, only her best friend's brother. She had enjoyed his company but she had no feeling of loss because the separation had come gradually as a result of the rift between their families after Cindy's disappearance.

There could never have been anything serious between them, she told herself. His real love was farming and although she was quite interested in what went on from day to day it wasn't the sort of future she wanted.

She had once told him she was planning a career in politics, and she knew that hadn't interested him in the least. When once or twice she had tried talking to him about it, he had dismissed the notion as being on the same level as Cindy's dreams of becoming a fashion star.

'You two have your heads in the clouds,' he'd told her. 'Why can't you concentrate on something practical like cooking or bookkeeping, something that might be of some use for the rest of your lives? You could even go in for nursing, something that would keep your feet on the ground.'

Rebecca remembered that she had told him he talked like an old man and that even her father had more modern ideas about careers for women than he had.

It brought her thoughts almost full circle, and once again she pondered about what had become of Cindy. And why she had disappeared so completely without a word to anyone, not even to her.

Twenty

Rebecca returned to Cardiff intent on applying herself to her studies. She felt she had done all she could to find out what had happened to Cindy and was both mystified and disappointed she'd had no success.

The time had come, she reasoned, to put all thoughts about Cindy from her mind and concentrate on studying for her exams.

She knew she had promised herself she would do this a great many times in the past few months, but now she was determined because she knew that if she didn't then she would never achieve the grades necessary for a first-class degree.

Her friend Grace Flowers had the same target as she did. They both wanted to be eligible for a fast-track teacher training course, and in order to achieve this they knew they had to have the right qualifications.

They'd agreed they would adopt a very serious approach to studying during the summer term, sometimes in tandem but more often in the seclusion of their own rooms.

They had also agreed that they would consider Saturdays as a day off and indulge in shopping or going to the pictures or a dance and thoroughly enjoy themselves.

It worked so well that they were both more than satisfied with their progress by the time the half-term vacation arrived. Even so, they decided not to go home but to stay in Cardiff and enjoy the various recreational opportunities and social occasions that were available.

Rebecca thought that perhaps a break from Shelston might help her to sort things out in her head about Cindy. Furthermore she enjoyed Grace Flowers' company. She was tall and slim, the same as Rebecca, but Grace had long, straight red hair, which she wore caught back in a ponytail, and bright-blue eyes that were a complete contrast to Rebecca's honey-coloured hair and grey eyes.

'I know it's a bit chilly for a trip to the seaside, but let's visit Penarth and Barry Island, and perhaps Swansea as well if we have time,' Grace suggested.

'When I'm at home in Liverpool,' she went on, 'I love to go to Southport or even New Brighton for the day and I'm feeling withdrawal symptoms as a result of not being able to see the sea.'

'What utter rubbish!' Rebecca laughed. 'Cardiff is right on the edge of the Irish sea. You can take a walk down to the Bay any Saturday you like.'

'I know, but somehow it's not the same.'

'New Brighton is on the Mersey and that's only a river—'

'It may only be a river but it opens out into the Irish Sea. And big boats – ocean liners, in fact – come down it and dock in the Port of Liverpool.'

'Don't worry, I'm only teasing you. I'd like to see Barry Island. I've heard so much about it, and Swansea as well if we can find the time. Where I live, in Shelston, we're landlocked and miles from the sea, so it's all new to me.'

'OK, let's do that then,' Grace agreed. 'You're quite sure you don't want to go home for the holiday?'

'No!' Rebecca suppressed a shudder and her grey eyes clouded as she shook her head. She had found the atmosphere in her own home as well as in the village depressing when she'd been there at Easter. What was more, she didn't want to revive any memories of Cindy and if she went back to Shelston, even for a few days, she knew she would.

She would never forget Cindy, of course, because she had been part of her life for so long. One day she would find her, she was quite sure of that. For the present, though, Rebecca felt it was more prudent to put the matter out of her mind.

Having agreed on their programme for work and recreation, the two girls worked hard and when Easter finally came they both felt they were in need of a break.

'Over the holiday we'll pack away our books and not even peep at them,' Grace said emphatically on the Thursday night, as she pushed back the strands of hair that had escaped from her ponytail and fallen over her face while she was concentrating. 'The next four or five days are going to be pure relaxation. Let's hope the weather keeps fine so we can really enjoy our sightseeing trips.'

Rebecca smiled. 'If it's warm enough, we might even manage to paddle.'

'I very much doubt it, but at least you'll know where you can persuade your family to visit next time they want a holiday without all the fuss and expense of going abroad,' Grace agreed, her blue eyes twinkling.

The day they went to Penarth was sunny but chilly and there was a sharp wind blowing in off the sea.

Nevertheless, they enjoyed their visit and were intrigued to be able to see the coastline of Somerset and Devon quite clearly on the other side of the Severn estuary.

'It makes me feel really close to home,' Rebecca said in surprise. 'We used to go on coach trips from Shelston to Weston-super-Mare when I was at school.'

'There's still time for you to go home for a couple of days if you're homesick,' Grace told her sympathetically.

Rebecca shook her head. 'No! I'm not homesick,' she declared emphatically.

Even as she spoke, her mind was full of memories of Cindy and herself at school, of the charabanc trips they'd gone on armed with a pack of sandwiches and a bottle of lemonade, all prepared to spend the day together.

'Come on!' She grabbed Grace's hand. 'Race you along the promenade.'

Their trip to Barry Island was a tremendous success. They took off their shoes and socks and wriggled their toes in the sand, but one dip in the sea was enough. Laughing and shivering, they scrambled back as waves licked their toes and decided it really wasn't warm enough for such an adventure.

After a meal of fish and chips, eaten straight out of the paper they were wrapped in, they went along to the fairground. The new season had only just started and the showmen were all offering cheap rates to drum up interest. The two girls took advantage of the offers and went on half a dozen rides until they were both completely exhausted.

To finish off the day, they went into one of the cafés near the sea front for a hamburger and fries, washed down with a glass of coke.

'Not very sophisticated, are we?' Grace laughed.

'Maybe not but it's been good fun. I wouldn't have missed out on today for anything,' Rebecca enthused.

'Shall we pay a visit to Swansea tomorrow?' Grace asked as they made their way back to Cardiff.

'Let's see how we feel in the morning. All that sea air has made me sleepy. Perhaps we should have a lie-in tomorrow and then go to Swansea the next day.'

'That might be a good idea,' Grace agreed. 'There's a good play on at the Sherman Theatre tomorrow evening and I'd like to see it.'

'Sounds good. Perhaps we could spend the day browsing round the museum or sitting in Cathays Park, then go to the play in the evening.'

Again memories of Cindy flooded Rebecca's thoughts. This was the sort of programme she'd planned for the weekend when Cindy should have come to stay. What had happened to her? How was it that no one had seen or heard from her after Jake dropped her off at Frome station? She must have gone somewhere. She'd have to eat and stay somewhere. Someone somewhere knew something about Cindy's disappearance.

Twenty-One

Life in Shelston had still not returned to normal, and when Rebecca didn't come home for the half-term break tongues once again began wagging.

Repeatedly, Sandra found customers were asking if Rebecca was all right or if she had gone somewhere else for the holiday.

When Sandra explained that Rebecca would very shortly be sitting her final exams and so had thought it best to stay where she was and concentrate on her studies, they smiled and nodded. But Sandra had the feeling many of them didn't believe her.

It became obvious that this was so when Lizzie Smith was heard commenting on Rebecca's absence. 'That's another girl from Shelston that's gone missing,' she added.

'Perhaps Rebecca has gone to see Cindy? After all, they were best friends,' someone suggested.

'No one knows where Cindy is or what's happened to her,' another observed.

'Well, we don't, but I suppose it's quite likely that Rebecca Peterson does,' Lizzie Smith remarked.

'That's possible because we all know those two girls were always the closest of friends,' Mary Roberts agreed.

The whispering and arguments spread around the village, becoming more and more malicious as the days passed.

Sandra tried to ignore them but found it increasingly difficult whenever customers commented on Rebecca's absence. When she explained why Rebecca had decided to stay on in Cardiff, they either raised their eyebrows or smiled dismissively.

In the end she became so nervy and bad-tempered that Bill took matters into his own hands and phoned Rebecca.

'Hello, Becky, look I know you decided to stay where you are over the break so that you could concentrate on your studies, but can you find the time to come home even if it's only for a day?' he asked.

'Why, Dad? What's happened?'

'It's for your mother's sake. She's in a right state. Folks are saying all sorts of things because you haven't come home and she's finding it very upsetting.'

'What sort of things?'

'Oh, you know. About them not seeing you around at all. Some are even hinting that you've gone missing the same as Cindy. That sort of thing.'

'Really! Well, you should point out that you haven't any pigs now, so you can't have fed me to them, not even to Moses,' she retorted with a sharp little laugh.

'I know, love, I know. They've nothing better to do with their time, that's the problem. Nevertheless, it's tearing your mother apart. She's as jumpy as a cat in a high wind and she's losing weight and she's that moody—'

'All right, Dad, I get the picture! Look, I can't do anything until the weekend but I'll come home then. It will be from late Friday night and then back here on Sunday. Is that all right?'

'Thanks, love, that will be fine, I knew you would understand. Not a word to your mother that I phoned you, though. I don't want her to know how worried I am about her. You understand?'

'Yes, Dad, I understand perfectly. Now stop worrying and I'll see you at the weekend.'

'What train will you be on? Let me know and I'll collect you from Frome Station,' her father asked, his voice tinged with relief.

'I've no idea. I'll phone you from the train,' she promised. 'Now don't worry and don't say anything to Mum about me coming home in case I can't manage to get away.'

'No, I won't. As I said, I don't want her to know I've phoned you. Do your very best. If you can't make it, then ring and let me know.'

As Rebecca put the phone down, she felt very concerned. She had never thought that failing to go home at half-term would revive all the malicious stories that had been spread about Cindy. But by the sound of things, it certainly had.

She knew her mother claimed she never listened to village gossip, but when you were the one involved it was a different matter.

She wondered what Grace would say when she told her they would have to postpone their planned trip to Swansea. She hoped she would understand.

Perhaps she could ask Grace if she would like to come to Shelston with her. There wasn't a lot to do in the village at weekends, or at any time for that matter, but since Grace had lived in a city all her life it might be a new experience for her.

It would also give her a reason for going home. It would mean that her mother wouldn't need to know that her father had phoned begging her to come home and show her face in the village in order to put a stop to all the gossip.

For several reasons, Rebecca kept putting off mentioning to Grace that she needed to change their plans for the following weekend.

For one thing, she knew Grace was very eager to go to Swansea and she hated having to disappoint her. Also, if she took Grace to Shelston she would have to explain the reason behind going there.

Telling her about Cindy's strange disappearance and the subsequent malicious gossip sounded so far-fetched, even to her ears, that she wondered if Grace would understand.

In bed that night, before going to sleep she ran the story over in her mind, debating which bits to leave out and exactly what to tell Grace. The next morning, when she woke up it all came flooding back and it all sounded so improbable that she put the matter to the back of her mind for another day.

On the Thursday night she knew she couldn't put it off any longer and vowed she would explain matters to Grace the next day.

She had the story all ready in her mind when they met at lunch time. But before she could say a word Grace said, 'Look, do you mind if we put off going to Swansea on Saturday? I've started a cold and I'm already aching and feeling unwell. By tomorrow it will be ten times worse.'

Rebecca felt so relieved that she had a hard job stopping

herself smiling. Now there was no need for her to tell Grace she needed to change their plans for the weekend or about Cindy.

Grace took her long silence for disappointment. 'I thought perhaps we could leave it until the following weekend,' she persisted.

'Yes, of course we can,' Rebecca assured her. 'After all, it's only a jaunt. We can do it any time.'

'Sorry if it's going to mess up your weekend,' Grace went on contritely. 'But as you know, when I get a cold it's usually pretty bad and I'm not the best of company for a few days.'

'I know. I'm sorry about the cold but I do understand,' Rebecca murmured. 'If there is anything I can do to help, do let me know.'

She crossed her fingers, hoping that Grace would refuse any offer of help. Then she would be free to go ahead with her own plans for going home.

'No, there's nothing you can do, thank you,' Grace mumbled. 'I'll go to bed and stay there until Monday morning. I should be fine by then.'

'What about your meals? You ought to eat to fight your cold.'

'I'll get in a stock of tissues and packets of soup and throat lozenges and pamper myself.'

'You don't want me to nurse you?'

'No, I most definitely do not. I simply want to suffer alone.' Grace grinned, her blue eyes twinkling.

Rebecca paused and then said, 'In that case I think I'll take the opportunity to go home for a couple of days. I know Mum was worried because I didn't go home for the half-term break, so this will set her mind at rest.'

'That's a great idea, it will make me feel less guilty about messing up our plans.'

Rebecca breathed a deep sigh of relief. She'd been reprieved from an awkward situation right at the eleventh hour. Now she could go home with a clear conscience, knowing that she wasn't letting Grace down in any way.

Furthermore, she hadn't had to tell Grace anything about Cindy being missing and the gossip and turmoil that was going on in the village as a result.

Twenty-Two

Rebecca was shocked by her mother's appearance. She had lost weight, her face was pallid, and her make-up that was usually so skilfully applied now made her look like a painted doll.

She clung on to Rebecca almost fiercely as they embraced, and her sigh of relief that Rebecca was there made her feel guilty she hadn't come home before.

The latest gossip had only started a week ago, she consoled herself, so her mother's decline must have started long before then. She looked as though she hadn't had a decent meal or a good night's sleep for weeks.

Normally she was impeccably dressed with everything coordinating. Today she looked as though she'd dressed in the dark and put on whatever had come to hand, without thought or care.

'I couldn't believe it when your dad took your call and said you were on your way home and wanted to be picked up from the station,' she said with a deep sigh.

'I didn't want to say anything earlier in case I couldn't make it. I've got to go back on Sunday, as I have an exam on Tuesday and need to spend Monday revising.'

'Oh dear, I do hope you're not working too hard.'

'Of course I'm not!' Rebecca laughed. 'It's what I expected. I must get good grades because I want to go on this fast-track course, then by next year I will be a qualified teacher.'

'What's a fast-track course?' her mother asked, frowning.

'It's a special course that condenses three years' work into one.'

'That sounds like even more hard work,' her mother said, shaking her head from side to side as if in disapproval. 'And I thought you wanted to go into politics.'

'I did when I started at university, but I've changed my mind. I mightn't be any good, and I can always take up politics later when I'm too old to be a teacher. This fast-track course is such a good opportunity. I know it means another year at university, but after that I will be working and earning my own living, instead of being a burden on you.'

'You're not a burden,' her father assured her. 'We want you to do well and we're both proud of the way you are working. Now, come on, you must be starving, so let's sit down and eat whatever your mother cooked while I was collecting you.'

As they ate, Rebecca broached the subject that had been worrying her, the malicious gossip in the village.

Normally her mother would have laughed and dismissed the topic but tonight she remained quiet, and as Rebecca looked up from her plate she saw that her father was shaking his head at her, trying to indicate that she should not pursue the matter further.

Taking the hint, Rebecca began telling them about some of the trivial happenings over the past few weeks and how her friend, Grace Flowers, was also planning to be a teacher.

'So does that mean you would both be going on to take the same crash course?' her father asked.

'That's right. One of the Liverpool universities runs a very good one, so we are both aiming for that.'

'Does Grace come from Merseyside or somewhere up that way, then?'

'Yes, she's from Liverpool,' Rebecca told them.

After she had helped her mother wash the dishes, Rebecca said she was tired and ready for bed.

'I am, too.' Her mother stifled a yawn.

'I'll get a good night's sleep tonight knowing you are home and in the next room,' she added with a smile as they kissed goodnight.

When Rebecca woke next morning she said nothing to her mother, but she had already decided she would go out and make a point of meeting Lizzie Smith, who was always to be found in the High Street on a Saturday morning.

Rebecca was convinced that Lizzie did this because there were usually more people about on a Saturday morning than at any other time in the week.

She would start off at the post office and then work her way down the High Street, going into every shop for some small item or other. The more people there were in the shop the happier Lizzie was, and she would forgo her turn time and time again in order to gossip with the people in the queue waiting to be served.

Rebecca carefully timed going out so that she would be in the general store at the same time as Lizzie. She immediately saw the surprise on Lizzie's face, so she smiled sweetly and said in a voice loud enough for everyone to hear, 'Hello, Lizzie, surprised to see me? I understand you've been spreading rumours that I've disappeared.'

For a moment the old woman seemed at a loss for words, then she retaliated sharply. 'Well, you didn't come home for half-term, did you?'

'No, I didn't because I had other things I wanted to do instead.'

'What were they then?' Her eyes narrowed. 'Was you visiting your friend Cindy Mason?'

'No, I wasn't visiting Cindy because I have no idea where she is. Do you?'

'Me!' the old woman's jaw dropped. 'Why would I know where she is?'

'Well, you seemed to have so much to say about it when Cindy disappeared that I thought you must know what had happened to her,' Rebecca retorted.

A dark flush stained the old woman's face. 'If you're referring to what I said about her being fed to the pigs you had up there at Woodside, then say so.'

The people in the store were all now listening with bated breath.

Lizzie leaned on her stick and thrust her wrinkled face towards Rebecca. 'After all, when her clothes were found rolled up and stuffed in a hollow tree and one of her shoes was found in the sty where you kept that great brute you called Moses, then what was one to think?'

'The very worst if they had a mind like yours, Lizzie. It was wicked to spread stories like that. Did you ever stop for a moment to think what damage you were causing to Cindy's family and to mine with such malicious lies?'

'I've heard stories all my life about folks being attacked and eaten by pigs,' Lizzie went on undaunted. ''Tis well known that they will eat anything at all. 'Tis also well known that the herd of pigs your dad kept up at Woodside were vicious beasts. They ruined more than one garden hereabouts, and they savaged one or two people when they tried to drive them off.'

By now a crowd had gathered to listen to their exchanges, and there were many murmurs of agreement and a great many angry mutterings on both sides.

Rebecca felt that airing the matter was good. It might bring to an end the sidelong looks both her family and the Masons were getting as well as bring an end to all the unpleasant insinuations.

The mutterings from the crowd gave way to actual opinions. It was soon clear that very few people had taken much notice of what Lizzie had said, although at the time they had appeared to do so and some had even goaded her into going into detail about what she thought had happened to Cindy.

The more level-headed among them, however, were of the opinion that Cindy had left home because she had a boyfriend that no one knew about, although no one could name him.

They felt sorry for the Masons and most of them thought it was irresponsible of Cindy not to contact them and at least let them know she was alive and well, even if she didn't tell them where she was.

'Waste of police time looking for her like they've done,' one man contended.

'I'm surprised they still haven't traced her, though,' another stated. 'After all, they know precisely the time she vanished and the last place she was seen.'

'True enough, but so many trains pass through Temple Meads station of a day it's like looking for a needle in a haystack. What's more, if she doesn't want to be found then she has only to change her name, dye her hair and go some place where she's not known and that's the end of it.'

They were still talking about it when Rebecca left the shop. She couldn't help wondering whether this would be the end of the matter, or whether she had perhaps stirred it all up again.

She thought about going up to the Masons' farm but wasn't

sure if they would want to see her, not even Jake, so she walked down the road to her parents' butcher's shop and spent the rest of the morning talking to her mother and father in between them attending to customers.

From the number of people who came into the shop and the size of the orders, she was pretty certain the worst of the scandal was over and that the village had settled down again and Cindy's disappearance was no longer the main topic of conversation.

Even so, she couldn't help wondering what had really happened to her friend. Deep down, she felt sure that one day they would meet up again.

Twenty-Three

The exams went well for both Rebecca and Grace. Their hard work had paid off and they both anticipated they would get very good degrees.

Subject to that happening, they knew their plans for being eligible for a fast-track teacher training course were possible and they waited for news in hopeful anticipation.

To some extent they felt free now that the onus of doing well in the exams was over. Their future seemed bright and they decided that celebration and relaxation were in order.

Their first excursion was their delayed trip to Swansea, and they enjoyed it so much that they planned to go there again before the end of their stay in Cardiff.

There were also a great many activities they now had time to participate in, both at the university and in Cardiff itself. The weather was mixed; some days bright and sunny, others showery or even dark and glowering.

They planned their activities accordingly. On fine days they would venture further afield or go on some outdoor project. They explored the Cardiff docks and, although the docks were now completely modernized, they could still find historic traces of when Cardiff was one of the largest ports in Britain, of the days when it was renowned for its exports of coal and visited by some of the biggest liners in the world.

They spent a whole day exploring Cardiff Castle, starting with the medieval castle and keep built on the mound to the rear. Then they toured the modern part, enjoying the historical aspects and the intricate carvings, as well as all the richness of colour and fabrics used in the interior.

They also went to St Fagans, on the outskirts of the city, to visit the Welsh Folk Museum, where they spent the day inspecting the reconstructed dwellings and furnished houses set out in the spacious park. They spent a whole day tracing the life, culture and traditions of the people of Wales dating back to the fifteenth century.

They found it hard to tear themselves away from the museum's costume gallery, where the different styles of dress worn by Welsh women over the past two and a half centuries were on display.

Rebecca reflected wistfully that Cindy would have been intrigued by the agricultural gallery with its farm implements, vehicles and machinery from the earliest days right up to modern times, especially the circular pigsties dating back to earliest days and the water-powered corn mill.

In complete contrast, the next day they visited the Big Pit at Blaenavon, once one of the leading coal mines in Europe but now a museum.

With an ex-miner as their guide, they were able to travel down 300 feet to the coalface in a cage, the same as the miners had once done, and saw the cramped conditions under which men had once worked.

They also visited the Blaenavon ironworks, and Rebecca felt it was like entering a cave as they went in through the rough stone entrance into the mountainside.

She wished she had been able to show all this to Cindy, because the contrast between the soft, rolling landscape of the West Country and the starkness of the mountain scenery and grim surroundings she and Grace were experiencing would have impressed her so much.

They bought each other a lovespoon as a keepsake. The spoons were elaborately carved, with twist handles. They had seen them when they visited St Fagans, both in the museum there and the individually furnished peasant cottages, and had been fascinated by them.

Now, as they exchanged spoons as a mark of their friendship they decided it would be nice to purchase one to take home for their mothers. Finding a different style from the ones they had bought for themselves took them further afield, but eventually they found exactly what they wanted.

Exchanging lovespoons also served to remind Rebecca of Cindy. She felt hot tears well up into her eyes and was tempted to buy another spoon and keep it until they met again, whenever that might be.

When their results finally came through, Rebecca and Grace found they were every bit as good as they'd hoped. They had both earned outstanding degrees.

Together, they waited to see if their applications for the teacher training course in Liverpool were successful. When they heard that they had both been accepted, their joy knew no bounds.

'Does this mean you will be living at home?' Rebecca asked hesitantly.

She enjoyed being with Grace and sharing what was happening in their lives. Although Grace would never take the place of Cindy, no one ever would, she was a tremendous companion and Rebecca knew she would miss her a great deal if they were parted.

'Of course not. We'll share a flat somewhere, the same as we've done here in Cardiff – unless you have other plans,' Grace added cautiously.

'No, if you're quite sure, then I'd like nothing better.'

'Shall I look for somewhere suitable as it's practically on my doorstep? Then you can come up and see if you like it before I sign anything,' Grace suggested.

'That sounds a great idea.'

'I'll get Mum or my brother to take a look as well before I make a decision. They're bound to spot any flaws.'

'That makes good sense. My mum and dad will probably want to see where I'm going to live, too. The three of us could stay overnight in a hotel, then meet up with your family for a meal or something after we've seen the flat.'

'That sounds reasonable.' Grace smiled, her blue eyes twinkled. 'I wonder how they'll get on? They mightn't be able to stand the sight of each other.'

'That's hardly likely and I think it would be great for them to get to know each other – what's more,' Rebecca added, 'you must come for the weekend or a few days and have a taste of rustic life.'

She rather hoped that Grace would refuse or say she would put it off to some other time, but Grace accepted with alacrity,

'That sounds a great idea!'

Rebecca nodded her agreement. She couldn't bring herself to speak. She felt she had done a foolish thing in inviting Grace to Shelston, because now she would have to tell her about Cindy.

Cindy was never far from her mind, no matter where she was or what she did, and several times she had thought of confiding in Grace about her former friend. At the last minute, however, she always stopped herself from doing so because Grace would be bound to ask questions about where Cindy was now.

Although she had vehemently rejected all the malicious gossip about Cindy disappearing with a married man, she supposed it could possibly be true. It was certainly far more likely than the rumour spread by Lizzie Smith suggesting that she had been killed and eaten by their herd of pigs. That really was so highly improbable she was surprised the police had even listened to such nonsense.

Deep down, however, although she still had no idea about what had really happened, Rebecca was sure that Cindy was still alive.

They had been so close ever since they'd been tiny tots that she was sure she would know if Cindy was dead.

She also felt certain that one day they would meet up again, although when or how she had not the slightest idea.

Twenty-Four

The end of term was a time for farewells and promises to keep in touch, although most of the students knew they probably wouldn't meet again except on graduation day or by accident at some time in the future.

Since Rebecca and Grace were going to the same university in the Merseyside area for their year of teacher training, their farewells were fairly perfunctory. They knew they would be meeting again and when that would be.

Both of Rebecca's parents came to the graduation ceremony and so did Grace's mother and father, so the two girls were able to introduce them to each other.

After the ceremony, during which the two girls were presented with their graduation scroll, Bill Peterson insisted that Grace and her parents should join them in a celebratory meal at the Castle Hotel, where they were staying.

Wine helped to ensure a relaxed mood and by the end of the evening they were all on very good terms.

Fred Flowers was a tall rangy man in his mid-fifties with thinning grey hair. He ran a shipping agency in Liverpool. His wife, Doris, was ten years younger, thin and nervy with tightly permed brown hair and large dark eyes.

'When Rebecca comes up to Merseyside, you must come with her for a few days so we can return your hospitality,' Fred Flowers insisted as they parted at the end of the evening.

'We've hired Nick Blakemore for a week, Becky, so me and your mother can spend a few days with you here in Cardiff,' her father told her.

'That's great, I'll really enjoy showing you around.' Rebecca kissed him on the cheek. 'See you in the morning. I'll come and find you at the hotel.'

The next two days were momentous. Rebecca revelled in showing off the city she had grown so familiar with. She also took them to the folk museum at St Fagans. Her father was so intrigued by some of the early agricultural appliances and the circular pigsties that they had a job tearing him away.

Before returning to Cardiff, they spent a couple of hours at Castell Coch, a picturesque small castle dating back to the eleventh century perched on a hillside midway between Cardiff and Pontypridd.

Her parents were so impressed by their visit to Cardiff that they assured her they would come back again some day.

Grace had already returned north with her parents, leaving Rebecca to spend her last few nights alone in their flat before returning the key to the letting agent.

Bill's idea of hiring Nick Blakemore for a week was to give Sandra an opportunity to have some time with Rebecca when she got back to Shelston. As it turned out, though, it was with Nick that Rebecca spent most of her stay.

He accompanied her to two annual shows that were being held in the area and they also did some sightseeing. Sandra was glad to see that they were enjoying themselves.

In no time at all, or so it seemed, it was time for Rebecca to once more pack her belongings and set off for another year at university.

In Merseyside, however, the course was quite different. Part of each term would be spent studying and part would be out teaching in an actual school. The schools would all be in the Merseyside area, but Rebecca and Grace had no idea in advance which they would be allocated to teach at.

The term work was far more intense than it had been at Cardiff, due to the fact that a three-year course was being condensed into one year.

Rebecca and Grace found there was little time for relaxation even at the weekends, although they were free from studies from midday on Saturday until Monday morning.

Since it was much too far from the West Country for Rebecca to go home for weekend breaks, she took to spending them with Grace at her home.

The Flowers made her very welcome, particularly Grace's brother Danny, who Rebecca discovered was a policeman. He was four years older than Grace, tall and good-looking with very black hair and vivid blue eyes. He had a ready smile and an infectious laugh, and he was a great dancer.

'I'm afraid I have two left feet when it comes to dancing,' Rebecca warned him.

He refused to listen but insisted that she must let him take her to the Tower Ballroom in New Brighton and he would bring along one of his friends as a partner for Grace. Rebecca was rather reluctant, but Grace persuaded her it would be a laugh.

By the end of the evening, Rebecca could hardly believe the difference as she found herself circling expertly in Danny's arms. When she danced with his friend Bob, however, it was quite a different story and she was eager to return to her previous partner.

'I think our Danny is falling for you,' Grace laughed at the end of the evening. 'He danced almost every dance with you.'

'Or else he was being kind because he could see I wasn't finding dancing with his friend very easy,' Rebecca said.

They both found that these weekend breaks fortified them for the strenuous studying during the week ahead and they were both greatly relieved when it was time to do some actual teaching.

'It will be like having a holiday after the way we've been working all term,' Grace commented.

'It very much depends on the sort of school we get sent to,' Rebecca pointed out.

'They can't expect us to work any harder than we have been.'

'I'm not sure about that, I don't think we'll find it easy. Depends on what sort of class we are given. They may all be little horrors and hard to control.'

'Rubbish!' Grace told her. 'Show them right from the start who's in charge and they'll behave.'

'But how do you do that? I've never had very much to do with young children.'

'They won't be very young children. We're being trained for secondary-school standard. Some of them won't be much younger than we are,' Grace said confidently. 'Anyway, we can always exchange ideas during the recreation periods or at lunch time and change our tactics if necessary.'

On the first point she was right. Both of them were given classes of fifteen-year-olds, so they could at least relate to them. On the second, she was wrong; they were not sent to the same school. They were not even sent to schools in the same area.

Grace was sent to a secondary school in Toxteth and Rebecca to one in Hoylake.

'Where on earth is Hoylake?' she asked Grace in despair. 'I've heard of it because of the famous golf course there, but I've searched the Liverpool map from top to bottom and I can't find it.'

'That's because it isn't in Liverpool, it's on the Wirral. That's the posh part on the other side of the Mersey. Danny took us over there to the Tower Ballroom in New Brighton. Remember?'

'Of course I do. We went across the Mersey on a ferry. Will I have to do that?'

'You could go over on the ferry, or you can take the train. I think there is one that goes direct from Liverpool Central, but you might have to change at Birkenhead.'

'I'm going to have to get up in the middle of the night to make a journey like that and be there by nine o'clock!' Rebecca moaned.

'No, not really. There are trains are every ten minutes, so it will only take you about half an hour. It will probably take me almost as long to get to Toxteth.'

Rebecca decided that since it was in a 'posh' area she would play safe and look smart. On her first day she wore a tailored navy suit teamed with a plain cream blouse. She used light foundation cream and a pale-pink lipstick. She was anxious to impress and hoped her honey-coloured hair didn't make her look too young and frivolous.

Grace decided that dark slacks and a T-shirt were more in keeping with the type of school she had been assigned to in Toxteth.

'They're probably all little hooligans or tearaways,' she explained. 'It's an area where a few months back they had riots,'

'Oh heavens! Are you scared?'

Grace shrugged. 'Someone has to teach them, I suppose. They're probably as bright, or even brighter, than the children you'll have in your class.'

'Well, that's something we both have to find out,' Rebecca said thoughtfully.

'True! See you tonight if we both survive, then we'll swop sordid stories.' Grace grinned as they set out in opposite directions, both of them feeling rather apprehensive about their coming encounters.

Twenty-Five

Rebecca felt very nervous as she set off for her first day of teaching. The journey was much simpler than she had anticipated, which helped boost her confidence, but as she approached the red-brick school building her heart was in her mouth.

The thought of standing up in front of a class of thirty children and holding their attention for a whole half hour was daunting. She knew her subject well enough, but what if her memory let her down or she found her voice was croaky? Or she dropped things and made a fool of herself?

Addressing a class of her peers, as she had done a great many times recently during her training, had been demanding but not nearly as scary as tackling a class of fifteen-year-olds.

Meeting the headmistress was the first ordeal, but she found Mrs Rankin, a middle-aged woman with grey hair and spectacles, far less forbidding that she had expected.

Somewhat reassured, she faced the next challenge: meeting the class she would be teaching with some degree of confidence.

They were a mixed class of boys and girls, all clean and neatly dressed, and they seemed to be as curious about her as she was about them.

By the time the lunch break came and she joined her fellow teachers for their midday meal, she felt far happier than she had at nine o'clock that morning.

The rest of her day was reasonably satisfying. She had one slight tiff with a boy of fourteen, who was bored by her lesson and inattentive. When she asked him a question during the course of the lesson, he'd said with a cheeky grin, 'What's the matter, Miss? Don't you know? Do you want me to take the class for you?'

Unsure of how to handle the situation, Rebecca ignored him and moved on to someone else, but she made a mental note to deal with him after the lesson was over.

Sensing this might happen, the boy made sure that the minute the lesson ended he absented himself from the classroom.

When she recounted this episode to Grace that evening, her friend merely smiled. 'You've been lucky, you should have had a taste of the class I've been given! They were absolute little horrors.'

As the week passed, Rebecca could see that she had been very lucky. The children she'd come into contact with were clean, bright and polite with very few exceptions. Grace, on the other hand, had been given a taste of teaching in a very poor run-down area, with a class of tough worldly-wise children.

It made Rebecca wonder what sort of class she would get next time, and whether she would be able to deal with them as efficiently as Grace appeared to be doing.

On her last day at the school in Hoylake, Rebecca finished early and as it was a nice bright day she decided that instead of going straight back to Liverpool she would spend an hour or so looking around the rest of Hoylake.

Danny had taken them to New Brighton, which was situated at the other corner of the Wirral peninsular and had a jolly seaside atmosphere. Hoylake was quite different and far more sedate.

She had heard a great deal from the pupils about Red Rocks, which seemed to be a favourite place for sea and sand and the ideal spot for flying kites.

After making several enquiries from local people, she located it and found that it was at the end of a quiet tree-lined road. The vista was breathtaking and she sat down on one of the great jutting red rocks to admire the view, the flocks of sea birds and the unbroken silence. Across the sand and sea and on the other side of the River Dee she could see the outline of mountains and the coast of Wales.

Her thoughts went back to the wide expanse of green fields

to be seen from certain points in Shelston, and for the first time since she arrived in Liverpool she felt homesick.

Life there had been so quiet and ordered, and she had known everyone and had been on friendly terms with everybody when she had been growing up. Cindy's disappearance had brought that to an end. It had caused such a furore that now that was what generally came into her mind when she thought of home.

Bringing her thoughts back to the present, she watched as the tide went out exposing a great expanse of sand. In the distance she could see the arrival of an enormous flock of seabirds.

Feeling hungry, she returned to the village centre and went into a small cosy-looking café, where she ordered a light lunch of scrambled eggs and salad.

After that, she decided that before catching a train back to Liverpool she would explore the rest of the village high street, where there were all sorts of independent shops and boutiques. She found most of them fascinating and resolved to suggest to Grace that they come over one Saturday for a longer look at them.

As she was hurrying towards the train station, she caught sight of a young woman wearing a bright-red jacket and found herself staring because the woman reminded her so much of Cindy.

Suddenly Rebecca felt a shiver go through her, as she continued to stare at the slim figure hurrying along in front of her.

It wasn't her imagination, there really was something familiar about the woman and from what she could see of the woman's face she was sure it was Cindy.

'What utter rubbish!' she told herself. 'What on earth would Cindy be doing in a place like Hoylake? I've spent too long sitting watching the waves at Red Rocks and reminiscing about home in the uncanny silence there and it has turned my mind.'

She stared again at the woman in the bright-red jacket as she followed her down the street. The woman seemed to sense she was being watched and turned to look to see who it was.

In that brief moment Rebecca was able to see her face even more clearly. Their eyes met for only a second before the woman hastily looked away.

Before Rebecca could call out to her, the woman had disappeared. Rebecca increased her pace until she was running in an attempt to see where she had gone. The woman had turned off the main street and vanished up a quiet road behind the shops.

Rebecca knew it was pointless trying to follow her. She was shaking as she went into the nearest café and ordered a strong black coffee to try to steady her nerves.

As she looked down into the dark liquid, she saw again the eyes of the woman as she had stared back over her shoulder at her and she was convinced there had been a spark of recognition in them. She was sure the woman had recognized who she was, just as she had known that the woman was Cindy.

So why hadn't she stopped to talk? What was she doing living in Hoylake?

The questions buzzed round and round in Rebecca's head, like trapped bluebottles, all the way back to Liverpool.

She wasn't sure whether to take Grace into her confidence or not. If she did, then it meant telling her all about the vile accusations that had been levelled at her and her family when Cindy had gone missing.

So far she had kept that part of her life a secret, and she wasn't sure whether she wanted to share it now or not.

Perhaps, she thought, it would be better to make another visit to Hoylake on her own and see if she could find the woman again. Her bright-red jacket was so distinctive that possibly someone might know from her description who she was if she asked about her in some of the shops.

What should she tell them if they asked her why she was trying to locate this woman? It was something she needed to think about, but for the moment she decided to keep the matter to herself.

Twenty-Six

For the rest of her first term teaching in Hoylake, Rebecca found herself scanning the road every time she went into the High Street, hoping that she might see the tall, slim young woman in the bright-red jacket again and find a chance to speak to her. She even made discreet enquiries, but most people looked at her blankly as if they didn't know who she was talking about.

Once or twice she considered mentioning it to Grace's brother Danny. As a policeman he would probably know how to go about tracing the woman, but she thought he would want to know why she was so anxious to talk to her. Also, he might discuss it with his fellow officers.

She wasn't sure what to do, so in the end she did nothing. She still kept watching out for her, however, because she was convinced it was Cindy.

When she went home to Shelston at Christmas, she was dismayed to find that the feud between the Masons and her own family had still not abated.

'We've no idea if there has been any news of her or not,' her mother told her with a deep sigh when she asked about Cindy. 'I often think about her and wonder what really did happen to her. Your dad refuses to discuss the matter. I think he would like to stop selling the Masons' produce, but to be honest we can't afford to do that and I don't think they could afford for us to do so either. Jake brings their stuff down early on a Friday morning and they send in a bill for it at the end of each month. We pay by return of post and that's the extent of our communicating.'

'What about if you see Mavis out, or Dad meets up with Tom in the pub?'

'I rarely see anything of Mavis. As far as I know she still shops at the new supermarket, and for things I can't buy locally I still go into one of the nearby towns like I've always done. It suits us both.'

'What about Dad and Tom Mason?' Rebecca repeated.

'They go to different pubs. Your dad still goes to the Red Lion because he and Jack Smart have been friends for years, and I believe Tom Mason goes to the White Hart because Harry Shepherd, the landlord there, is his cousin. It works well for both of them.'

Rebecca was tempted to mention to her mother about the girl she had seen in Hoylake but she was sure her mother would only think she was being fanciful so she said nothing.

They were extremely busy in the shop in the days leading up to Christmas. For the festive spread, most families bought turkeys or capons or joints of beef or ham.

'We've had fewer orders than usual this year,' Bill commented as they closed up late on Christmas Eve. 'I suppose we have that damn supermarket to thank for that.'

'There's not as much money about anywhere this year as there was last year,' Sandra pointed out.

'Either that or Tom Mason is going behind our back and supplying people direct.'

'No, I don't think he would do that,' Sandra assured him. 'He would know that it would get back to us, and he would have lost his market for their butter and cheese as well as their poultry and he couldn't afford that.'

Although her father nodded in agreement Rebecca could see he wasn't wholly convinced, and not for the first time she wished she could find out exactly what had happened to Cindy and set all their minds at rest. It would be such a relief to bring an end to all the ill-feeling there was between their two families and to scotch the malicious gossip that still went on in the village.

On Christmas Day they had a surprise visitor. To Rebecca's delight, Nick Blakemore turned up mid-morning with gifts and wine.

'Well, this is an unexpected surprise,' Rebecca smiled.

'I didn't tell you I would be popping in because I've been working as a relief manager at a shop in Bristol and I wasn't sure if I would be able to get here.'

'Busy night, last-minute rush of customers was it?' Bill laughed.

'Very much so. I didn't finish until half past eleven last night. But I managed to catch a very early train this morning, so here I am.'

'You kept that very quiet,' Rebecca commented as she went through into the kitchen to help her mother prepare their meal.

'Not really,' her mother told her. 'I asked him weeks ago, but I didn't say anything because he wasn't sure if he would be able to manage it.'

It certainly made Christmas special for Rebecca. More than once she found herself comparing Nick and Danny Flowers. They were so completely different not only in looks and colouring but in character as well, and at this moment Nick was far more to her liking.

She felt much more at ease with Nick than with Danny. Perhaps it was because Danny was a policeman and whenever they were together she felt he was on duty, mentally if not physically. With Nick, she felt she could relax and was far more comfortable and at ease.

Overnight they had a light fall of snow, and on Boxing Day she took Nick for a long walk to show him how lovely Shelston looked with its pristine white covering.

As they returned through the woods at the back of Woodside, it was Nick who brought up the subject of Cindy.

'Even the tree where we found your friend's clothes looks less sinister with its covering of snow,' he commented.

'Did you ever find out what had happened to her?' he went on when Rebecca remained silent.

'No, not really.' She hesitated for a moment, then began to tell him about the young woman in the red jacket she had seen in Hoylake.

He remained silent when she'd finished and, giving him a sideways glance, she noted the deep frown on his face.

'You think I'm mad, don't you?' she said with a small self-deprecating laugh.

'No, not at all. But I am a little worried though because obviously you are still very concerned about her.'

'You think I imagined it was Cindy?'

'Perhaps you were thinking about her and it was a sort of thought transference? You saw this girl, about the same age as Cindy, and because she was wearing a bright-red jacket you immediately thought it was Cindy.'

'No, it wasn't only that. It was the look of recognition in her eyes as they met mine.'

'Are you quite sure that was what it was? It might have been surprise or unease because you were staring at her so hard.'

'Then why did she rush off and disappear as if she was afraid I was going to speak to her?'

'She probably was afraid. After all, if you were a complete stranger, she might well have been scared of you.'

'I could understand that if it had been a man following her.'

'I don't know about that, but . . .'

'Ssh!' Rebecca put her finger to her lips. They were approaching her home and she saw that her father was collecting logs from the shed in the garden to take indoors. She didn't want to talk about Cindy in front of either of her parents.

Nick seemed to understand immediately. He said no more and hurried over to the shed to help Bill Peterson to carry in the logs.

Next morning Rebecca tried to have a moment alone with Nick before he left for Bristol, where he would be working over the New Year.

'Perhaps we'll have a chance to see each other at Easter if you are coming home for the holiday break this year?' he said as they said goodbye.

'I think I might be doing that,' she smiled.

'You'll be able to bring me up to speed about Hoylake then,' he murmured quietly as he kissed her on the cheek and they wished each other well.

Twenty-Seven

When she went back to Liverpool after the Christmas break, Rebecca found herself caught up with her studies and kept so busy that she did not have time for anything else.

Her next teaching assignment was with an inner-city school, which proved to be very different from the one she had been sent to before in Hoylake.

The Liverpool school was mixed in every respect. On her first day the headmaster, Jeffrey Wilson, handed her a sheet of paper on which was printed a head-and-shoulders photograph of every child in the class she would be teaching with the name of the child below it.

The class consisted of so many different nationalities that Rebecca looked at it with dismay. The only thing they seemed to have in common was that they were all about fourteen years of age.

'They're all such individual characters that I'm sure you will soon be able to tell them apart,' the headmaster told her curtly. 'If you have difficulty pronouncing any of their names, ask one of the staff to help you.'

It was certainly hard work teaching them. Some of them were exceptionally bright and grew impatient when she repeatedly had to stop to explain things to the ones who were slower.

There were also a few who appeared to be so uninterested that she found it difficult to hold their attention.

When she mentioned this to Grace, she admitted she'd had the same problem.

'So what did you do?'

'In the end I simply ignored the ones who didn't want to learn.'

'I don't think it's right to do that. After all, that's what teaching is about, isn't it? We're supposed to be helping them understand things they don't know but which they ought to know.'

'But it's not right to bore the more intelligent ones or those who are keen to acquire knowledge just because of a few who aren't.'

'Are you still ignoring the ones who don't want to learn?' Rebecca asked.

'No, thank goodness, I don't need to in the school I'm at this term,' Grace said smugly. 'At the school I'm teaching at in Wallasey they're all average to bright, so I don't have any problems when it comes to holding their attention. They're much better behaved in every way than the children were at my last school.'

'In fact our positions have been reversed,' Rebecca sighed. 'I had an easy class last term and you've got one this time.'

'Makes you think we'll have to be very careful when we're applying for jobs after we've qualified and make sure we don't end up in the wrong sort of school.'

By the end of each day, Rebecca found she was so completely

exhausted that it was hard work preparing material for lessons the following day. There was certainly no time to think of anything else of a personal nature, not even about Cindy.

It was almost as if by confiding in Nick Blakemore about the young woman in the red jacket she'd seen in Hoylake that she had cleared all the memories of Cindy from her mind.

On the one or two occasions when she did think about her, she decided that the girl had probably taken fright because she had stared at her so hard, and that was why she had scooted out of sight so quickly.

She was glad she hadn't told Danny Flowers about her, or mentioned her suspicions to him.

Danny was still very keen on taking her out, she reflected, but she was hesitant and usually made some excuse not to go.

She had gone to the pictures with him one weekend and to a dance at the Tower Ballroom in New Brighton. But she had only done so because Grace was keen on his friend, a fellow police officer called Bob King, and begged her to make up a foursome.

When she went home at Easter, Rebecca was disappointed to find Nick Blakemore wouldn't be coming to visit them over the holidays.

'He's working in Bath and they want him for two weeks so the owner and his wife can go away on holiday,' her mother explained. 'We're seriously thinking of doing the same thing later on, as we haven't been away for years.'

'That's because Dad would never close the shop and there was never anybody he felt could run it except him.'

'I know, but it's different now we can rely on Nick. Your Dad is quite happy to leave him in charge.'

'So what's stopping you?'

'Nothing at all really. We'll have to make up our minds soon because Nick is getting so booked up that he won't be able to fit us in.'

'I thought he would have found himself a permanent job by now,' Rebecca commented thoughtfully.

'Well, I think he regards what he is doing as a permanent

arrangement. He seems to be fully booked up and, as he says, he likes the variety of working in different places.'

'I meant start his own business.'

'Well, he probably will one day when he settles down. At the moment, as I've just said, he likes freelancing as a relief manager because it gives him an opportunity to move around and see so many different places.'

'Has he got a girlfriend?' Rebecca felt hot blood flooding her cheeks and avoided her mother's eyes as she asked the question.

'Not as far as I know. He's never mentioned one. In fact he's always joked about the fact that he's fancy-free and has no family ties of any kind, so will eventually be able to settle down wherever he wishes.'

Rebecca quickly began talking about something else, but her heart beat just that little bit faster.

'So when are you thinking of taking this holiday?' she repeated in what she hoped was a nonchalant way.

Her mind was already working overtime, wondering if she could manage to get home for a couple of days while her parents were away. It would be a wonderful opportunity to have Nick all to herself when he had finished working in the shop for the day.

'That's the problem,' her mother said rather tetchily. 'As I keep telling you, I can't pin your father down to any sort of date.'

'Why not? You say he is quite confident about Nick Blakemore's ability to run things on his own.'

'He seems to think we ought to wait until you've finished at university and you have a job.'

'Whatever difference does that make?'

'Well, your dad thinks we shouldn't spend money on a holiday until we know where you will be working'

'Why ever not?' Rebecca asked in astonishment.

'He says we ought to wait until we know that you are settled in a flat or a small house or something.'

Rebecca frowned. 'I don't understand?'

'Well, we may be needing the money for that.'

'In that case I think you should persuade him to take you on holiday as soon as possible, even if it is only for a week,'

Rebecca said, smiling. 'After all, I might be living at home if I can get a posting to a school nearby.'

'I've already put forward that argument,' her mother said, shaking her head dolefully. 'He said if that happens then we'll need the money to buy you a car because the buses around here are so infrequent. He's quite right, of course, and I can understand what he means but I do so want a holiday.'

'Shall I have a word with him?'

Sandra's face brightened. 'Well, I suppose there is just a chance that he might listen to you, though I doubt it. All the same, it might be worth giving it a try.'

Twenty-Eight

It was one of the hottest days of the year, baking hot even for early July. It had been exceptionally warm all week, but today it was overpowering and Rebecca felt so exhausted she was relieved it was Friday.

There were less than two weeks to the end of her course and she couldn't wait to finish and get away from the classrooms and lecture rooms and be out in the fresh air. She longed for the countryside and the sweeping open vista of Shelston.

She had been planning a trip across to New Brighton with Grace when classes ended, but Grace had skipped the afternoon session and gone to bed with a migraine.

New Brighton didn't appeal to her on her own and it would be packed with noisy day-trippers, but she was desperate for fresh air. Then on the spur of the moment she suddenly thought of Red Rocks. There the view out over the Dee towards Wales was almost as reviving as the view across the Blackmore Vale at home.

It seemed unfair to leave Grace on her own when she wasn't feeling well, Rebecca thought rather guiltily as she changed into a thin cotton dress. But there was nothing she could do for her and, after all, they weren't joined at the hip.

She made a pot of tea and took a cup up to Grace before she

left, with the intention of telling her she was going out. But she found Grace asleep, so she left the tea on the bedside table and crept out as quietly as she could.

The train from Liverpool Central was packed and airless, which made the expanse of sandy shore and lapping water all the more inviting when she reached Red Rocks. It was unusually crowded, mostly mothers with children, but she managed to find a secluded spot.

There was a pleasant breeze, clean and refreshing, coming off the water. She settled back against a sand dune and watched the activities going on along the sandy stretch between her and the water's edge. The lapping waves of the incoming tide looked so cool and inviting that she wished she had brought a towel so she could paddle.

She would have stayed there longer, but she remembered that they were out of bread and milk and Grace had asked her to get some. As she scrambled to her feet and made her way to Hoylake village, she wondered if she would find any shops open that late in the afternoon.

Hurrying down the main street, she remembered there was a supermarket and guessed they would keep open late.

Inside the store she found the milk and then rummaged among the bread still left on the shelf for the kind they liked.

As she stood waiting to pay for her purchases, she saw a tall, slim figure in a startling jazzy dress of orange covered with swirls of red, black and white ahead of her at another till at the checkout.

Rebecca smiled to herself, remembering how she had once ordered the very same dress from a catalogue and how grotesque it had looked on her although it had looked so glamorous in the book. She wondered how many other people had been caught out in the same way. Cindy had thought it gorgeous and it had certainly gone well with her colouring, so she had swapped it with Cindy for a pale-green one.

She stared anew at the girl, who had now been served and was already through the checkout. She was loaded down with numerous bags of shopping and as Rebecca walked through the checkout the girl was struggling to carry them out of the shop.

'Here, let me help you.'

Before the girl could protest, Rebecca had picked up one of the heavy bags.

'No, it's all right, I can manage . . .' The girl looked up as she spoke, and then froze as her eyes met those of Rebecca.

'It is you, Cindy, isn't it?' Rebecca gasped in a low voice. 'Come on, let me help you with this lot. We're in everybody's way here and we can talk as we walk.'

Not waiting for Cindy to answer, she went on ahead with the bag she had picked up and started to walk down the High Street in the direction she'd seen her go before.

Cindy followed, but no matter how often Rebecca slowed down Cindy still remained several paces behind her.

'Come on, catch up so we can talk.' She stopped walking and waited for Cindy.

Cindy hesitated and shook her head. 'I've been told not to talk to people. They've forbidden me to talk to people when I'm out,' she said in a scared voice.

'They? Who do you mean? Who are these people?'

'The family I live with. If any of them saw me talking to you, they would punish me.' There was such fear in her voice that Rebecca felt a shiver of apprehension.

'Are you some sort of prisoner?' she asked, frowning.

Cindy hesitated and then admitted in a pathetic voice, 'Yes, I suppose I am.'

'Well, there's no one else about at the moment, so tell me what's happened to you and why you're living here and why you mustn't be seen talking to me.'

Cindy looked over her shoulder nervously. 'I can't, Rebecca, someone might see us together. Let me have my shopping. I must get back before they come looking for me.'

'Then tell me when and where we can meet again. Make it somewhere where we can talk, so you can tell me what happened that day when you were supposed to be coming to Cardiff and you simply vanished.'

Cindy stared back at her wide-eyed. 'That was so long ago, it was another life,' she said in a small wistful voice.

'Becky, I've missed you so much,' she sniffled, her dark eyes filling with tears. She stretched out a hand and grasped Rebecca's arm. 'Is it really you, or am I going mad and imagining things?'

Twenty-Nine

Two days later, Rebecca met Cindy at Red Rocks. It was an overcast day and the place was almost deserted.

They found a secluded spot where they were sheltered from the light wind, with a view of the River Dee and the Welsh coast beyond.

Rebecca unpacked two glasses and a bottle of red wine from the carrier bag she'd brought with her and set them down on a shelf of rock. She poured out the wine and handed a glass to Cindy.

They sat in silence for a moment, as if neither knew quite what to say. Rebecca finally raised her glass towards Cindy, took a sip, and then asked, 'So what happened that Friday afternoon when you were supposed to be coming to Cardiff?'

Cindy suppressed a shiver and took a gulp of wine. 'I think I should start before then. You need to know what happened after you left Shelston to go to university.'

'The day I left for university, you were going for a trial on one of the checkout tills at the supermarket. Start from there,' Rebecca told her.

'That's right!' Cindy giggled. 'You were with me when I asked Bruno for a job, weren't you?'

'Bullied him into giving you a trial, you mean,' Rebecca responded, her eyes twinkling.

'Yes, I suppose I did,' Cindy admitted. 'Well, he gave me a job and I started working on the till the following week. I enjoyed it and proved I could do the job easily. I got to know Bruno better and we started dating.'

'You mean you went out with Bruno Lopez? The manager?'

'That's right. After a couple of months he promoted me to Staff Manageress. Some of the others didn't like it, and claimed it was favouritism because I was going out with Bruno.'

'I bet they did!' Rebecca gasped, staring at Cindy in disbelief. 'Quick work, wasn't it?' she added with a laugh.

'Well, yes . . .' Cindy took another drink of her wine and stared at Rebecca defiantly.

'Was he the married man you were supposed to have run away with?'

'To make matters worse,' Cindy went on, ignoring Rebecca's question, 'a few months later he promoted me to Assistant Manager of the whole shop.'

Rebecca's eyes widened. 'That's unbelievable in such a short time. You must have been the latest one to be employed there and yet you were getting promoted over everyone else's head.'

Cindy nodded. 'The trouble is that when everything seems too good to be true it usually is.'

'What do you mean?'

'The company became suspicious of such a quick promotion. I think there were also complaints from some of the members of staff who were jealous.'

'I can well believe that,' Rebecca said dryly as she refilled their glasses. 'So what happened next?'

'They sacked Bruno.'

'Oh, heavens! What about you?'

'No one said a word to me. But Bruno just vanished overnight. No one knew where he had gone, whether he was still with the company, or what had happened to him. A middle-aged Scottish man was sent in as a temporary manager. My promotion was never mentioned and I found myself back on the checkout, where I started.'

'Didn't you question it?'

'How could I? It had all happened so fast. I had nothing in writing to say I had been promoted, only Bruno's word. Now that he'd gone it didn't count for anything.'

'How humiliating!'

Cindy nodded, took a long swig of her drink and then said, 'That wasn't my worst problem though.'

Rebecca frowned. 'What do you mean?'

'I had no idea what had happened to Bruno or where he had gone. And no one, not even the relief manager, seemed to know either.'

'Did that matter?'

'Very much so! I was pregnant.'

'Pregnant! You mean with Bruno's baby?'

Cindy nodded.

'Oh, Cindy! What did you do?'

Cindy picked up some pieces of loose shale and slid them from one hand to the other. Then she dropped them on the ground and brushed her hands together. 'I phoned the top man of the supermarket chain and told him my plight and asked him for Bruno's new address. He said he couldn't help me but thought it was better if I left the company and gave me a week's notice.'

'Cindy!' Rebecca looked utterly shocked. 'That's illegal, they couldn't do that. Didn't you kick up a fuss?'

Cindy shook her head. 'I didn't know that, I thought they could. I hadn't signed a contract or anything when Bruno gave me the job.'

'Why on earth didn't you tell me all this at the time?' Rebecca demanded. 'Cindy, I found your clothes in the woods. I was terrified for you.'

Cindy looked crestfallen. 'I left them there one day when I was going on a date with Bruno. I couldn't let my parents know I was dating him, so I snuck out there after visiting the pigs and swapped clothes.'

'Oh Cindy, you should have told me all this! We always shared our problems and between us we always managed to find the right solution.'

'How could I? You weren't around. You were all wrapped up in your life in Cardiff.'

'Now you're making me feel guilty,' Rebecca groaned.

'There was probably nothing you could have done, except to have appeared shocked,' Cindy told her dryly. 'Anyway, the big white chief obviously did know Bruno's address and I learned much later that he had told Bruno of my predicament. But of course I wasn't aware of that at the time.'

'Oh, Cindy. What a drama!'

'It was the same time you asked me to Cardiff for the weekend, and I thought that was a great idea because it would get me away from Shelston for a few days while all the gossip circulated. I hoped, too, that I'd have an opportunity to tell you about what had happened and it would give me a chance to sort things out in my head and decide what to do about the future.'

'So why didn't you come to Cardiff?'

Cindy let out a long sigh. 'That's another story.'

'Go on, tell me what happened,' Rebecca insisted. 'I need to know. Why did you leave me in the dark worrying my head off about what could have possibly happened to you when you didn't turn up?'

'I'm sorry about that. I simply wasn't thinking clearly.'

'My family as well as yours were beside themselves with worry. Even to this day there is a rift between them and they don't speak to each other. There were some terrible stories going round – one of them was that you had run away with my dad! Lizzie Smith was even telling people we had killed you and fed you to the pigs, and heaven knows what.'

'Oh, I am sorry!' Cindy held her hands to her face in dismay.

'It caused such a rift between our families that even now they are not reconciled and barely speak to each other.'

As Rebecca saw the tears well up in Cindy's eyes, she stopped berating her. 'Never mind about that, tell me what happened afterwards.'

Cindy looked at her in silence.

'Come on, I still need to know why you didn't come to Cardiff that Friday afternoon. Jake insists he took you to Frome station and you knew exactly the time of your train and so on, so why didn't you turn up?'

Cindy drained her glass and held it out for a refill. 'That's a very long story,' she said quietly.

'That's all right. I have plenty of time.'

'You might have, but I haven't.' She stood up. 'I must run. They'll be wondering where I am and there'll be trouble.'

'You can't go until I've heard the rest of what happened,' Rebecca told her, grabbing hold of her arm.

'Please, Becky, I must!' She sounded so anxious that Rebecca let go of her arm.

'Then when can we meet again?' she asked as she collected up her own things ready to walk back to the High Street with Cindy.

'I'm not too sure. Soon, I promise you. Don't desert me now, Becky, because I really do need your help.'

Before Rebecca could say any more, Cindy was running over the rocks towards the road. She was tempted to follow but thought that perhaps it was better not to do so. Someone, somewhere, was frightening Cindy, there was no doubt about that. She suspected it was Bruno, but couldn't understand how he had such a hold over Cindy that she was scared of what might happen if she disobeyed.

'Cindy, meet me here again tomorrow at the same time,' she called after the fleeing figure.

Cindy hesitated. 'Very well, but not here. I'll see you in the High Street,' she called back over her shoulder.

Thirty

Rebecca felt more confused than ever after Cindy had gone. She reproached herself for not following her instincts earlier, from the first time she saw her she had been sure it was Cindy.

It certainly seemed that she was some sort of prisoner. As she made her way to the station to catch a train back to Liverpool, she wondered once again if she ought to tell Danny Flowers and ask him what she ought to do. But some inner sense warned her that this could be dangerous for Cindy. She must wait until she had seen Cindy again and heard more of her story.

Thank heavens it would be Saturday tomorrow and there were no lectures, so there would be no problem about meeting Cindy at half past ten. She had to get to the bottom of this. Cindy was obviously in deep trouble.

She must help her, but until she found out why Bruno was treating Cindy this way and who else was involved it was best to do nothing.

It was a hot, sticky night and Rebecca slept badly. She tossed and turned for hours, then towards morning fell into a deep sleep.

She was sleeping so soundly she didn't even hear the alarm clock, and when she finally woke with a start it was to find that it was after nine o'clock. It meant she was going to have to skip breakfast if she was to get to Hoylake in time for her assignment with Cindy.

Although it was a tremendous rush, she found time to pick out a pretty pale-blue cotton dress and a bright-red lipstick and pop them into a carrier bag to take along with her.

As she hurried down the main street, she spotted Cindy waiting near the supermarket. She had intended to see if she could persuade Cindy to change her mind about going to Red Rocks because it would be so lovely and cool there, but she was so hungry she decided it would be best if they went into one of the many small cafés in the High Street.

'Sorry I'm late,' she said a little breathlessly.

'I was worried,' Cindy told her. 'I was afraid someone might see me hanging about here.'

'I know,' Rebecca gave her an understanding look.

'I mustn't be out too long. I have some shopping to do.'

'I thought we could go to one of the cafés for a coffee,' Rebecca suggested.

Cindy smiled with delight, then her eyes clouded and she shook her head. 'I would like to do that, but I am so afraid someone will see me.'

'I've thought of that.' Rebecca held out the bag. 'I've brought you a dress. There are some public toilets a few yards down the road. Go in there and get changed, and put the one you're wearing now into the carrier bag out of sight. Meet me at the Bluebell Café. It's just a couple of yards further down the road.'

For a moment Cindy stared at her in silence. Then her hand shot out and she almost snatched the carrier bag from Rebecca's hand.

Rebecca gave her a couple of minutes start, then walked leisurely towards the Bluebell Café.

She went inside and ordered coffee and toasted teacakes for both of them, then found a table near the window where she could watch out for Cindy.

The slim young girl in a cool pale-blue cotton dress, her dark hair flowing loosely on her shoulders, looked so different from the girl in the jazzy red dress with her hair scraped back in a ponytail that even Rebecca was surprised by the transformation. It was as if she had her old friend back at last.

'This feels wonderful,' Cindy murmured as she slipped into the chair opposite Rebecca. She smiled as she looked across at her. 'I feel like I'm in a dream. Remember how we used to swap clothes when we were both living in Shelston?'

'Of course I do. Now, relax. I want to know what has been happening to you. The whole story, Cindy,' she added severely.

The arrival of the waitress with their order gave Cindy a moment's reprieve, but as soon as the waitress moved away Rebecca demanded, 'Come on!'

Cindy picked up her cup of coffee and although it was very hot took a mouthful as if gasping for a drink.

'You said you were being kept prisoner. What did you mean?' Rebecca persisted.

'I am.' Cindy's voice was bitter and unhappy. 'I am their slave. I have to be up at six each morning to make all the breakfasts, then I have to clean the house, cook the midday meal, do the shopping and prepare a meal again in the evening, then clear up and wash up before I go to bed. All the time the old woman grumbles. She hates me. She accuses me of slovenliness, of not doing things her way.'

Tears were now trickling down Cindy's cheeks, but she brushed them away with the back of her hand.

Rebecca opened her handbag and brought out a pack of tissues, took one out and passed it over to her. Cindy took it and dabbed her wet cheeks.

'I'm sorry,' she snuffled. 'I have never spoken of this to anyone and now it's too much for me.'

'Why do you stay there, then?' Rebecca asked in a bewildered voice.

Questions were tumbling from Rebecca's lips like leaves off a tree in autumn, she was so anxious to get to the bottom of the mystery concerning Cindy's disappearance.

'Because of the baby!'

'What baby?' Rebecca looked at her in bewilderment, then she gasped, 'Oh Cindy, not yours?'

'Of course it's mine. I told you that was why I was so anxious to find Bruno. I was pregnant. I didn't know what to do, Becky. I didn't dare tell my mother and you weren't around, so I had no one to confide in, no one to ask for advice.'

'You knew where I was, you could have phoned me.'

'No, as far as I was concerned you were in another world leading a different life. You wouldn't have understood.'

'You never gave me the chance.'

'I was going to. I was going to tell you all about it when we met in Cardiff.'

'But you never came to Cardiff! You simply vanished. You ran away with Bruno,' Rebecca said accusingly.

'In a way I did, but not the way you're thinking it happened.'

'Go on then, tell me what did happen.'

Cindy hesitated, took a long drink of her coffee. 'All right,' she said in a flat voice, 'but hear me out.'

Rebecca nodded. 'I'll order two more coffees first and then I want to hear your story. All of it.'

Thirty-One

'Come on, Cindy, you promised!' Rebecca said the minute the waitress had placed fresh coffees in front of them.

'I didn't run away that Friday when I was supposed to be coming to see you in Cardiff. I was accosted on the station then bundled into a car and brought up here to Merseyside.'

'By complete strangers?' Rebecca knew she sounded horrified. She couldn't believe what she was hearing.

'Couldn't you have screamed or fought them off? Or called out for help?'

Cindy gave a sigh that was almost a cry of anguish.

'It all happened so quickly. As I went up on to the platform a man came up to me and said that Bruno was outside and wanted to speak to me.'

'The man who'd been manager at the supermarket in Shelston, the chap you were trying so hard to contact?'

'That's right. I was mystified but I went with him. We went down some steps to a back entrance and at the bottom this man suddenly grabbed me by the arm and shoved me into the back of a car. The car engine was already running and we roared off before I could do or say anything.'

'Was the driver Bruno?'

'No, of course he wasn't. He was involved, though. His real name is something quite different. They drove non-stop up here to Merseyside, to a house in Liverpool where he was waiting for me. He seemed so different. He wasn't the man I had fallen in love with, the man who was the father of the baby I was expecting.'

Cindy paused and wiped her eyes. 'I asked him to let me go but he simply laughed at me. He said he'd decided that I would be his when he first saw me in Shelston, that day when we both went to the supermarket and I asked him for a job. Now that he had me in his home I would never go free again and I could forget all about Shelston and my family and friends.'

Rebecca stared at her in dismay. She was about to say something when Cindy started to speak again, so she remained silent.

'I was so scared, Rebecca, and so shocked that I didn't speak to any of them for almost a week. I tried every ruse I could to get free and each time they punished me, beating me until I couldn't stand up for days afterwards.

'Then one night Bruno came into the small room where I slept, which was little more than a store cupboard. It was so small there was no way I could escape from him and he forced me to make love.

'It was then that he told me Bruno Lopez wasn't his real name but simply one he had used when he was in Shelston.'

'So he isn't Spanish at all, as we had been led to believe?' Rebecca murmured in astonishment.

'No, and I've no idea what nationality he is. That's why there would be no point in my going to the police even if I did manage to escape, because he is an illegal immigrant and they have no record of him in this country. He forged his details to get the job in the supermarket.'

For a moment Rebecca stared at Cindy in shocked silence. 'Even so, you can't let them treat you like they're doing, you can't stay there,' she protested lamely.

'What else can I do?' Cindy asked with a hopeless gesture of her hands.

'Well, for a start, why don't you run away?'

'Not without my baby. Not without little Poppy,' Cindy gulped. 'I care too much about her and they get angry with me for paying too much attention to her. If I answer back or argue or do something wrong, they take her away from me. I can hear her crying but I can do nothing about it.'

'Oh, Cindy, this is terrible,' Rebecca exclaimed and reached out to take Cindy's hand and hold it in hers.

'They know that I care about her so much that I will never leave her, so whenever they send me out to do the shopping they insist that she stays at home with them.' Her voice caught in a stifled sob and Rebecca could see the unhappiness and fear in her eyes.

'They allow you out, though, so why don't you go to the police and ask for help? Tell them what you've told me and they will help you.'

Cindy gave a hopeless little shrug. 'You don't understand, it's not that easy. I must go now,' she said, looking round anxiously. 'If they see me talking to you, they will punish me.'

'How? What will they do?'

'They won't let me see the baby. I won't even be allowed to feed her or nurse her for several days, perhaps for as long as a week.'

'That's blackmail!' Rebecca exclaimed. 'Oh Cindy, whatever has happened to you? Who are they? Who is this old woman who has such a hold over you?'

'Bruno's mother. She speaks no English but she understands every word that is said. His brother also lives in the house, he was the driver of the car that brought me here from the West Country. There's also another man, but I'm not sure who he is.'

'Was he the man who spoke to you at Frome station?'

'Yes, I think he's some sort of bodyguard. He's always very respectful to the old woman.'

Rebecca remained thoughtful for a moment, her brows drawn together in a frown as she tried to work things out.

'You said that when they first brought you here it was to a house in Liverpool. Why did they all move to Hoylake?'

'It was a safety precaution. They thought that you or my parents would report me missing to the police, and that someone might have seen what happened at the station and noted the car's number plates or a description of the driver and manage to trace them. Because they've no right to be in this country, they're very careful about their movements.'

'So how do they live? Has Bruno got a job of some kind, or do the other men work?'

Cindy shrugged helplessly. 'I don't know. Sometimes one or the other of them will disappear for days at a time, but mostly all three of them are in the house. Since I've been here I've always been the one sent out to do the shopping, so no one ever sees anything of the others.'

'Do they never have any visitors?' Rebecca asked in a puzzled voice.

Cindy shook her head. 'No one. They wouldn't even send for a doctor when I went into labour.'

'Oh Cindy! What happened?'

'The old woman acted as midwife and delivered the baby,' Cindy said in a low voice, shuddering at the memory.

'After that I couldn't leave, could I? I was so afraid of what they would do to the baby. They never allowed me to be alone with her for one minute and I couldn't run away and leave her with them, they are so evil. Oh, Becky, little Poppy is so lovely and so helpless that I can't leave her with these terrible people.'

'I do understand that, but it's hideous!' she said with a shudder. 'I've been thinking of you ever since I saw you in that jazzy old dress I gave you years and years ago. I certainly don't intend on leaving you here like this.'

'Oh heavens! Is that the time?' Cindy gasped in horror as she looked at the clock on the café wall. 'I must go!'

Cindy drained her coffee cup. The teacake lay on her plate, limp and unpalatable.

'I must go,' she insisted. 'I'll go and change back into my own dress and meet you outside the supermarket.' She ran a hand over the cotton dress Rebecca had brought for her to wear. 'This has been like a wonderful dream,' she murmured gratefully.

Rebecca remained sitting at the table for several minutes. When they met up outside the supermarket, Cindy had changed back into the jazzy dress and scraped her hair back into a ponytail. She looked utterly different from the girl who had been sitting opposite Rebecca in the café only a few minutes earlier

Yes, Cindy was right, she reflected, it was like a dream. A very disturbing one.

Thirty-Two

In the train on the way home, Rebecca went over in her mind all the things that Cindy had told her.

The revelation that Cindy had been ill-treated by Bruno was horrifying. When she met him at the supermarket in Shelston he had appeared to be the perfect gentleman, and she could understand Cindy falling for him. But to be dragged away and kept prisoner and to cause so much distress to both their families was beyond belief!

She was quite sure everything Cindy had told her was true. She looked cowed, she was frightened, and her concern over her baby was very understandable.

What she couldn't comprehend was why Cindy stayed there. Why didn't she run away? Why didn't she take the opportunity to go to the police when they sent her out to do the shopping?

Of course, there was her fear that they would harm the baby. But surely they only said they would do that to keep her there?

Or perhaps it wasn't merely a threat? Rebecca remembered a terrible report she had read in the newspapers about how a foreign family retaliated when their sister refused to marry the man they had chosen for her. They seemed to regard death as being something of no consequence. Yet to kill a baby, that really was beyond belief.

She recalled how Cindy had shuddered as she described how Bruno ill-treated her and his threats of what the consequences would be if she disobeyed him.

Rebecca knew she must do something to help Cindy, to get her away from Bruno and make sure Cindy and her baby were safe. But she had no idea of how to go about it.

She thought of telling her own parents and seeing if they could help. Or telling the Masons. At least it would mean that they knew that Cindy was still alive. But would the details horrify and distress them even more?

And if they went the wrong way about trying to rescue Cindy, then they might do more harm than good. Bruno had already proved he could be both cruel and violent and that Cindy was powerless when he turned on her.

The only person she could think of who might know how to deal with the situation was Danny Flowers. The trouble was that he was a policeman and Cindy had been so adamant that Bruno would harm both her and the baby if the police ever became involved.

She was still wondering what was the best way to handle the situation when she arrived home. Grace was waiting for her, a scowl on her pretty face.

'Where have you been?' she demanded crossly as Rebecca walked in. 'You promised we would spend today revising for tomorrow's exams. We were going to test each other, remember?'

'Oh, Grace, I'm so sorry. It went right out of my mind.'

'So it seems,' Grace retorted ungraciously, flouncing back into the kitchen.

'We'll get started right away, if you like,' Rebecca volunteered in an attempt to placate her.

'Can't you see I'm cooking? I'm starving and I can't study on an empty stomach.'

'So am I,' Rebecca admitted. 'Shall we eat first, then? It certainly smells appetizing. Afterwards we can settle down for a concentrated session.'

Grace didn't answer, but busied herself taking plates out of the cupboard and banging them down on the worktop then rattling knives and forks loudly as she took them out of the drawer.

'I'll lay the table,' Rebecca offered, taking the cutlery from Grace's hands.

'You'll wash up as well since I've done all the shopping and cooking. Where have you been anyway? What was so important that you didn't even take the trouble to let me know you were going out?'

Rebecca hesitated, then as they sat down to eat she made up her mind and began to tell Grace about Cindy.

Grace listened in appalled silence. Several times she paused with a forkful of food halfway to her mouth and stared at Rebecca in disbelief.

'What are you going to do to help her?' she demanded when Rebecca finished.

'That's the trouble, I don't know. Cindy is so cowed and frightened she won't take any chances. She won't try to escape or even go to the police because she is so afraid that if she does the baby may be harmed.'

Grace frowned. 'If these people are living here in Britain illegally, then surely the police will have a good reason to visit and interrogate them?'

Rebecca shook her head. 'I still think it's dangerous. Bruno might suspect that Cindy had informed on them or had something to do with it, and he'd take it out on her before they could stop him.'

'Talk to Danny and see what he says,' Grace urged. 'You don't have to tell him where they live or who they are. Anyway, the names they are going under aren't their real names, nor is the name this bloke called Bruno is using, so I doubt if Danny could trace them even if you did accidentally drop their names into the conversation.'

'I know you're right and I will think about it,' Rebecca promised as they cleared away the remains of their meal and washed up together.

'When are you seeing her again?' Grace asked.

'The day after tomorrow.'

'By the way,' Grace went on, a frown creasing her brow, 'have you told her family or your own that Cindy is still alive?'

Rebecca shook her head.

'Don't you think you should put them out of their misery? Her mother must be going out of her mind with worry. And she's a grandmother now by the sound of it. Surely she would want to know that?'

'That's another problem,' Rebecca admitted, pushing her hair back behind her ears. 'I know they would be relieved to hear that Cindy is alive and so would my own family. The trouble is

I'm sure they would take matters into their own hands and I'm worried about what they might do. If they were to insist on knowing where she is and turn up on the doorstep, then Bruno and his family might do Cindy some dreadful harm.'

Grace nodded. 'Yes, there is always that possibility,' she admitted. 'In fact, it's all the more reason for you to tell Danny. He would know exactly how to deal with it all.'

'Danny couldn't do it single-handed, though, so it would mean he would have to tell others. And the more people who know what's going on, the greater the danger for Cindy.'

They finished clearing up in silence, each absorbed in her own thoughts.

'Come on,' Rebecca tugged at Grace's arm. 'Let's get down to this business of testing each other in readiness for tomorrow's ordeal. Let's get the exam over first, then we'll decide what's the best thing we can do to help Cindy.'

Thirty-Three

Rebecca and Grace both felt exhausted at the end of the exam. It had been gruelling and they arrived back at the flat thankful it was over and looking forward to a quiet evening.

They were still discussing the different questions they had been asked and comparing their answers when the doorbell rang.

'Who on earth is that?' Grace exclaimed. 'Were you expecting anyone?'

'No, I most certainly am not. All I want is a cup of tea and a couple of rounds of hot buttered toast and a quiet evening at home.'

As the doorbell rang again, Grace stood up. 'It's probably Danny,' she murmured as she went to answer it.

Rebecca listened to the rise and fall of voices. It certainly wasn't Danny's voice, although it did sound familiar.

'There's someone to see you,' Grace announced as she came back into the living room followed by a tall fair-haired man.

'Nick!' Rebecca's voice was a mixture of amazement and pleasure. 'This is a surprise.'

'A pleasant one, I hope?' he said with a smile.

'Very much so, I'm delighted to see you. Grace, this is my friend Nick Blakemore,' she added smiling as she introduced them to each other.

As they shook hands there was another ring at the doorbell.

'More visitors?' The two girls looked at each other in surprise.

'I'll answer it this time and leave you and Nick to get acquainted,' Rebecca offered.

As she had half-expected, it was Danny Flowers who was standing there. He was in civilian clothes – a very smart grey suit with a white shirt and a red-and-grey striped tie.

'Come on!' he greeted her cheerfully. 'I'd like to take the pair of you out for a meal to celebrate the end of your exams.'

'Oh Danny, we'd love to but we are both extremely exhausted. It was a very gruelling exam.'

'Yes, and the very last one you have to take, so it's time to celebrate,' he insisted.

As they entered the living room, he pulled up short. 'Sorry, I didn't know you had a visitor.'

'This is a friend from Shelston, Nick Blakemore,' Rebecca told him as Danny stretched out a hand towards the other man.

'I heard what you said about taking these two out to celebrate,' Nick said, 'and that is exactly the reason why I'm here. Shall we join forces?'

'Sounds good to me,' Danny agreed.

Rebecca and Grace looked at each other. 'How can we refuse?' Rebecca said with a laugh.

'Good! You've got five minutes to get ready then,' Danny told them, looking at his watch as if he was timing them.

Twenty minutes later the four of them were entering a restaurant in the centre of Liverpool. Both girls had changed into pretty dresses and there was no sign of tiredness on either of their faces or in their animated chatter.

Over their meal they talked about the future and the girls fantasized about the type of school they hoped to teach at. Grace wanted to stay in the Merseyside area so she could live at home, but Rebecca was hoping for something either in

Cardiff, as she had liked the city so much, or somewhere in the West Country near to Shelston.

'You can't leave Merseyside until you've sorted out what you're going to do about your friend Cindy,' Grace remarked.

'Cindy? Do you mean Cindy Mason?' Nick asked in surprise.

Before Rebecca could reply, he went on, 'Do you mean you have found her or know where she is?'

'Both,' Rebecca murmured, her face red with embarrassment.

She avoided Nick's eyes and looked at Danny. 'I need your help, or advice,' she told him.

'Danny is a policeman,' she explained, looking back at Nick.

Danny frowned. 'Go on.'

Haltingly at first, and then more fluently as she got into her stride, Rebecca told them about finding Cindy and a little about the terrible life she was leading.

'I'm meeting up with her tomorrow,' Rebecca ended. 'I'm going to try again to make her see sense and run away. I'm sure they are only threatening to hurt her baby because they know it will stop her trying to escape their clutches.'

Danny shook his head. 'You're taking a great risk,' he warned her. 'These people think differently to us and they can be vicious. This really is a job for our undercover team to handle.'

'I think you should listen to what Danny is saying,' Nick told her worriedly. 'Those sort of people can be very dangerous. Isn't that right, Danny?' He looked across at Danny for confirmation.

'Precisely.' Danny's tone was authoritative and his face grave. 'Why don't you leave it to us to handle things, Rebecca?'

'I promised Cindy I wouldn't go to the police. She was afraid not only for her own life but for her baby if Bruno or his family found out.'

'I understand that,' Danny nodded. 'But if she was caught talking to you, then they might retaliate in the worst possible way. As I've said, they're dangerous people.'

Nick reached out and took Rebecca's hand. 'Listen to what Danny's saying,' he implored. 'I don't want anything to happen to you.'

'But what are we going to do about Cindy? I must do what I can to rescue her and the baby. I must meet her tomorrow like I promised. I won't stay talking to her a minute longer than necessary.'

'What are you going to talk to her about?' Nick asked. 'Have you any sort of plan?'

Rebecca shook her head. 'No, not really. I was going to ask Danny for advice,' she added lamely.

'My advice is to hand the whole matter over to the experts,' he told her crisply. 'Men who have experience of these sort of people and know how to handle them. This sounds like a particularly serious situation needing very delicate handling.'

Rebecca looked from one of them to the other, shaking her head, not knowing what to think. She felt she owed it to Cindy to meet with her and give her some sort of comfort. She hoped she might be able to persuade her that telling the police was not only the right thing to do but the only hope there was of her ever getting away from the clutches of these people.

'Promise me you won't attempt to persuade her to do anything if you meet her on your own tomorrow,' Danny persisted.

'Are you hinting that you want to come with me?' Rebecca asked in alarm.

'Heavens no! If they saw her talking to a man, even if I was in civvies and they didn't know I was a policeman, they'd harm her.'

'So what are you telling me I should do?'

'Go and see her tomorrow as you've promised, but say nothing about telling anyone. In the meantime, I will inform the right authority.'

'What that does mean? What will happen?'

'Since these people are illegal immigrants, they may deal with it from that angle. Once I tell them about Cindy being kept prisoner and about the baby, they will be very discreet and handle the operation in such a way that they ensure they don't get hurt.'

Rebecca chewed on her bottom lip. She didn't know what to do for the best. She felt that by telling Danny about it she had betrayed Cindy's confidence, yet she could see the sense of his argument.

'Look,' she said at length. 'If I tell you all I know and give you the address where they live and so on, then when I meet Cindy tomorrow can I warn her what is about to happen?' Cindy had mumbled the name of a street last time they spoke. It was as close to an address as Rebecca could get from her.

Danny looked doubtful and she thought he was about to refuse, but Nick came to her support.

'I think Rebecca owes that much to Cindy,' he said quietly. 'Cindy is very sensible and level-headed and she will probably be able to deal with the situation better if she is forewarned. It should work out all right.'

Danny still looked uncertain.

'Rebecca will feel easier in her mind if she lets Cindy know what is happening,' Nick went on.

Danny shook his head as if uncertain whether or not this was advisable.

'Once Cindy has accepted that this is the only possible way to get her life back, then knowing what is going to happen will give her hope.'

'Yes, but if she reacts in the wrong way it could jeopardize the whole operation,' Danny argued.

'I don't think you need be afraid of her doing that. Tell her what you want her to do and how to behave, and she'll follow your instructions. She will feel hopeful that things are going to work out all right for her in the end, so she'll do whatever you tell her to do.'

Danny shook his head. 'I think you should wait before you say anything to Cindy. Give me a chance to speak to one or two of my colleagues first, and give them a chance to decide exactly how they are going to proceed.'

Thirty-Four

For the first time in many months, Rebecca's thoughts weren't about Cindy when she went to bed that night but about Nick Blakemore.

She had thought him attractive the very first time they

met. She had felt comfortable in his company and he had seemed far more mature than Jake Mason or any of the other boys she knew in Shelston.

Ever since then her feelings had grown, but she had no idea if he felt the same way about her. That would be wishful thinking, she told herself.

Once they had finished eating with Danny and Grace, they had gone for a stroll on their own and wandered down to the Liverpool waterside.

For some it would not have been the most romantic ending to a pleasant evening, but for her it had proved a turning point, she thought complacently.

They had held hands as they stood looking out across the water towards Wallasey. Nick had placed an arm around her shoulders and then drawn her into his arms and kissed her very lightly on the lips.

She had held her breath, almost wondering if she was dreaming. When she responded he kissed her more deeply, only releasing her when they were both gasping for breath.

'I've waited so long to do that,' he told her huskily. 'You've been in my thoughts ever since the day we first met.'

'Oh Nick!' She felt she was bursting with happiness. She had thought about him so much but somehow had never imagined that he returned her feelings.

As they gazed up at the Liver Birds dominating the pier head it was as if Liverpool was suddenly sparkling in the moonlight – a magic city full of hope and promise, a place where dreams came to fruition.

He took her into his arms again and kissed her passionately, then fingers entwined they made their way towards where she lived.

'I have to catch a train in half an hour,' he told her. 'I'll see you home, then make a dash for Lime Street Station.'

'I wish you could stay,' she said softly.

'So do I, but it's not possible. Work tomorrow.'

'I'll be back in Shelston again in a few days.'

'Good, it will be easier to meet there. I have several bookings coming up in succession, all within a twenty-mile radius of Shelston.'

By this time they'd reached her flat. Although every fibre in her being cried out for him to stay, she knew he had to go and as they embraced once again she felt tears dampening her eyes.

'See you soon,' she whispered.

'Very soon,' he promised.

When she woke next morning, Rebecca wondered if it had all been a dream. Lying there cocooned in the warmth of her bed, she went over every detail of what had happened after they left Grace and Danny and recalled every moment.

She could hardly wait to get back to Shelston and see Nick again. First, though, there was the problem of Cindy. She couldn't simply leave her stranded on Merseyside without a friend in the world.

She thought over everything Danny had said about letting the police handle things. It certainly made sense, and it would solve her own problems as well as Cindy's if they did it quite soon. They could travel back home to Shelston together, and if necessary Cindy could stay with her at Woodside until they had been to see her parents and knew that they accepted her and her child.

Cindy's child! She must not forget about the little girl that Cindy referred to as Poppy. She had never seen the child and didn't even know how old she was.

She lay there for several minutes trying to work out how old Poppy might be, but everything was so jumbled in her mind. She knew exactly when Cindy left Shelston, but didn't know how pregnant Cindy was when she left – which had obviously been before anyone realized she was pregnant, since not even her own mother had noticed.

It must have come as a great shock when she learned that Bruno had left the supermarket and vanished almost overnight without a word.

Knowing Mavis Mason as she did, Rebecca knew she would have been irate to find her daughter was pregnant. Tom Mason might even have turned her out.

Still, what had eventually happened was much the same, she supposed. Cindy had ended up homeless in a strange city where she knew no one and was completely without friends.

As she caught the train from Liverpool to Hoylake, Rebecca tried to make up her mind about whether or not she should give Cindy a hint of what might be about to happen.

If she said nothing, then when the police arrived at the house, no matter how discreet they might be, Cindy was bound to be frightened. If she had advance notice, then at least she could cooperate, knowing it was to her benefit to do so.

She still hadn't resolved what to do for the best when she arrived at Hoylake and was walking up the High Street. The train had been late getting in and, knowing how much Cindy worried about any of the family seeing her, she hoped she had managed to find a way of waiting without it being obvious that she was waiting for someone.

The High Street was very quiet and there was no sign of Cindy. Rebecca walked from one end to the other, looking in shops and cafés in case Cindy had gone into one of them to kill time rather than wait out on the street.

She went into the supermarket and walked down every aisle, but there was no sign of Cindy. Then, as she emerged back in the High Street she caught sight of a tall figure in a red jacket ahead of her and hurried to catch up.

'Cindy!'

The figure half turned and slowed a little but kept on walking.

'What's the hurry?' Rebecca asked as she caught her up.

'Keep walking and don't look at me in case anyone sees us together,' Cindy said in little above a whisper. 'I was seen last time we met. I said you were trying to persuade me to take out a subscription to a magazine but Bruno gave me a beating all the same.'

'Oh Cindy, this has got to stop,' Rebecca said quickly. She was about to explain to her what was going to happen but Cindy interrupted her.

'I must go. We had better stop meeting, I can't see you again,'

Before Rebecca could say anything, Cindy was running down the road away from her.

Rebecca stood where she was for a moment. She knew she dare not run after her but the fear in Cindy's voice had cut her like a knife and now she was all the more eager for the police to act.

They really were the only people who could help, she reflected grimly.

When Rebecca reached home she told Grace what had happened, and Grace was as angry as she was that Cindy was being treated so badly. But when she wondered if she ought to let Danny know about this latest development, Grace said she didn't think there was much point in doing so.

'Danny knows how serious it is and he will have acted as soon as he got to work this morning,' she assured Rebecca. 'If you like, you can tell him if he comes round or phones to let us know how things are progressing, but I don't think there's much point in contacting him especially.'

'I'm sure you are right,' Rebecca agreed. 'It's just that I feel so helpless. I wish I had mentioned it to him sooner, but Cindy was so much against it that I felt I had to listen to her.'

Thirty-Five

Although they had now finished at university and both Grace and Rebecca knew where they would be teaching the following September, they were reluctant to give up their Liverpool flat until they knew what was being done about Cindy.

'Although I've never met her, I feel almost as anxious about her as you do,' Grace told Rebecca as they washed and dried the breakfast dishes together. 'I wish Danny would come and tell us what's happening.'

'I feel the same,' Rebecca agreed. 'I'm tempted to go over to Hoylake and see if I can see Cindy again, but common sense tells me not to in case I get her into even more trouble.'

'Yes,' Grace agreed thoughtfully, 'I think we should do nothing until we hear from Danny. It's the baby I'm worried about.'

'Poppy! Poor little love!'

'How old is she?'

'I'm not too sure.' Rebecca frowned. 'I've tried to work it out and think she must be about three years old now.'

'Can't you fix it from the time Cindy was coming to visit you in Cardiff? She must have been pregnant then,' Grace pointed out.

'I'm not sure how pregnant she was then. It couldn't have been more than about three months because none of her family knew anything about it, so she obviously wasn't showing at all.'

'Well, take it as three months and see if you can work it from there,' Grace said practically.

'That's what I've done, and that's why I think Poppy must be about three. Why, what does it matter?'

'Well, if she was still a tiny baby, only a few months old, she wouldn't be aware of what's going on. But at three she will understand if she is stopped from going out with her mother. She probably cries whenever Cindy is sent shopping and she's not allowed to go with her.'

'Yes, you're probably right,' Rebecca agreed. 'That makes Cindy's situation even worse. We've got to help get her away as soon as possible. Can't you get in touch with Danny and find out what progress they're making?'

'I don't think I can,' Grace said worriedly. 'He hates me phoning him at work unless it is terribly urgent.'

'Well, it is, isn't it?' Rebecca pointed out.

'Yes, but there is the added problem that someone may overhear the conversation. Often their calls are recorded, so they would know he's been discussing Cindy's situation with you.'

'Would that matter?'

'It would to Danny. He's always considered it unprofessional to talk about things connected with his work.'

'I understand,' Rebecca acknowledged with a sigh. 'So what can we do?'

'Nothing except wait for him to come and tell us how things are progressing, I suppose.'

The sound of the doorbell startled them both and they looked at each other expectantly.

'Do you think it could be Danny?' Rebecca asked hopefully.

'We'll soon know,' Grace said as she headed for the door.

It wasn't Danny, it was Nick Blakemore. Rebecca was very surprised to see him.

'Just a flying visit to see if you have any fresh news about Cindy,' he told her.

'No, I'm afraid not,' Rebecca shook her head. 'We were hoping it was Danny calling to tell us what was happening.'

'I was afraid you would be out. I thought you might have gone over to Hoylake on the off chance of seeing Cindy.'

'I'm very much tempted to,' Rebecca admitted.

'I tell you what,' Nick suggested, 'my car is outside, so why don't we all three go over there? If there is no sign of her, then you can take us to Red Rocks. You're always talking about it, Rebecca, and I've never been there. Have you, Grace?'

'I think I went there once when I was very small, but I can't remember anything at all about it.'

'Come on then. Let's do that,' Nick enthused. 'It's a lovely day.'

'Are you sure you want me to come?' Grace asked. 'Don't say yes just to be polite.'

'No, we really do want you to come,' Nick assured her.

Half an hour later they were travelling through the Mersey Tunnel. It was a glorious day. As they emerged on the other side, it was sunny and warm.

'What are we going to do first? Take a walk along the main street and see if there is any sight of her, or go straight to Red Rocks and look for Cindy afterwards?' Nick asked, looking from one of them to the other as he parked the car.

'I don't mind which we do,' Grace smiled.

'Why don't we go to the High Street and have a coffee and a toasted sandwich first, then go to Red Rocks afterwards?' Rebecca suggested.

'Splendid idea,' Nick agreed.

'If we can manage to get a seat by the window, we might see Cindy if she walks down the street,' Rebecca pointed out.

Rebecca took them to her favourite café where she had taken Cindy. They were lucky and managed to find a table by the window. Nick went to the counter and placed their order.

The High Street was quite busy, but there was no sign of Cindy. When they had finished their snack, Rebecca suggested that it might be worth walking to the road where Cindy turned off, in case they could catch sight of her there.

'It's only a short way down the road and it won't delay us more than a couple of minutes.'

'Sounds good sense to me,' Nick agreed. Grace nodded, indicating that she thought so too.

'You've never actually been to the house, then?' Nick said thoughtfully as they walked along.

'Heavens no! Cindy wouldn't have dared risk letting me do that. Look what happened when she was seen merely speaking to me. She ended up being punished.'

'You are pretty sure, though, where she lives?'

'Oh yes, just a couple more roads down on the right. We're almost there.'

When they reached the turning, they found one half of the street was barricaded off by blue police tape. They looked at each other in consternation.

'I wonder what's happened?' Rebecca asked in alarm.

'Perhaps the police have already made a raid,' Nick suggested.

'It certainly looks that way,' Grace agreed. 'I wonder how we can find out.'

The street had seemed deserted when they turned into it, but Rebecca spotted a middle-aged woman weeding the scrap of garden outside her door and went over to her.

'Has there been an accident or something?' she asked, smiling at the woman in a friendly manner.

'Not an accident, luv. The police have been here ever since early this morning, with cars and vans and heaven knows what. In fact they've only just gone.'

Rebecca shook her head from side to side and waited for the woman to give her more information. Nick and Grace had now joined her and, nodding towards the cordoned-off area, Nick asked 'What happened?'

'The police came and raided the house,' the woman told him.

'Really? I wonder why?'

'It seems there were illegal immigrants living there – men, women and even a small child. Poor little love, only about three years old and she seemed frightened to death. Well, so did the younger woman but she went along with them without any fuss. It was the old woman who kicked and struggled and made a terrible to-do. There were three men as well, and all three of them were handcuffed and bundled into a big van. They took the two women and the little girl away in cars. Not together, mind you. I think the old woman was making such a fuss that they were afraid to put them in the same car.'

'Were they local police?' Nick queried.

'From Liverpool,' the woman told him. 'I think some of them were armed,' she added. 'Had to be to keep that lot under control.'

'So they will have taken them back to Liverpool?'

'Reckon so. My husband said they will charge them and either send them to jail or back to where they've come from.'

'So there's no one left in the house, then?' Grace asked.

'No, luv. It's all locked up and sealed, and they've left this blue tape all round the place to keep folk from going in and prying. Probably sending some of their detectives over later on to go over the place and see what they can find.'

They thanked the woman, then turned back into the High Street and walked in silence to where Nick had parked the car.

'Do you still want me to take you to Red Rocks?' Rebecca asked as Nick opened the car door for them.

Grace and Nick both shook their heads. 'No, I don't think so,' Grace said firmly. 'I think we should go straight home and wait for Danny to contact us.'

Thirty-Six

Danny was waiting for them when they arrived back at the flat. Rebecca was the first one out of the car and rushed up to him, calling out 'What news have you?' even before she reached him.

'Shall we go inside?' Danny suggested.

Nick switched on the kettle in the kitchen before joining the girls, who were waiting impatiently for Danny to tell them his news.

'Coffee everyone?' Nick asked.

'Great idea,' Danny said. He pushed his fingers through his red hair. 'Then we can all sit down and I can tell you the whole story.'

Rebecca and Grace took over in the kitchen and made the coffee and put some biscuits on a plate. Nick carried them through to the sitting room, where Danny had collapsed into an armchair as if he was exhausted.

As they drank their coffee, Danny related all that had happened.

'We raided the house at three o'clock this morning. There were four of us and we had other officers on standby in case they were needed. They all tried to resist arrest except the young woman, who I take it was Cindy. She was distraught at first, because she thought she was going to be separated from her child. Once she found that the little girl was remaining with her, she was as docile as could be. Eager in fact for us to take her in.'

'Where is she now?' Rebecca asked.

'She was taken to hospital with the little girl to be checked out—'

'Is she still there?' Rebecca interrupted him.

'Yes, and she's under police protection. I'll tell you all about her in a minute.'

'What happened to the men?' Nick asked.

'They've been taken into custody and charged with being illegal immigrants, and also with drug running.'

'And the old woman?'

'She's in custody, but so far she hasn't been charged with anything.'

'She was the one who was treating Cindy so badly and threatening her and keeping her separated from her child,' Rebecca reminded him.

'We must wait until we have had a statement from Cindy and we haven't taken one yet,' Danny told her.

'You said that Cindy and Poppy . . .'

'Poppy?' Danny frowned, his green eyes questioning. 'Is that the little girl's name?'

'Yes. How old is she?'

'About three, I think. She's a pretty little thing.'

'Can we go and see Cindy?' Grace asked.

Danny hesitated. 'As I told you, she's in hospital and under police guard. They've agreed to let you visit her but you won't be allowed to stay very long. We still need to interview her, so they may say you'll have to wait until after that has taken place. On the other hand, they may decide that seeing you might help Cindy to relax and speak out.'

'Then let's go!' Impatiently Rebecca jumped up and held out a hand to Nick. 'You'll drive us there, won't you?'

'Of course! But I do have to get back tonight for work in the morning, so I can't stay very late.'

'If you take us there in your car, I can see Rebecca and Grace home,' Danny told him.

As the four of them went into the hospital, the uniformed porter stepped forward as if about to bar their entrance. Then he saw Danny's uniform and hesitated. 'Do you know where to go?' he asked.

'Yes, thank you,' Danny said curtly.

He led them up to the second floor and along to a room at the far end where a uniformed policeman was standing guard. He nodded at Danny and let them pass without saying anything,

It was a good-size room with a bed and cot in it. Poppy was in the cot, fast asleep. She was so small and white-faced that Rebecca thought she looked like one of the china dolls she and Cindy used to push around in their doll's prams when they were little girls in Shelston.

Very gently she stroked the sleeping child's face. Poppy stirred and Rebecca drew back quickly, not wanting to disturb her.

Cindy lay propped up by pillows. Her eyes were closed as if she too was asleep, but she had one hand stretched out towards the cot, grasping the side of it as if to protect the sleeping child.

Rebecca drew in her breath sharply as she saw the cuts and bruises on Cindy's face and the dark shadows under her eyes. One of her arms was bandaged and there was a metal cage over her legs to prevent the bedclothes resting on them, so Rebecca assumed one or both of her legs had also been injured.

Rebecca wanted to hold her in her arms and reassure her that everything was going to be all right, but she was afraid to do more than gently take Cindy's free hand and hold it between both her own for fear of hurting her.

As Rebecca bent over her, murmuring her name softly, Cindy opened her eyes.

For a moment there was a look of terror on Cindy's face and she seemed to shrink into the bed. Then as she recognized Rebecca, she let out a deep sigh of relief.

Rebecca bent down and kissed her tenderly on the brow. 'You're going to be all right now and so is little Poppy,' she said softly. 'As soon as you are well enough, you're coming home with me. Understand?'

Cindy nodded and gave a wan smile. 'Today?'

Rebecca shook her head. 'You need to stay here in hospital for a few days until . . . until your cuts and bruises have healed.'

'Oh, Becky, I'm so afraid . . .' Her voice trailed away in a sob.

'There's no need to be,' Rebecca told her quickly. 'There's a policeman on guard outside your door, and Bruno and all the other men are in custody. They can't hurt you anymore.'

Rebecca felt Danny's hands on her shoulders gently but firmly moving her away from the bed.

'Cindy, we need you to make a statement. Do you feel strong enough to do it now?'

Cindy closed her eyes wearily and moved her head from side to side. 'Not now,' she whispered.

Danny looked at Rebecca. 'Can you persuade her?'

Before she could answer him, a nurse carrying a tray of medicinal equipment came bustling into the room. She frowned in annoyance at finding them there.

'I hope you haven't tired my patient,' she said sharply. 'She needs all the rest she can get.'

As she spoke, she placed the tray on the locker beside the bed. Then, having taken Cindy's pulse, she quickly cleaned a spot on her arm with a damp swab, selected a syringe from the tray, and held Cindy's arm firmly while she injected her.

Wincing, Rebecca turned her face away and clutched at Nick as she saw Cindy flinch as the needle pierced her flesh.

'I must ask you all to leave,' the nurse said sternly as she pulled the covers up over Cindy.

Danny's green eyes hardened as he returned the nurse's stare. 'Very well,' he said crisply. With a curt nod towards the door, he shepherded Rebecca, Nick and Grace out into the corridor.

He stopped to give some instructions to the policeman on duty before ushering them all out of the hospital.

They stood in a huddle for a few minutes outside. The sun had gone and it was overcast, and there was a light drizzle falling.

Danny told them that he had given Rebecca's name and telephone number to the hospital as a contact should they need it.

He had also informed them that when Cindy was ready to be discharged she would be going to stay with Rebecca. He had not given any details about Cindy's parents or their address, but the arrangement could be changed if Rebecca or Cindy wished it to be.

Rebecca was more than delighted by what he had done. 'On no account tell them Cindy's home address. It would distress her so much if any of her family found out what has happened to her. They know nothing about Poppy, and that piece of news as well the state Cindy's in would break Mavis Mason's heart. So let's leave things exactly as you have arranged.'

Danny had to go back on duty, but he was anxious to see Rebecca and Grace safely home first.

'I have time to drive them back to the flat,' Nick told him, checking his watch. 'So there's no need for you to come as well.'

'That would be a great help,' Danny said with a smile of relief.

'I'll leave you to keep an eye on them, though, until I'm able to visit again,' Nick told him as they shook hands and said goodbye.

Thirty-Seven

Over the next couple of weeks Danny called in most days to check that Rebecca and Grace were all right and to give them the latest news on Cindy's progress.

Both girls were on edge and anxious for Cindy to be released from hospital so that they could make sure she was safe and settled before they started their new teaching jobs. Although Grace would still be near Liverpool, Rebecca would be in Dorset.

They had intended giving up the flat and going to their own homes during August, but because Danny had arranged for Cindy to come to stay with them when she was discharged from hospital they had taken a further three-month lease on the flat.

Even so, they spent time at their own homes during the month and several times Rebecca was on the brink of confiding in her mother about Cindy. But she felt it might be betraying her friend and was not at all sure what her mother's reaction would be. Her main fear was that Sandra might tell all to Mavis Mason because, despite the rift that had existed between them over the malicious gossip regarding Cindy's disappearance, the two of them had been close since childhood.

There was so much that the Masons didn't know, Rebecca reflected. In fact there was still a lot she didn't know, but hints dropped by Danny had confirmed that Cindy had had a terrible time at the hands of Bruno and his family.

It was almost three weeks before Cindy and Poppy were allowed out of hospital. They were both very quiet and extremely nervous when they arrived at the flat. Rebecca explained who Grace was, and when she said she was Danny's sister Cindy visibly relaxed.

Cindy had only the clothes she stood up in, so for the first couple of days it was like old times as she tried on various garments from Rebecca's wardrobe.

There was nothing suitable for Poppy, of course, so Grace suggested they all go shopping together and buy her some clothes.

'It's impossible,' Cindy told them. 'I haven't a penny piece to my name.'

'Then we will have to pay for some clothes for you and Poppy,' Rebecca told her. 'Thank goodness it's summer and the sales are on, so we can pick up some bargains.'

Cindy shook her head. 'No, I am indebted enough to both of you as it is.'

'Then a bit more won't make any difference and you can pay us back when you're fit and well and have got your life back,' Grace told her in a very practical tone.

The next day, when Nick arrived, Cindy listened in silence when Rebecca told her that they had got to know each other when he came to work in their butcher's shop in Shelston.

'Is he still working in Shelston?'

'No, he's not there at the moment. Why?'

'He might say something and give my whereabouts away. I haven't been in touch with my family since I left, so they know nothing about what has happened to me.'

'And they won't until you want them to. I hope that when you're feeling stronger you'll want to put the past behind you and get in touch with them,' Rebecca told her quietly. 'But not until you are ready,' she added quickly as she saw the look of terror on Cindy's face.

'I don't think I ever will be.'

'You don't have to tell them everything, but they deserve to know you are safe. Your mother has been terribly upset, and your father and Jake have done everything in their power to trace you.'

Cindy shook her head and hid her face behind her curtain of dark hair, but Rebecca knew from the way her shoulders were moving that she was crying.

'I think they'll be delighted to know they have a granddaughter, and Poppy will benefit from their love and affection,' Rebecca added.

Cindy brushed back her hair with her hand and stared at her in amazement. 'Delighted? You mean shocked, don't you?' she said bitterly.

'I said delighted and that's what I meant. Poppy is adorable and your mum and dad won't help but love her. Grace and I would like to keep her forever, she's certainly won a place in our hearts.'

Over the next ten days the three of them, Rebecca, Cindy and Grace, had a good many heart to heart chats. As Cindy revealed more and more of the terrible things she'd had to endure, it was as if the poison was leaving her mind and body.

Poppy was the catalyst. She was now talking and her pretty ways wound tendrils of love, binding them all tighter and tighter together. Even Danny and Nick, on his occasional visits, were drawn into the charmed circle of their affection.

Like Rebecca, Nick felt that Cindy must repair her relationship with her family, and offered to take her and Poppy down to Shelston when she was ready.

'It could be the answer to all our problems, Cindy,' Rebecca told her. 'There's only a week left before Grace and I will have to get ready to start work at our new schools and you don't want to be left here on your own, do you?'

'But I feel safe here,' Cindy murmured, biting down on her lower lip to stop herself crying.

'You feel secure because we're here with you,' Grace said gently. 'But Liverpool can be a lonely place when you're living alone. Give it some thought, Cindy.'

'Look, why don't I smooth the path for you by telling my mother where you are?' Rebecca suggested. 'I'll just tell her that I've found you and know where you're living.'

'Nothing more,' she added quickly as she saw the fear in Cindy's eyes. 'I'll make her promise not to tell your mother and then let you know her reaction.'

'Better to let Rebecca's mother tell your mother rather than for her to read about it in the newspapers when the case comes to court,' Danny pointed out.

'Comes to court? You mean it will be reported in the newspapers?'

'Of course it will.'

'All the details? Things I've told the police in confidence?'

'They'll try to keep a lot of it out of the papers, but I'm afraid we can't stop the reporters doing their job.'

'I'm not blaming you, Danny, you've been wonderfully kind,' Cindy said quickly, giving him a little smile.

Rebecca noticed that Danny looked a trifle embarrassed, and was blushing as Cindy reached out and touched his arm.

'Think about it, Cindy,' she told her. 'I'm going to Shelston with Nick at the weekend, so if you want me to I can go up to the farm and let your parents know where you are, or simply tell my own mum and dad. Or, of course, you can come with us and do it yourself if you wish.'

'No, no! I doubt if I could do that . . . I will think about it, though.'

'You'll be here on your own at the weekend,' Grace warned her. 'I have to visit my new school and sign the lease for the flat I'm taking over.'

'On my own?' The alarm and fear were back on Cindy's face.

'Don't worry, I'll be around,' Danny reassured her. 'So you won't be completely on your own.'

Thirty-Eight

After Danny and Nick left, Rebecca and Grace spent a lot of time trying to persuade Cindy that she must let her family know she was safe, even if she didn't tell them where she was.

'You ought to tell them about Poppy as well, they deserve to know that they have a granddaughter,' Grace said bluntly.

Cindy was adamant that she didn't want them to know, not yet anyway. She said she needed more time to get herself together. She wanted to feel strong enough to face up to their shock when they heard about Poppy and to be able to bear the shame she knew she was bringing on the family because she had an illegitimate child.

'That's ridiculous,' Rebecca told her. 'Your mother and father love you too much to criticize or bear a grudge against you because of that. They nearly went out of their minds when they heard you were missing, and they tried every possible way they could to get some news about your whereabouts.'

'But I'm bringing disgrace on the family by having a child out of wedlock,' Cindy insisted.

'All the more reason to make sure they know about her and meet her and get to know her and love her,' Grace pointed out. 'What do you think would happen to Poppy if you died? Or if you were so ill you couldn't look after her?'

Cindy went white but she still shook her head at the idea of letting her family know where she was or of mentioning Poppy to them.

It wasn't until Nick and Rebecca were on the point of setting off for their weekend in Shelston that Cindy capitulated. As they were leaving the flat she called after them, 'Becky, do what you think best if you see my mum.'

Rebecca stopped in her tracks. 'You mean I can tell her where you are? Tell her everything?'

Cindy hesitated, brushing her hair back behind her ears and squaring her shoulders before answering.

'Yes, all right. Tell her whatever you feel is right.'

'Can I tell her about Poppy?'

Again Cindy hesitated then she said in a rush, 'If you have to, if you think she will understand and take it all right.' Then before Rebecca could say any more she slammed the door shut.

'Well, what do you make of that?' Rebecca asked, staring at Nick who was looking equally baffled.

'I'm not sure what to say,' he said. 'Probably the best thing you can do is play it by ear. See what your mother has to say first and then follow your instincts. It's like walking on eggshells! But I agree with you and Grace, Cindy's family ought to know she is safe and they ought to know about Poppy.'

'Next week, or very soon,' he went on, 'the case will go to court and it may well get splashed all over the newspapers. No matter how hard Danny tries to keep Cindy's name out of things, it's unlikely that he will succeed. Journalists are past masters at digging and this will be a very sensational story.'

'I hope they won't try to interview Cindy,' Rebecca said, shaking her head.

'They most probably will. In fact it would be better if her family not only know where she's been all this time but what the outcome has been, and take her back into their home. She would be much safer from bombardment from the press if she was in Shelston rather than here in Liverpool.'

'Yes, you're right,' Rebecca nodded. 'Grace and I won't be with her at the flat as we are at the moment. Grace might manage to get along there from time to time, but her school is some distance away and she will be kept very busy for the first few weeks.'

'Then you must make an effort to tell Cindy's mum everything and see if you can persuade her to have Cindy back living with them,' Nick told her.

For the rest of the journey Rebecca said very little. She was busy sorting out in her own mind what she was going to tell Mavis Mason and how she would approach it in the first place.

As they neared Shelston Nick gave her a sideways glance and asked, 'Planned the attack?'

'I'm going to confide in my mother and then take her advice on how to go about things. She's known Mavis since they first started school and they are more like sisters than friends, so I'm sure she will be able to tell me what to do.'

'Why don't you leave it until this evening – until after we've had a meal and listened to their news and they've listened to ours? I'll suggest taking your dad out for a drink and that will give you the opportunity to talk to your mother.'

'Great idea!' A smile transformed Rebecca's face and she squeezed his arm affectionately. 'It will be a lot easier if there's just the two of us. I've got it worked out pretty clearly what I am going to say, and if I can do it without any questions or interruptions I won't lose my train of thought.'

Bill and Sandra Peterson came to the front door of Woodside together to meet Rebecca and Nick.

'My, you two are organized! You picked Becky up from the railway station en route, did you, Nick?' Bill Peterson asked him.

'Nick has been staying with me in Liverpool for a couple of days, so we motored down from there,' Rebecca said quickly.

'You mean you've been working up there?' Sandra questioned. 'I didn't know you went to shops as far afield as that,' she added before Nick could answer.

'No, I took a couple of days off,' he told Sandra. 'I wanted to spend some time with Rebecca before she becomes too engrossed in her new job to have any time for any of us.'

There was a moment's silence as he caught the exchange of looks between Bill and Sandra, and hoped he hadn't given then the wrong impression. It was obvious that Rebecca hadn't told them he was staying in Liverpool with her.

'Well, come along in and tell us all your news,' Bill said, giving Nick a hearty slap on the back as they went into the hallway.

'Yes, come on, the meal is all ready and waiting and I expect you're both starving after such a long journey,' Sandra added.

'OK. We'll leave our cases in the hall and we can take them upstairs later,' Nick said.

They exchanged news as they tucked into the meal that Sandra had prepared for them. Rebecca listened with interest to some of the local news, and Bill and Nick exchanged opinions about changes in the retail butchery business.

'You seem to keep yourself far more up to date on new legislation than I do,' Bill said grudgingly.

'Well, I have to with moving about. Some of the larger businesses are red hot on such matters, and so they should be. It's no good the government making changes in the law for the betterment of our trade and our customers if we don't play our part and follow them through.'

'No, you're quite right,' Bill agreed. 'I must try to make sure I keep in touch with things more in the future. The trouble is I'm not getting any younger,' he added with a grin.

As soon as their meal was finished and they had helped Sandra to clear away, Nick suggested a trip to the pub for a pint.

'I've missed the local brew that they serve at the Red Lion,' he told Bill with a knowing look.

'In that case we'd better stroll along there and see if it's as good as you remember. Can we bring you girls back anything?' he asked, looking at Sandra.

'No, you two cut along and leave us in peace. We've got plenty of chatting to do ourselves. I want to know where Rebecca bought those lovely shoes she's wearing and dozens of other fashion tips that I miss out on down here in the country.'

Thirty-Nine

As soon as the door closed behind Bill and Nick, Sandra Peterson went over to the glass-fronted sideboard and brought out a bottle of cream sherry. She placed it on the table and put two glasses alongside it.

'I think we'll probably both need a glass of this after you've told me your news,' Sandra said looking at Rebecca rather sternly.

'What do you mean?' Rebecca frowned.

'You've obviously got something serious to tell me and that's why Nick's taken your dad out for a beer. You planned that he would do that once we'd eaten, didn't you?'

'Yes, as a matter of fact we did because Nick thought it would be easier for me to tell you the news I have for you if we were on our own.'

'Come on then, let's get it over; tell me the worst. It concerns you and Nick, I suppose. I had no idea he was staying with you in Liverpool,' she added censoriously.

'He only stayed for a couple of nights. We weren't sleeping together, if that's what you're thinking,' Rebecca said with a short laugh. 'Nick slept on the sofa and Grace was in the house as well, so it was all quite proper.'

'So what is this news, then?'

'It's not about me, it's about Cindy.'

'Cindy! You mean you know where she is?'

'I do, but I'm not sure whether or not to tell her mother. Cindy said she would leave it up to me.'

'Of course you must tell her, Becky. You must do so right away. She'll be over the moon. Why wouldn't you tell her?'

'It's not that simple, Mum. You see, Cindy has a little girl. She's called Poppy and she's adorable,' she added quickly when she saw the look of horror on her mother's face.

'You mean she's married?'

'No, she's not married.' Rebecca paused. 'Pour us both a glass of sherry and then I'll explain everything. I need to tell you the whole story right from the beginning.'

Sandra listened in stunned silence as Rebecca related how she'd first spotted Cindy in Hoylake when she'd been sent there as a trainee teacher. She went on to explain how she had found out that Cindy was virtually a prisoner, because they were threatening to harm the baby if she tried to escape or informed the police about them.

'She even got a beating because she was seen talking to me one day.'

'You haven't said who it is that's keeping her a prisoner,' Sandra said as Rebecca paused to take a sip of sherry.

'Bruno and his family. Only that isn't his real name, of course.'

'Bruno?' her mother looked puzzled.

'The chap who was the manager of the supermarket here when it first opened.'

Sandra still looked puzzled. 'But he left here some time before Cindy disappeared. So she didn't run away with him. You mean she followed him?'

'No, it wasn't like that. He and another man, I think it was his brother, waylaid Cindy at Frome station the day she was on her way to Cardiff to spend the weekend with me.'

'You mean they grabbed her after Jake had dropped her off?'

'That's right.'

They were silent for a moment as they sipped their sherry.

'So now that she has got away from them, or at least I assume she has, why doesn't she come home?'

'Because of Poppy.'

'Her little girl?'

'That's right. She feels she will be bringing shame on her family and that they would probably prefer her to keep away.'

'What rubbish!' Sandra looked shocked. 'Mavis and Tom will be over the moon at finding her, and for that matter so will Jake. He's always felt in some way to blame because he was the last person to see her. He's said time and time again that he wished he'd gone up on to the platform with her and seen her on to the Cardiff train.'

'So you think Cindy's mother will accept little Poppy?'

'I'm quite sure she will. She might feel a trifle hurt that Cindy hasn't come straight home. I take it she is living with you now?'

'Oh yes. At the moment she's in our flat in Liverpool. But she can't stay there because we are both moving out. Grace is going to a school near Chester and I'm going to one in Blissford.'

'Blissford? Why that's less than twenty miles from here!' Sandra exclaimed, her face lighting up with a smile. 'Why didn't you say so earlier?'

Rebecca smiled but didn't answer. She didn't want to be drawn into a discussion about her own future at the moment.

'So Cindy will be homeless when you two move away?'

'Yes, unless she can come back here. Though we might be able to make some sort of arrangement for her. Maybe she could go and live at Grace's home. Grace's brother Danny has been one of the policemen involved in the case—'

'Policemen? The police are involved?'

'Yes, that's the other problem. The case will be going to court soon and it's more than likely that it will be in all the newspapers. Cindy's not at all sure what her family will think about that.'

'I think you must have missed out a lot of your story,' her mother told her sharply. 'Why are the police involved? What has Cindy done?'

'Cindy hasn't done anything. The people who were holding her prisoner turned out to be illegal immigrants and they've all been arrested. Cindy and Poppy were sent to hospital so that their injuries could be treated, and they were only discharged a couple of weeks ago.'

'Dear, oh dear! This story gets worse in the telling,' Sandra exclaimed as she reached for the sherry bottle and topped up their glasses.

There was silence for a moment, then Sandra put down her glass.

'Let me get this straight. Cindy was abducted by that chap Bruno and his gang, and then kept prisoner. She had a baby, presumably it is his, and then they allowed her out to do the shopping but wouldn't let her take the baby with her and threatened to harm it if she tried to run away. Have I got that right?'

'Yes, but they also used to keep the baby from her as a form of punishment and they ill-treated both her and the baby.'

'Was there no other woman in the house?'

'Yes, a very old woman who also treated Cindy badly. They wouldn't even let Cindy have a doctor or a nurse when she gave birth to Poppy. The old woman delivered it.'

'That's scandalous! I hope she's all right.'

'I think she is, although they kept her in hospital for several weeks and she's never really told us why.'

'Of course she must come home,' Sandra bristled. 'What a silly girl to think her mother and father won't welcome her with open arms.'

'And her little girl?' Rebecca asked.

'She's their grandchild, of course they'll welcome her.'

'Even though she's illegitimate?'

Sandra shuddered. 'Yes, even if she's illegitimate. I would do the same for you.'

Rebecca grinned. 'I know you would. In fact, I think that's what you thought I was about to tell you, that I was expecting a baby and wanted to come home.'

Sandra blushed. 'Well, when your daughter who is living away from home turns up with a boyfriend and says he has been staying with her, Mum is bound to think the worst.'

'Really!'

As their eyes met, they both started laughing.

'You'll understand better when you are a mother yourself,' Sandra told her.

She drained her glass and put it down on the table. 'Come on, get your coat. We're going up to the Masons' farm right now to give them the good news about Cindy.'

Forty

The late evening sun was sinking over the horizon like a huge golden-red ball as Rebecca and Sandra set out for the Masons' farm.

'Do you think we should have left doing this until the morning?' Rebecca asked anxiously.

'No, not a bit of it! I wouldn't be able to sleep knowing what I do and aware of how worried Mavis and Tom still are over Cindy's disappearance. No, we owe it to them to put their minds at ease just as soon as we can'.

'I hope you're right,' Rebecca murmured. 'By the way, are you and the Masons friends again now?'

'More or less. I think Mavis still sometimes blames us for Cindy vanishing. If she hadn't been coming to see you, then she would have been safe and sound on the farm as usual. Leastways, that's the way Mavis looks at it.'

'All those dreadful accusations against Dad, though. Does she ever regret them?'

'She wasn't the one who started those terrible rumours,' Sandra defended. 'That malicious gossip was started by old Lizzie Smith and her cronies.'

'Yes, I know, but the Masons didn't do very much to stop the rumours, did they?'

'True, but they were so upset about Cindy disappearing that I don't think they were thinking rationally at the time.'

'So everything is more or less all right between you now?'

'Yes, perfectly all right,' Sandra said firmly.

Mavis Mason was shutting up the hens for the night and Tom was making sure the other animals were all comfortably bedded down when Sandra and Rebecca arrived at the farm.

'What's up? You don't usually come calling at this time of night,' Mavis remarked in surprise.

'Bill not with you?' Tom asked with equal surprise.

'He's gone for a drink at the Red Lion with Nick,' Sandra told them.

'Then I think I'll go and join them and leave you women to your chatter.'

'No, wait,' Sandra said. 'There's something I have to tell you . . . Both of you. Can we go inside?'

'Sounds serious,' Mavis commented as she led the way into their sitting room. 'There's something wrong, isn't there?'

'Is it to do with our Cindy? Have you heard something, Becky?' Tom asked, looking at her.

'Yes, she has,' Sandra told him. She looked at her daughter, 'Do you want to tell them or shall I do it for you, Becky?' she asked.

'Let Becky do the talking since she must be the one who knows what's been going on,' Tom said as he led them into the comfortably furnished sitting room. 'Come on, sit down and let's hear what it is you have to say. Come straight out with it, girl. After all this time we can take just about anything.'

'She's not dead, is she?' Mavis asked, her voice shaking.

'No. No, she's not dead. She's alive and well and I can tell you where she is. But there's just one very important thing you need to know first. Cindy has a little girl and—'

'Our Cindy's had a baby!' Mavis exclaimed, the colour draining from her face. 'Are you sure about that, Becky?'

'Yes, I'm quite sure. She has a little girl called Poppy and she's adorable.'

'Then why hasn't she brought her home to see us?' Tom asked in a bewildered voice.

'It's a long story,' Rebecca told them. For the second time that night she found herself recounting all that had happened to Cindy since the evening she disappeared.

The Masons sat in stunned silence, then bombarded her with countless questions. Some she could answer, but several she didn't know the answer to and she felt almost as bewildered as they were by the time she had finished explaining everything she did know.

'Well, this is wonderful news and calls for a celebratory drink,' Tom insisted as he fetched a bottle of port and filled glasses for each of them.

Rebecca was about to say she didn't want any more to drink as she had already had two glasses of sherry. But she felt they might find it hurtful if she refused, so she joined in the toast as they raised their glasses and drank to Cindy's safe homecoming.

'What I can't understand,' Mavis said as she drained her glass and put it down on the table by the side of her armchair, 'is why Cindy didn't come home with you today. Why leave it to you to tell us all that's been happening?'

'I think she was afraid to in case you were upset by all that has gone on,' Rebecca said lamely. 'She didn't know how you would feel about her having had a baby when she isn't married.'

'How I would feel about my own grandchild! What sort of person does she think I am? As for not being married, well whose business is that except ours?'

'You mightn't feel that way when Lizzie finds out and starts spreading malicious gossip in the village,' Sandra warned.

'That foul-mouthed old hag! I don't worry about her or any of the other gossips who join in with her,' Mavis said dismissively.

'The other thing that's worrying Cindy is what may be said in court and what they will put in the newspapers.'

'It might only get into a couple of papers, and I doubt if anyone in the village will hear about it if it does,' Tom reassured them.

'Don't be too sure about that. Journalists can make these sort of cases seem really dramatic.'

'Well, let them, see if we care. As long as our Cindy is safe and sound, that's all that matters.'

Tom nodded. 'Our Jake will be that relieved. He's always felt he was in some way to blame.'

'Yes, I was telling Rebecca, Jake's always said he wished he had gone on to the platform with her and seen her safely on to the Cardiff train.'

'If only he'd done that, then none of this would ever have happened! Those men wouldn't have been able to bundle her into their car and take her away,' Mavis added with a sigh.

'Let's forget all about that now,' Tom said. 'Cindy's safe and sound, and what I want to know is when she is coming home. I'd like to go and get her right now.'

'I don't think that would be a very good idea, it might frighten her if you suddenly turn up after all this time,' Sandra warned him. 'No, let Rebecca go back and tell her that you now know everything and then bring her home in a day or two's time.'

'Yes, I suppose you're right,' Tom agreed. 'It will give us time to get used to the idea as well.'

'It'll give me time to get her room ready for her, and we'll need to see if the cot we had for our two is still in the attic. First thing tomorrow, Tom, you must get it down, then I can clean it up and find some bedding for it. I'll have everything ready and waiting for the pair of them, so bring her home as quick as you can, Becky.'

'I'll tell her everything you've said and that you want her home,' Rebecca promised. 'I'll ring you and let you know which day we're coming.'

'That's a good girl,' Mavis told her, flinging her arms round Rebecca and hugging her. 'Make it as soon as you can. I still feel like I'm imagining all this, so bring her back here before I wake up and find it's all a dream.'

'I think we'd better be going,' Sandra said. 'It's getting dark, and Bill and Nick will be back from the pub and wondering where we are.'

'They'll have a damn good idea, I imagine,' Tom agreed. 'Come on then, if you're ready to go, I'll walk down to your place with you.'

Forty-One

When Rebecca and Nick arrived back at the flat in Liverpool, they found that Cindy looked as though she had been crying and her first words the moment they went through the door were 'Well? What did they say?'

'They're over the moon that at long last they know you are safe and where you are,' Rebecca told her.

She stared at them for a long moment in silence, almost as if she hadn't heard what they said or if she had then she didn't believe them.

'Do they want to see me, though?'

'Of course they do. And little Poppy,' Rebecca told her. 'They're thrilled to bits about having a grandchild.'

Cindy looked doubtful. 'Are you sure?'

'Quite sure,' Nick affirmed.

'Did you tell them everything?'

'Absolutely everything, from the time you vanished at Frome station right up to the present moment.'

'Rebecca even warned them there would be a court case coming up soon and your name may be mentioned,' Nick added.

Cindy went white. 'So what did they say to that?'

'They want you to be home with them safe and sound before that happens,' Rebecca assured her.

'They are so eager to have you back that your father would have driven up here tonight to collect you, but we felt you needed a day or so to come to terms with the idea of going home.' Nick told her.

'When we left, your mum was planning to bring down the cot she used for you and Jake when you were little from the attic and get it all cleaned up ready for Poppy,' Rebecca said with a smile.

Cindy still didn't seem to be completely convinced. She shook her head from side to side, pushed her hair back behind her ears and fiddled with the belt of her dress as she looked from Rebecca to Nick and back again.

'So what do you think I ought to do?' she burst out.

'Get down to Shelston and see them, of course,' Nick told her.

'When they see me again, they might think I've changed and maybe they won't want me back.'

'Oh for goodness sake, Cindy, pull yourself together,' Rebecca said impatiently, 'We've been to see your parents. We've told them everything there was to tell them, and they want you back.'

Cindy nodded and smiled weakly. 'Sorry, I just can't believe it's true! But I . . . I'm afraid to face them. Will you come with me, Becky? I'd feel better if you did.'

'Of course I will. Not tonight, though,' Rebecca grinned. 'What about tomorrow?'

'Oh yes, yes, that would be wonderful!' Cindy flung her arms round Rebecca and hugged her.

'Hold on a minute,' Nick said quickly. 'How are you going to get there? I can't take you, I have to be at work tomorrow morning.' He looked at his wristwatch, 'In fact, I ought to be setting off within the next half hour if I'm to get to the lodgings I've reserved before midnight.'

'We'll figure something out,' Rebecca said confidently. 'We can always go by train.'

'Or perhaps Danny would take you down if he's off duty?' Grace suggested.

She had been sitting quietly nursing Poppy and listening to all that had been said.

'I couldn't ask him to do that, it would take him all day,' Cindy demurred.

'He'd jump at the chance of spending a whole day with you,' Grace said with a smile.

Cindy blushed but said nothing. She suspected that it was true. Danny had been calling at the flat more and more frequently and he always seemed concerned about how she was. It had been due to Danny's intervention that she had been allowed to stay with Grace and Rebecca after she came out of hospital, and she would always be grateful to him for that. Even so, to expect him to spend his free time driving her down to Shelston was asking rather a lot, she thought.

'I would feel much happier if I knew that was what was happening,' Nick said. 'I don't like the idea of you travelling all that way by train, with Poppy to look after and having to change trains and so on.'

'Danny will take them, I'm sure of that,' Grace stated.

'I don't think we could get there and back in a day,' Cindy muttered.

'Why do you need to come back here?' Grace looked puzzled.

'That's right. You could stay down there and we can bring all your things down later on,' Rebecca suggested.

Cindy still looked undecided, but did seem ready to go along with their suggestions.

'I've got to leave, I'm afraid,' Nick said finally. 'Will you phone me later on, Rebecca, when you've decided what you're going to do?'

'I will,' she promised as she went to the door with him, leaving Cindy and Grace still volubly discussing the pros and cons of Danny driving her to Shelston.

In the privacy of the hallway, Nick took Rebecca in his arms and kissed her. 'This wasn't the way I intended our weekend to end,' he said ruefully.

'Never mind!' She hugged him close. 'We have plenty more weekends to come.'

'A whole lifetime, I hope,' he said tenderly as once again he kissed her deeply and passionately.

When Danny came round to the flat later that evening after coming off duty, Grace put the question to him about driving Cindy down to Shelston to see her parents.

'Of course I will,' he said eagerly, his face lighting up with the pleasure. 'When do you want to go, Cindy?'

'As soon as possible. But are you sure you want to drive all that way? It will take hours.'

'I don't mind if it takes days. I've got three days' leave coming up at the end of the week, so we could go then.'

Cindy's face registered delight, then clouded. 'That's two days away. Perhaps I ought to take the train?'

'Two days is no time at all,' Rebecca told her. 'You need time for me to let my mum know what is happening, and for her to tell your mum and for your mum to get things ready for you and Poppy.'

'Yes, I suppose you're right,' Cindy agreed. 'The thing is, the longer I put it off the worse it seems. I'm so scared they won't want me when I get there.'

'You do talk a whole lot of nonsense sometimes,' Grace told her bluntly. 'Don't forget we have to give up this flat in ten days' time, then you'll have nowhere to live. Rebecca is going down south, I'm going to a school near Chester, and we've got a lot of preparation and planning to do—'

'All right, Grace, don't make a meal of it!' Danny said

reprovingly. 'I can understand how Cindy feels and I only wish I could get away earlier. But I can't, so that's that. I certainly don't want you travelling all that way by train,' he told Cindy firmly.

'Very well,' Cindy said meekly. 'Thank you for agreeing to take me, Danny, I didn't mean to sound ungrateful. There's just one other thing,' she went on slowly. 'Can Rebecca come with us? I'd like her to be there when I meet my family.'

'Of course she can, but will she have time? There's all the clearing up here for her and Grace to do before they hand back the flat.'

'Don't worry, I'll help them do that,' Cindy said quickly.

'Right, then. That's fine by me, as long as Rebecca doesn't mind coming with us.'

Forty-Two

They left Liverpool at eight o'clock. Danny was driving, with Cindy sitting alongside him and Rebecca in the back of the car with Poppy safely strapped into a car seat that Danny had managed to borrow from a fellow officer who had small children.

Packed in with them were several of Poppy's soft toys to keep her amused during the long journey.

'She will probably sleep once we get moving,' Danny prophesied. 'That's what usually happens with young children, so I'm told. I've put a soft cushion and a blanket in there for her, and you can cover her up and make her comfortable if she nods off.'

Danny was quite right. Poppy did sleep for most of the journey. Although it was a long way, they only stopped once to have a break at a roadside café.

'With any luck we should be in Shelston by midday,' he said as they returned to the car.

It had been dull and overcast when they left Liverpool, but by the time they reached Shelston the sun was out and it was pleasantly warm, a perfect early-September day.

As they approached the village, Danny pulled into the side of the road. 'Perhaps you and Cindy should change seats, Rebecca,' he suggested. 'You know where to go and you can direct me. Are we going straight to Cindy's home?'

'Cindy knows the way there as well as I do, probably better,' Rebecca objected. But she followed Cindy's example and changed seats.

'I don't want to go straight to the farm,' Cindy said. 'Can we go to your place first, Becky?'

'Of course. That's what I thought we would do.'

Seated next to Danny, Rebecca directed him off the main road and up the small side road to Woodside. When they had stopped at the café, she had quietly slipped away and telephoned her mother so she knew she would be there waiting for them.

Everything was as she had planned. Sandra welcomed Cindy with open arms and then turned her attention to Poppy, making a great fuss of the little girl as she led them indoors and into the kitchen where the table was already laid for a meal.

Within minutes Bill Peterson arrived home from the shop for his midday break, and by the time Rebecca had introduced him to Danny and Bill had made a fuss of Poppy, their meal was ready and waiting on the table.

'Now, as you know, your dad and me have to get back to the shop. So I'll leave you to take Cindy up to the farm,' Sandra Peterson said as she and Rebecca cleared things away and tidied the kitchen.

'Thank you, Mrs Peterson,' Cindy said, giving Sandra a hug. 'Would . . . Would you mind phoning my mum and telling her we're on our way?'

'Of course I will, if that's what you want me to do. But she knows you are coming today, so wouldn't you rather it was a surprise for her?'

Cindy looked hesitant then, after exchanging looks with Danny, she nodded and said, 'Very well, we'll do that.'

Ten minutes later they were all up at the farm. Rebecca went to knock on the door, but before she could reach it Mavis and Tom were out in the yard, holding their arms out to Cindy, hugging and kissing her and exclaiming how happy they were that she was back with them.

While all this was going on, Danny and Rebecca stood holding Poppy's hands. She was staring mesmerized at what was happening, and when Cindy turned and held out her hand and called her name she clutched shyly at Rebecca and hid her face.

It took Rebecca a minute to persuade Poppy to go to her mother, and then when she did she grabbed at Cindy's leg and buried her face against her.

Cindy picked her up and cuddled her, and gradually Poppy turned to look at Mavis and Tom and then quickly hid her face again.

'Let's go inside,' Mavis suggested. 'Perhaps she'll feel more comfortable with us if we're all sitting down.'

'I think I know what will make her smile,' Tom said as he left the little group and strode across to one of the barns.

By the time they were indoors and sitting down, he was back carrying a small bundle of fur, which he placed on the floor near Poppy. 'There you are my little darling,' he told her, 'a baby like yourself. Someone for you to play with. Try stroking her.'

Poppy stared fascinated as the tiny bundle uncurled itself and moved towards her. Gingerly she stretched out a hand and touched its soft silky fur. The kitten purred and arched its back, then moved close to Poppy, waving its little tail like a flag.

Poppy scrambled down from Cindy's lap and sat on the floor with the kitten, laughing as it began to climb over her and paw playfully at the tassel on the belt of her dress.

'I think those two are going to be good friends, don't you?' Tom laughed, looking round.

He turned and held out a hand to Danny. 'Rebecca said on the phone that you would be driving them down. That was very good of you. I wanted to come up to Liverpool the minute I heard that my Cindy had been found, and was safe and well, and bring her back here, but the missus persuaded me to have more sense. That's the trouble with running a farm, you have to be there twenty-four hours a day in case something goes wrong with one of the animals. What do you do for a living, Danny?'

'I'm a policeman,' Danny told him as they shook hands. 'My sister Grace has been Rebecca's flatmate since she's been up in Liverpool, so I got to know Cindy through them,' he added.

'It's thanks to Danny that I was rescued and that I'm here now,' Cindy told them. 'I owe my freedom to Rebecca and Danny,' she added, smiling at Danny.

'Yes, we gathered from what Becky and her friend Nick told us that there has been a lot going on,' Tom Mason said solemnly. 'They told us all they knew but we will be looking forward to hearing more about it from you, Cindy, when you feel you are ready to talk about it. You seem to have been having a pretty harrowing time.'

'Would you all like a drink?' Mavis invited. 'I was going to offer you tea, but you young ones might want something stronger.'

'Tea would be lovely, Mrs Mason,' Danny told her. 'I have to drive back to Liverpool, so I had better not have anything stronger.'

'You're driving back right away?' Mavis looked astonished.

'Well . . .' Danny hesitated.

'You said you have three days off,' Cindy reminded him. 'Surely you can stay for a couple of days?'

'We have a spare bed,' Tom assured him. 'Our son Jake has got himself married and left home, so you can have his room.'

'Yes, of course. That came as rather a shock,' Cindy admitted ruefully.

'Well, if it won't be putting you out, then I would happily stay overnight. It will give Cindy a chance to decide whether she is going to stay or come back to Liverpool.'

'Oh, there's no question of that,' Tom said with feeling. 'Now we've got her home, we have no intention of letting her out of our sight again.'

'All my things and Poppy's are up in Liverpool, I've only brought an overnight bag,' Cindy told him.

'Never mind about that, you are staying right here, my girl, and no argument,' her father said firmly. He looked across at Rebecca. 'You can sort out all her stuff and get it down here, can't you, Becky?'

'Yes, I suppose I can. I might be able to get Dad to come and collect me and take me to my new place in Blissford for the start of the new school term, and we can probably bring Cindy's stuff with us.'

'Or I can bring it down for you,' Danny interposed. 'I'd like to,' he added quickly when he saw that Tom was about to decline his offer. 'I'll want to know how Cindy and Poppy are and make sure they've settled in.'

Forty-Three

For the next few days, life in their Liverpool flat was hectic for Rebecca and Grace. They had not only to pack up their possessions for their move to the new schools they'd been allocated to but also to pack up all Cindy and Poppy's belongings ready for them to be taken back to Shelston.

Then the two of them cleaned, polished and dusted every inch of the flat in order to make sure it was in pristine condition for the end of the week, when they were due to hand the keys back at the end of their lease.

By the time bedtime came, both of them were so exhausted they were sure they wouldn't be able to sleep. They had a final drink together, wished each other well, and promised to keep in touch and that they would meet up in Shelston at half-term.

'That means Cindy as well,' Rebecca said. 'You don't want to lose touch with her, do you?'

'I think that's unlikely,' Grace said dryly, 'especially since Danny will no doubt be visiting Cindy to make sure she's all right.'

'Well, if he comes to Shelston at half-term then you must come too,' Rebecca insisted. 'Promise now!'

The next morning, as the final parting came they both knew their lives were changing and that they could only hope the future would turn out well.

* * *

When Rebecca went home at half-term she not only found that Cindy and Poppy had settled in very happily, she also discovered that Danny was a regular visitor at the Masons' farm.

Old Lizzie Smith had plenty to say on the matter when she met Rebecca.

'That young policeman seems to be checking up on Cindy Mason almost every weekend. What sort of trouble has she been in that he needs to do that?' she asked, her dark eyes bright with curiosity.

'None at all, Lizzie,' Rebecca told her sharply, 'so watch your tongue!'

'Well, then, why does he come down here so often?'

'He's a friend of Cindy's, that's why. He just happens to be a policeman.'

'You can make it all sound innocent, Rebecca Peterson, but I spotted some of the details in the newspaper a few weeks back. Some scandalous goings on by the sound of it, and your friend Cindy was in the thick of it.'

'If you want the details, Lizzie, then go up to the Masons' farm and ask them about it,' Rebecca snapped and pushed her way past, leaving Lizzie muttering until she was out of earshot about criminals and wrongdoers and young girls who went off the rails.

'Lizzie Smith is a malicious old crone!' she told her mother when she got home.

'Take no notice of her, no one ever does.'

'That's the whole point, though,' Rebecca argued. 'People say they don't take any notice of what she says, but you know as well as I do that they do listen and they always think there's a grain of truth in what she says.'

'That's true enough, but don't worry about what she's saying about Cindy. Tom has spelled out the true story down at the Red Lion and it has circulated in the village. Everyone I've spoken to is as relieved as we are that she's back home safe and sound.'

'What about Poppy, though? What are they saying about her?'

'That she's an adorable little girl and everyone who has met her thinks so. I hear them talking among themselves in the shop while they're waiting to be served and I've not heard one bad word either about her or about Cindy.'

'So you think everything has settled down?'

'Absolutely. And Mavis and Tom are like new people. They were so glum and miserable that folks were starting to shun them, but now they're both back to their old selves.'

'Do Tom and Mavis like Danny?' Rebecca asked.

'Very much. The same as we like Nick,' Sandra said archly.

Rebecca felt the colour flooding her face.

'He's coming to work here all next week,' Sandra added.

'Really?' Rebecca looked surprised. 'Why is that?'

'Your dad has a series of hospital appointments for tests on his heart. Now, tell me all about this new school, you haven't said very much so far.'

'I'll do that when you tell me more about Dad. What's wrong with his heart?'

'Nothing you need worry about. We think he's been doing too much recently, and he's had one or two dizzy spells and small blackouts. He thinks it happens when he's lifting carcasses and doing heavy jobs like that.'

The rest of her half-term holiday seemed to fly past but it was harmonious enough. While Nick was working in the shop, she saw a good deal of Cindy and Poppy. They had both settled happily at the farm, almost as if they had never known any other sort of life.

Cindy was helping her mother with the dairy work and the general running of things. Poppy loved it there and was fascinated by all the animals.

Tom was always picking her up and taking her to see a new-born calf or some other happening. The kitten that Tom had given her on her first day in Shelston had grown considerably but was still as playful as ever. It was Poppy's constant companion and followed her everywhere.

Danny was a regular visitor and it was difficult to say who enjoyed his visits the most, Cindy or Poppy.

Rebecca was almost sorry when the half-term break was over and she had to return to Blissford. The only thing she had been disappointed about was the fact that Grace hadn't found time to come with Danny, after all.

When she asked him why that was, he grinned broadly and explained that Grace had a new boyfriend and that he lived in Chester, where she was working. 'I'm surprised she hasn't told you about him. They went away on a short cruise for the half-term break.'

As Nick drove Rebecca back to Blissford, he told her he had some special news to tell her.

'Oh yes, what's that?'

'I'll tell you when we get to Blissford. We're in good time, so let's stop and have a drink before I take you to your lodgings.'

'Why can't you tell me now as we're driving along?'

'I need all my attention on the road,' he told her, grinning.

Twenty minutes later, when they stopped at the Golden Crown, Rebecca turned to face him. 'Come on, what's your news?'

'I've got a new job. I've been offered a partnership.'

'You mean you won't be travelling all over the place any more but settled in one town? That's good, isn't it? Where is it?'

'It's in a village, not a town.'

Her face fell. 'Oh, only a small place.'

'Yes, but it's a very busy little shop.'

'Are you happy about it? Is it far from here?'

'I'm very happy,' he told her, 'and it's not far from here.'

'Come on, if we're going to have that drink before you leave then we'll have to hurry up.'

Inside the pub she found a corner seat while Nick ordered their drinks at the bar. When he brought the drinks over and set them down, she raised her glass. 'To your new job and let's hope it will be a success.'

He raised his glass and clinked it against hers.

'You haven't told me where it is,' she reminded him.

He grinned. 'Can't you guess?'

She shook her head.

'Your dad has offered me a partnership,' he said quietly.

She stared at him wide-eyed. 'Oh no!' She put her glass down, her hand was shaking too much for her to hold it.

'What's wrong?' Nick frowned. 'I thought you'd be pleased. It means—'

'It means that his heart problem is worse than my parents have told me,' she said in a shaky voice. 'Did you know he went to the hospital for a check-up? That's why they asked you to come and work at the shop this week.'

'Of course I knew. He was told he has to take things easier. His heart will be all right as long as he doesn't overexert himself, so he has to stop lifting heavy things, like whole carcasses and so on.'

Rebecca took a drink from her glass and they stared at each other in silence for a while.

'You are telling me the truth?' she asked at length.

'Yes,' he said solemnly. 'Your dad is going to be OK, especially if I am there to do all the heavy work and the butchering. It will mean your mother can ease up too. She won't be needed in the shop if she doesn't want to come in, because your dad will be able to deal with customers when I'm working out the back.'

'So it means things are going to be better all round,' Rebecca murmured. She drained her glass. 'You'll be there whenever I can get home,' she added with a warm smile. 'It might even be worth coming home at the weekends in future.'

Forty-Four

Rebecca found her new school at Blissford extremely challenging. Several times during her first week she was almost in tears from frustration.

Her class of twenty-eight pupils, all over eleven years of age, knew all the rules and regulations and, of course, the school layout too. They were also well aware that not only was she a new teacher in their school but that it was her first experience as a qualified teacher. Many of them played on this to undermine her authority.

She tried her best to deal with the many problems she came

up against without resorting to going to the headmaster for help or advice. By the end of the first week she knew she needed guidance.

'I'm surprised you've lasted this long,' Tim Heath, the headmaster, told her, staring at her over the top of his horn-rimmed glasses. 'Children can be very cruel and by the sound of things they have been testing you. From what I hear from your colleagues, however, you've done well. Don't despair. Another few days, a week at the most, and you will have them under control and they'll respect you all the more for not having brought me into the affray.'

Although Tim Heath was right, Rebecca found exercising her authority over an unruly class extremely exhausting.

Added to her tension was the fact that she had not been able to see Nick. He, too, was enduring a life-changing situation. When the agency he worked for learned that he was leaving them, they sent him to work out his month's notice at a butcher's shop a long way from home. As a result he was unable to visit Shelston, even for one night.

'Never mind,' he assured her when they spoke on the phone, 'I'll soon be in Shelston permanently and we'll be able to see each other every weekend.'

'By the look of things we won't see each other until half-term,' Rebecca sighed.

'By then you will have resolved all your problems and I will be free and working with your dad,' he consoled her.

Half-term couldn't come soon enough, Rebecca thought, and wished she hadn't been so adamant in telling her parents that she didn't want to come home at the weekends, at least not for the first few weeks.

'I'll need the weekends to prepare lessons for the coming week,' she explained. 'It's all pretty new to me, so it will probably take me quite a long time to do that. Once I get established, things will be easier.'

She wondered how Grace was getting on in her new school, and when she phoned her found that Grace was experiencing many of the same problems. That made her feel better, and from then on it seemed that her renewed confidence was apparent to her class and she had no further trouble from them.

By half-term she really had things under control and was congratulated by the headmaster. She knew her pupils and their various abilities. She knew which ones were bright and eager to learn; which ones wanted to learn but found it hard work; and which ones were either lazy or plain naughty and wanted to disrupt the class.

'You've done wonders and far quicker than I expected,' Tim Heath told her. 'I've even heard compliments about you from one or two of the parents. They said you seem to bring the best out in their children and manage to make your lessons so interesting that they talk about them at home.'

Rebecca found that Nick had already taken up his position as partner in the butcher's shop just before she arrived back in Shelston for half-term. She had expected him to drive over to Blissford to collect her, but it was her mother who came instead.

'They were so busy in the shop that it made sense for me to come and collect you,' she explained. 'Having Nick working with us full time has made a terrific difference already. He's doing all the heavy work and butchering, and your dad is looking so much better already.'

'Has Nick managed to find somewhere in the village to live?'

'Not yet, so he is staying with us at Woodside. It means you'll be able to see a lot more of each other,' she added archly.

Rebecca didn't answer. She was too busy wondering if this was such a good idea. She always looked forward so much to seeing Nick and wondered if it would take away some of the excitement if he was there all the time.

They drove direct to Woodside, and while Rebecca unloaded the car Sandra went indoors and made them both a cup of tea.

'Are you going back to the shop now?' she asked he mother as they finished their tea and she carried the tray back into the kitchen.

'No, I'm going to start getting the meal ready for tonight,' her mother told her as she took down her apron and fastened it round her waist. 'I usually come back home about this time in order to do that. Got to feed the lodger, you know,' she added with a smile. 'Why don't you go down to the shop and meet your dad and Nick? I'm sure they'd both be pleased to see I managed to get you home safe and sound.'

After dinner that evening, as they sat making plans for the following week Bill insisted that Nick must have some extra time off to go out and about with Rebecca while she was at home.

'We managed without you before and we can do so again for a few days,' he insisted when Nick argued that it wouldn't be fair to take time off when he'd only just started working there.

'You're as much the boss as I am now, you know,' Bill blustered, 'so why shouldn't you take time off when you need it?'

In the end Nick gave in, but only on the promise from Bill that he wouldn't lift any heavy carcasses and that, wherever possible, he would leave large joints that needed cutting for Nick to do the next morning before he and Rebecca went off for the rest of the day.

The arrangement worked well. Rebecca found herself relaxing after the gruelling term she had just experienced and by the end of half-term she felt ready to face her class no matter how rebellious they might be.

Rebecca enjoyed her vacation. She and Nick went for long walks, went to the pictures in one of the nearby towns, and even went dancing on the Saturday night.

She also managed to see Cindy and Poppy and was delighted by how happy and settled they were.

'Poppy follows Dad everywhere, she's like his shadow,' Cindy laughed. 'They get on like a house on fire. She has no time for me when he's around.'

'Or when Danny is here,' her mother added.

'Danny? You mean he's been down to see you, Cindy?'

'Down to see her, I'll say he has. I never knew a policeman who had so much time off,' Mavis Mason chuckled. 'He might as well move in here.'

As Nick drove her back to Blissford on the Sunday night at the end of her half-term break, Rebecca was happy in the knowledge that the partnership between her father and Nick was working out well. The two men not only seemed to understand each other but also seemed able to work together amicably.

Furthermore, her mother was clearly pleased with the arrangement because it meant she didn't have to work in the shop so much and this gave her more time for her own interests. She was once again her old glamorous self and not the worried-looking woman she had been when Rebecca was last at home.

'Are you happy in your new position?' she asked Nick as he took her in his arms and kissed her before saying goodnight.

'Completely,' he assured her. 'I've only one more ambition to achieve and I hope I will manage that pretty soon.'

'One more ambition?'

He laughed and kissed her again, then placed a finger on her lips to silence any further questions.

Forty-Five

After half-term, Rebecca didn't go home again until the school broke up for the Christmas holidays. Nick came to see her several weekends and talked enthusiastically about how well the shop was doing and the various improvements he had either made or intended to make.

'I think you need to take things slowly,' she warned him. 'Dad is not good about anyone changing things in the shop. He even used to get cross if Mum rearranged a window display he'd done.'

'Don't worry, he's fine about things. I usually manage to put the ideas to him in such a way that by the time they are carried out he's convinced they were his idea not mine,' Nick said with a laugh.

When Rebecca phoned to let them know which day she'd be coming home, she found that they were so busy in the shop neither Nick nor her mother could spare the time to come and collect her.

'In that case I'll leave it for a couple of days. I'd like to go and see Grace and her family. I haven't seen them for ages.'

Grace and her parents were pleased to see her and made her

very welcome. Grace was very interested in comparing what she was doing at her school and the routine at Rebecca's.

'So are you going home for Christmas?' Mrs Flowers asked as she brought them some fresh coffee and joined them for a chat.

'Of course! Nick and Mum are so busy in the shop they couldn't come to collect me, so I decided to pay you a visit first. I'll get the train home from here.'

'Well, in that case why don't you let Danny take you down to Shelston? He's going there to collect Cindy and Poppy and bring them back here for Christmas.'

'Really!' Rebecca looked surprised.

'Our Danny is on duty over Christmas and can't get down to Shelston to stay, so they're coming here. I'm looking forward to having a young child in the house, I can tell you.'

'I'm sure you are. How do the Masons feel about it?'

'Oh, they're being very understanding. Danny and Cindy are getting engaged at Christmas, so it is only right they should be together. We did invite Tom and Mavis up here, but as Tom explained you can't just take off and leave all those animals unattended. By the way, don't say anything about them getting engaged, not yet.'

'No, of course I won't,' Rebecca promised. 'I'm very pleased, though. I know Danny is very fond of Poppy.'

'Yes, but wait until one of them tells you. I suppose I shouldn't have said anything but I'm almost as excited as he is.'

The rest of the day passed all too quickly. Mrs Flowers had the meal ready and waiting when Danny came off duty. As they ate, she mentioned that Rebecca was on her way home and wanted a lift.

'Great! It's a long drive, but with someone to talk to it will pass twice as quickly.'

When they reached Shelston, Rebecca asked Danny to drop her off in the High Street. As she got out of the car and he handed her her suitcase, she heard a sharp cackling laugh and swung round to find Lizzie Smith standing there watching them.

'So you're pinching Cindy's boyfriend now are you?' she commented. 'Nice sort of friend you are and no mistake.'

Rebecca ignored her. Danny had heard what Lizzie had said and he raised his eyebrows and grinned then drove off in the direction of the Masons' farm.

When Rebecca walked into the shop, she was surprised to find everything looked different. For a start, she had never seen so many people waiting to be served. Both her parents were so busy dealing with them that they didn't even notice her come in.

As she looked around her, there were so many changes she hardly recognized the place. As well as a new glass-and-chrome floor-to-ceiling display cabinet for chutneys, relishes, sauces and spices, there was a separate display of produce from the Masons' farm, including cream, eggs, cheese and butter. There were also new chill-cabinets, a bigger counter and an incredible display of meat, poultry and bacon, all neatly wrapped in cling film and labelled with weight and price.

Many of the people waiting to be served were looking these over and selecting what they wanted to buy, so the turnover of customers was surprisingly speedy.

Rebecca edged her way through the waiting customers to the office. This too had changed considerably. A new computer took pride of place on the desk, which was completely clear of its usual mound of files and ledgers and scraps of papers. There was a new filing cabinet in one corner and the rather uncomfortable high stool that her mother always used had been replaced by a smart leather swivel chair.

As Rebecca sat down in it and twirled around, she wondered why they hadn't done all this years before. Perhaps she should have taken more interest and made suggestions, she thought a trifle guiltily. Yet if she had done, she doubted whether her father would have taken any notice. He had always been king in his little kingdom and no one – not even her mother, although she worked alongside him – had ever managed to persuade him to make any changes either to his display or to his method of working. Now it seemed everything had changed and, judging from the number of customers and the purchases they were making, had changed for the better.

* * *

Rebecca's parents and Nick were busy in the shop right up until late evening on Christmas Eve.

They declined her help in the shop, but her mother asked her if she could prepare something hot for their supper. She suggested soup.

'That will be easy to keep hot, as I've no idea exactly when we'll be home. There are still dozens of orders to deliver and a good many turkeys and gammon and beef joints still to be collected.'

As it turned out, it was almost eleven o'clock when they returned to Woodside. All three of them were exhausted. Rebecca was glad she had done as her mother asked and made soup, because they were far too tired to eat anything more substantial.

They followed it up with some mince pies, and coffee laced with whisky as a nightcap. Leaving Rebecca to clear up, Sandra and Bill went straight off to bed.

Nick and Rebecca sat in front of the roaring fire entwined in each other's arms as he told her about the success the shop had become.

'I think you can say we've taken on the supermarket and won hands down. Your dad says that most of the old customers are back with us, and we have some new ones as well. He is more than pleased.'

'I bet he is, but why have they come back?'

'I started putting ready-for-the-oven joints on view, wrapped in cling film so people could pick them up and look at them. That way they can see if they are lean enough or big enough for their needs. I also marked the price on them, so they would know what they cost.'

'You think that's made such a big difference?'

'Oh, it has. People say they like to have an idea of what they're going to spend. Previously when they asked for a particular cut they often found it was too small or too big for them or not a price they could afford, and they didn't always like to say so when there were other people waiting to be served.'

'Mm. I can understand that.'

'I also sent out leaflets to several hotels in the nearby towns, and that's brought us in a lot of extra trade. We have to deliver, of course, so that means your mum has had to start helping out again. If it's a heavy load then I normally take it, but if she wants to do some shopping in the town where the hotel is then she usually says she'll make the delivery. We all work well together and we make sure your dad doesn't do anything too strenuous.'

'He certainly looks better than he has done for a long time,' Rebecca agreed.

'Right. Now you know all that is going on in the shop, how about telling me what you're planning for us to do over Christmas?'

Rebecca looked up at him smiling. 'Not a lot, the most important thing is just being together.'

He smiled down at her, then their lips met and there was no need for any further discussion.

As the grandfather clock in the hall struck twelve, Rebecca pulled away from Nick. 'Did you hear that?' she asked. 'It's midnight, it's Christmas Day.'

'So it is!' He fumbled in the pockets of his jacket, which he had placed over a nearby chair, and brought out a small brown-paper package.

'My first Christmas present,' Rebecca exclaimed and stretched out her hand to take it.

'Hold on, not so fast!' he teased, raising his arm so that she couldn't reach it. 'You have to answer a question first.'

There was a moment's silence as he regarded her solemnly. 'Rebecca, will you marry me?'

'Marry you! Oh, Nick, of course I will. That's if you're sure.'

'Oh yes, I'm very sure,' he told her. He waved the small package. 'I bought this in the hope you would say yes.'

He tore away the wrapping paper to reveal a small jewellery box, and as he opened it she gave a cry of excitement. 'Oh, Nick, it's beautiful!'

He took out the ring that was inside and placed it on her finger. The ruby flanked by a small diamond on either side sparkled in the firelight. He kissed her hand, then gathered her in his arms and murmured her name before kissing her again, very slowly and passionately.

Forty-Six

At Woodside they all slept late on Christmas morning. Sandra, Bill and Nick because they were so exhausted by all the work they'd done during the weeks leading up to Christmas and on Christmas Eve itself.

Rebecca was almost too excited to sleep. She found it hard to believe that she and Nick were engaged, and kept fingering the ring he had slipped on to the third finger of her left hand as if reassuring herself that it was true.

At breakfast, when she showed the ring to her parents they were delighted by the news.

'I could see it was going to happen, of course,' Sandra said as she hugged them both.

'I'm pleased about it, too,' Bill confirmed as he shook hands with Nick and gave Rebecca a bearlike hug. 'I couldn't have chosen a better man to hand my daughter over to,' he added with a broad grin.

After breakfast they opened their presents. Nick had bought a beautiful cashmere stole for Sandra and a dark-red waistcoat for Bill.

He handed Rebecca a small flat package. She frowned as she took it. 'I thought I'd had my present,' she told him, splaying her hand so that her new ring gleamed and sparkled.

'Well, yes, you have really. That's why I've only bought you a little Christmas present.'

Mystified, she undid the wrapping. Inside, on a small velvet pad, was a key – a Yale key.

Rebecca stared at it bemused. 'What's this key for? she asked. 'It looks like a door key, but I already have a key for Woodside.'

'Oh, it's not for Woodside,' Nick told her. 'Nothing quite so grand I'm afraid. No, it's the key for a small cottage in the village of Millham and I hope we will soon be making it our home.'

'Our home!'

'Yes, our home,' he repeated. 'Now we're engaged we need to make plans for our future, and I thought this would be a good start. It's small but big enough. It's detached and has a pretty little garden around it. And it's empty. We can go and see it whenever you're ready.'

Rebecca couldn't wait. She was out of her chair, collecting her coat and hat. 'Come on then, let's do it now. We can all go. The turkey is in the oven and it's too early to put the vegetables on to cook.'

'No, you two go and look at it and we'll see it later,' Sandra demurred. 'We're both tired out. We'd sooner take it easy this morning, and we've promised the Masons we'll keep an eye on their farm as they've gone to spend the day with Danny and his family.'

'All that way, just for one day?' Rebecca said in surprise.

'Well, they can't stay longer because of the animals,' Bill explained. 'As it is, the cows won't be milked until they get home and heaven knows what the poor beasts will make of that. Poor old Tom will be up until midnight getting them sorted out.'

'It was a last-minute arrangement,' Sandra added. 'I know they very much wanted to be with Cindy and Poppy for Christmas.'

'I'll go up there this morning and feed the hens and check the cattle, and you two can go up this afternoon and make sure the hens are locked up for the night,' Bill told them.

'We'll expect you back here by midday and I'll have everything ready for our Christmas dinner, so don't be late,' Sandra called after them as Rebecca and Nick set off.

Millham was about six miles away, almost halfway between Shelston and the school at Blissford where Rebecca was teaching. It had only two shops, a pub, a church, and a village school. The main street consisted of ten houses along one side and twelve along the other, with a small garage and filling station in the middle of them. There were four or five outlying farms, and the two larger ones had cottages for their workers.

The cottage they were going to see was at the far end of the High Street, detached from the other cottages by a garden that went right round it with fairly high hedges. It was Victorian, had a thatched roof, and consisted of one large living room and a medium-size kitchen downstairs and a large bedroom and a smaller one upstairs. There was no bathroom and the only water supply was a cold-water tap in the kitchen. At the side of the cottage was a wooden lean-to with a galvanized roof, which housed an Elsan toilet.

'I'm afraid it's a bit primitive. Looks as if it hasn't had anything done to it for a good many years,' Nick warned. 'Even the decorations are in a poor state. It does have potential, though. And when I've had time to work on it, it will be transformed.'

Rebecca nodded, although she felt doubtful that such a miraculous transformation could ever be achieved. She liked the living room; it had windows on both sides, one looking out on to the front garden, the other on to the back garden and the fields and trees in the distance. The main bedroom had a similar aspect.

Yet for all that, it was very primitive and she couldn't see how Nick thought he could convert it into anything like the modern comforts she enjoyed at Woodside.

It was theirs, though, and she found that exciting. Their very own place. And if he could make it habitable, they could furnish it and decorate it to their own taste. They could shut the front door and be alone if they wanted to, or invite friends to visit without having to consult anyone to check if it was convenient to do so.

Although it was a cold day they walked all round the garden, noting how much space there was and how many fruit bushes and fruit trees were packed into it. Many of them still bore traces of fruit, half eaten by the birds or lying in heaps on the ground where it had fallen.

'I think my first task will be to clear this lot up,' Nick said as he kicked some rotten apples along the ground.

'I'm sure you can find someone in the village who would be happy to do that as a spare-time job.'

'Yes, you're probably right. I'll see if I can find a chap who knows more about gardening than I do. That will leave me all my free time to work on the house. I don't want anyone else doing that.'

'You might find you have to call in professional help. There's an awful lot to be done.'

'It will get done, don't worry. Wait until next time you come to see it. You won't recognize the place, it will have been transformed,' Nick promised as he locked the door and they set off back to Woodside.

As they enjoyed their Christmas dinner, Nick repeated his determination to transform the cottage.

'Sounds promising,' Bill Peterson agreed. 'I think I know the place. An old couple lived there for years and years. He died about five years ago. Then she stayed on and managed all on her own. She died about three months ago. I can't recall their names.'

'It was Woodley,' Nick told him.

'Yes, that's right. Well, I hope you will both be very happy there.'

'We will, when it's modernized,' Rebecca smiled.

'You won't be living there, though, not until you are married,' Sandra said quickly.

Rebecca looked rather taken aback.

'In that case, we'd better fix a date,' Nick said quickly before she could speak.

'Easter would be rather nice,' Sandra suggested.

'I'm not sure I can get everything done by then,' Nick frowned.

'I certainly don't want to get married in the middle of a school year,' Rebecca told them. 'No, August or September would be much better.'

'Well, you don't have to decide this minute, you've only just got engaged,' Bill said quietly. 'Think it over and decide which is the best for both of you.'

Forty-Seven

When she came home at half-term, Rebecca was eager to visit the cottage at Millham, but Nick didn't want her to.

'Is this because you haven't done any work on it?' she asked, frowning anxiously.

'No, it's because I don't want you to see it until the work is more or less complete. The state it's in at the moment would only depress you.'

'If I had my own transport, I'd go anyway,' she retorted when he refused point-blank to take her. 'Will you take me, Dad?'

Bill Peterson shook his head. 'I'm not getting involved, it's nothing to do with me.'

'I'll ask Mum then.'

'Be patient,' Nick told her. 'Wait until Easter.'

'If we're getting married at the end of August, I need to see the place as soon as possible. So I can decide what we will require in the way of curtains and so on—'

'So you've decided to make it August, have you?' Bill interrupted. 'Any particular date?'

'We can't decide that until we know if the cottage is going to be ready for us to move in,' Rebecca told him.

'It will be,' Nick said confidently.

'I'd still like to see it and make sure,' she persisted. 'Dad, is my bike still up in the rafters of the garage? If so, could you get it down for me? Six miles isn't all that far to ride.'

'Your bicycle? That old thing! I gave it away years ago,' her father laughed.

'Why did you do that?'

'You hadn't ridden it since before you went to university, and it was rusting away. I gave it to one of my customers for her little girl a couple of years ago. Her dad had to spend hours cleaning it up and oiling it, and he had to buy new tyres before she could use it because the ones that were on it had perished.'

'There are too many big lorries on that stretch of road to cycle along it, anyway,' Nick told her. 'What you need is a car.'

'Very funny, seeing that I can't drive,' Rebecca said waspishly.

'You could learn. I'll get some L-plates for my car, and take you out and see how you get on.'

'That sounds like a very good idea to me,' her father agreed, nodding approvingly.

'Once you've got the hang of it, you can book some lessons and by Easter you should be driving,' Nick added.

'As soon as that? I doubt it very much. I don't have that much spare time and it would have to be early evenings.'

'Well, maybe you won't have passed your driving test by Easter, but you would be able to drive and that's a start.'

Rebecca said no more on the matter, although she was peeved by Nick's refusal to take her to the cottage.

A few days later, while Nick was busy working in the shop, she went up to the Masons' farm to air her grievance with Cindy, who was now back from her visit to Liverpool.

'I didn't know you had a cottage. How lovely!' Cindy said.

'Nick told me about it on Christmas Day. We went to see it then, and it's lovely but it is a bit derelict.'

'Where is it?'

'Millham, which is about six miles away. That's the problem, I can't get there and Nick won't take me. He wants me to wait until he has renovated it.'

'Well, there's no hurry, is there?'

'Yes, there is. We're getting married in August and I need to be able to—'

'Getting married in August?' Cindy interrupted. Her dark eyes were saucer-wide with surprise 'You never told me. When did you decide on that? I didn't even know you were engaged!'

'It all happened on Christmas Day. Nick proposed to me at midnight on Christmas Eve and gave me this.' Rebecca held out her hand to show the diamond-and-ruby engagement ring. 'Then on Christmas Day he gave me a Yale key – the key to the cottage in Millham.'

'That's wonderful,' Cindy told her, hugging her and kissing her.

'So we've fixed our wedding day, because there's no point in having our own place and not being able to live there and my mum won't hear of us living together until we're married.'

'We're getting married in August as well,' Cindy told her.

'You and Danny?'

'Who else would I be marrying?' Cindy laughed.

'What date?'

'We haven't fixed the exact date yet, but it will be at the end of August when Danny has some leave.'

They stared at each other in silence for a moment and then

both of them said in unison, 'Why don't we make it a double wedding?'

They fell into each other's arms, laughing and overjoyed at their decision. For the next hour they talked of nothing else. Where it was to be, the exact date, the people they would invite, who would be best man and who would be bridesmaids.

'We'll have to have Poppy, of course, and she'll look so sweet,' Rebecca enthused.

'We'll have to have Grace.'

'Well, that's great!'

'I agree. Grace will be able to keep an eye on Poppy, and as Poppy adores her she'll do what Grace tells her and will be no trouble at all.'

'All we have to do now is tell our respective families and start making firm preparations.'

'Where will we hold the reception?' Rebecca asked.

Cindy's face clouded. 'That might be a bit of a problem. I think my mum is expecting to hold it here, but I don't suppose your mum will want to do that.'

'No, I don't suppose she will,' Rebecca said thoughtfully. 'I tell you what, why don't we say we want to hire a hall somewhere, either the village hall or at one of the pubs and hold the reception there?'

'Great idea! Then if they want to do the catering themselves they can work out between them who does what, or they can ask the pub to do it or call in caterers.'

'I don't think that should be too difficult. It's a small detail to settle once we know where it is to be. The great thing is that we have fixed a date.'

'Have you bought your dress yet?' Cindy asked.

'Heavens no! Have you?'

'No, of course I haven't,' Cindy laughed. 'Don't forget I'm going to have to shop for two dresses, as Poppy will have to have a special dress for the occasion.'

'I take it we are both going for white with a veil and all the usual paraphernalia?'

'Of course!' Cindy agreed. 'Do you want us to go shopping together?'

Rebecca considered the idea for a moment, then shook her

head. 'No, I don't think that's a good idea. Anyway, I'm sure Mum is looking forward to helping me choose my dress and I wouldn't like to disappoint her.'

'Probably the same goes for my mum, too.'

'In that case, let's keep what we're wearing a secret from each other until we turn up for the ceremony. I suspect half the villagers will be in attendance as well,' Cindy added with a laugh. 'It will give old Lizzie Smith enough to gossip about for months to come.'

'I'd better be getting back and let my parents and Nick know the date we've decided on,' Rebecca smiled.

'Yes, I don't think we had any intention of planning our weddings when you came up to see me!'

'You're right, I came to tell you that Nick was trying to persuade me to learn to drive and I wanted to know what you thought about the idea.'

'Great idea. I'm planning to take lessons soon. I can't afford a car of my own, but I will be able to drive the family car and Danny's so it could be very useful.'

'Do you want to set a date for us passing our driving test? And see if we can do that together as well?' Rebecca asked with a smile.

'No, I don't think that is quite as important as our wedding day, do you?'

Forty-Eight

When Rebecca phoned to tell Nick the date the school would be closing for the Easter break, he promised to come and to pick her up.

They hadn't seen very much of each other since Christmas because he was spending every spare moment he had working on the cottage.

She was eager to see what he had been doing there, and as they set off from Blissford she was determined to go to Millham and see the cottage before going home.

To her surprise, instead of trying to deter her, Nick gave her a mischievous smile and agreed.

As they approached the turn-off for Millham she felt tense with excitement, then her mood changed as he drove straight past it. Before she could say anything he stopped and began to back the car up, giving her an amused sideways glance as he did so.

'You thought I'd forgotten!' he chuckled.

'I was about to scream at you,' she told him with an answering grin.

When they drew up outside the cottage, she was out of the car almost before he had put the brakes on. She ran round the car to the garden gate, then stopped and stared in utter amazement. What had been an overgrown wilderness the last time she'd been there was now a neat and lovely front garden. The borders that flanked the path leading up to the front door were a blaze of golden daffodils, and beneath them primulas, snowdrops, polyanthus and violets were bursting into bloom. The lawn on either side was mown and the edges neatly trimmed.

Rebecca couldn't believe what she was seeing, and her eyes were sparkling with delight as she turned to Nick.

'Like it?' he asked. 'Looks pretty, doesn't it?'

'It's wonderful,' she breathed. She reached up and kissed him, and his arms went round her holding her close as he kissed her back.

'I didn't do it, I'm no gardener and anyway I had other things I wanted to do,' he confessed.

'Well, you certainly found someone who knows how to make a garden beautiful,' she told him.

'Come on, I can't wait to see what you've done inside,' she said eagerly as she pulled away and took his hand, dragging him towards the cottage.

Then she stopped. 'It looks different. It seems bigger than I remember.' She stared again. 'Yet it's just the same.' She turned and looked at him. 'What's happened?'

Nick grinned knowingly. 'You'd better come inside, then perhaps you'll find out.'

As they went inside, Rebecca again felt that somehow it

was different. She looked into the living room first. That seemed to be the same. The two big windows facing each other, the inglenook fireplace and the exposed beams across the ceiling were all still there. She turned towards the kitchen, and as she pushed open the door she gasped. The room was three times as big as she remembered.

'What have you done?' she exclaimed in awe.

'Enlarged it. We now have a kitchen-diner almost as big as the one at Woodside. And what's more, at the end there is a small cloakroom with a toilet and washbasin.'

'Heavens, that's wonderful!' Rebecca exclaimed.

'There's also another window, in case you haven't noticed. It looks out on to the garden at the side, and I am proposing that we have the kitchen area with all the equipment we still have to buy at the far end and use the front part as a dining room. What do you think?'

'That sounds marvellous.' She wandered round, touching the walls, peering through the windows, and finally opening the door at the far end and exclaiming in delight at what she saw there.

'Now come upstairs and see what I've done there,' Nick invited.

Upstairs, what had been a small second bedroom was now large enough to take a double bed, and next to it there was a bathroom with access from the landing.

Nick then took her into the main bedroom, which now had a built-in wardrobe running almost the full length of one wall. Alongside it was another door and he pushed Rebecca towards it.

'Open that door and see what's inside,' he told her.

Gingerly she pushed the door open, then gasped in amazement as she stepped into a fully fitted bathroom.

'Happy?'

'Happy! I feel as if I've stepped into a dream. It's fantastic. You couldn't possibly have done all this yourself, though,' she said, shaking her head in disbelief.

'I designed and planned it all,' he told her, 'but I admit I had to call in professional help to do the work. It needed skilled builders and plumbers to do the job properly, and the cottage is so old that it needed someone who understood what they were doing. Anyway, it's done now and you are the first to see it in all its glory.'

'I can't wait to bring Mum and Dad to see it. And Cindy will be amazed. I think she thought we were mad to buy such an old place, but when she sees how you have transformed it she'll be green with envy.'

'I reckon we should leave showing it off until it is completely finished,' Nick cautioned.

'What else is there to do?'

'Select all the fittings for the kitchen, and the carpets, curtains and furniture for the whole house. I'm counting on us being able to buy all of these while you're at home for Easter. By the time you come home again at half-term, they should all be installed and it will be ready for when we get married in August. Agreed?'

'It sounds wonderful, but can we afford all this? The work you've already had done must have cost the earth, not to mention buying the cottage in the first place.'

'I used the money my parents left me to buy the cottage and do the work so far. I've enough savings left to pay for the fittings and furniture, so we're not running ourselves into debt,' he assured her. 'I can afford to pay for all the kitchen equipment we are going to need and for it to be installed. I have a list here. Cooker, washing machine, dishwasher, new sink and worktops . . . Anything else?'

'I would like a microwave.'

'Right, I've added that to the list. Is that the lot?'

'Yes, I think so.'

'Well, smaller items like a toaster and so on we can get as we go along. I'll leave all that and the pots and pans to you.'

'Of course. We'll also need an electric iron and an ironing board. And a vacuum cleaner,' she murmured thoughtfully.

'The other big items are the carpets and the furniture. We ought to shop for them together to make sure we choose what we both want. I've been thinking in terms of a hardwood floor in the kitchen and dining area. Then carpets throughout the rest of the house. I thought these should be in just one colour and texture, so it makes the place appear more spacious. If we pick a fairly neutral shade of grey or beige, then you can change the look of each room with curtains and cushions in different colours and fabrics.'

'Whew!' Rebecca took a long breath. 'There's an awful lot still to do, isn't there?'

'True, but think how nice it will be when it's all completed.'

Rebecca didn't answer, her eyes were full of tears as she flung her arms round Nick's neck and kissed him.

'Hey, what's this all about?' he said as he took out his handkerchief and gently brushed away her tears.

'I'm so happy,' she whispered. 'So very, very happy.'

Forty-Nine

For Rebecca, the Easter holiday proved to be one long round of excitement. She could hardly wait to get to Woodside to tell her parents about the work Nick had carried out on the cottage, so slightly reluctantly he agreed that they would take them there so they could see the transformation for themselves.

Sandra was enchanted and Bill was full of admiration for all the work Nick had done.

'No wonder you've been walking round with your head in the clouds for the past few weeks. You must have been scheming and planning in your sleep,' Bill joked. 'You certainly managed to find some first-class workmen to carry out your ideas. You've transformed the place. I'd go as far as to say that you've doubled its value.'

'Perhaps I have, but it's not for sale so don't think of buying it and retiring,' Nick told him.

When Rebecca took Cindy to see it, she was equally enthusiastic in her praise.

'I thought you'd made a bit of a mistake when I first saw it,' she admitted. 'It was a nice enough cottage but so decrepit. I wondered how you would ever manage to live here without a proper bathroom and so on.'

'Well, now it's as modern inside as any house could be,' Rebecca replied.

'Oh, I agree with you about that. In fact, I'm quite envious. The farm is comfortable enough – don't get me wrong – and I'm very happy there, but when I see this place, well, it's like something out of a magazine.'

During the Easter break Rebecca went to Salisbury three separate times on shopping sprees. The first time, she went with Nick to buy carpets and to choose the essential fitments for the kitchen, such as a cooker, washing machine and dishwasher.

Although they looked at furniture for the dining area and sitting room, they decided to leave buying it and also a bed for the moment.

'We're not moving in until August, so we have plenty of time,' Nick pointed out. 'Once the carpets are down we'll have a much better idea of what is suitable.'

Two days later Rebecca went to Salisbury again with her mother to buy kitchenware, and the following day she went with Cindy to choose curtain fabric and arrange for the curtains to be made up.

She was disappointed that none of her purchases could be delivered before she had to go back to Blissford for the start of the new term. She so much wanted to see them actually in the cottage and to know that she had made the right choices.

Nick promised that as soon as any of them were in place, particularly the kitchen fitments and the carpets, he would come and collect her and bring her back to make sure she was happy with them.

Rebecca returned to school with her mind still on her furniture and furnishings and all the things that were being done at the cottage. She found it difficult to settle down to the regular routine of classwork and looked forward to the end of the school year, in July, when she would be able to devote all her time to making sure everything was as she wanted in their cottage.

There was also the wedding to plan. Because it was to be a double wedding, she had less to worry about. Since her mother and Mavis Mason would be busy organizing everything, there was really no need for her to do anything. All she would have to do was find a wedding dress at half-term. She knew her mother was looking forward to shopping with her for it. In fact, Sandra had already mentioned that she had seen one or two she thought suitable, so Rebecca suspected she would have very little choice in what was eventually chosen.

As soon as the kitchen fittings were installed, Nick came over to take her to Millham to see if she approved. Not only were the fittings in place, but the hardwood floor had been laid in the kitchen and dining area.

Her first impression was one of delight. It was difficult to recall the tiny drab little kitchen with its shallow sink, wooden draining board and stone floor that had been there when she had first seen the cottage. Now it was all modern and gleaming, and she ached to be able to start using it.

By half-term the carpets had been laid in the sitting room, on the staircase and in both bedrooms. They were a warm mushroom shade and gave a cosy feel to the entire cottage.

Nick had retained the services of the gardener, an elderly man called Bob who lived in one of the cottages in the main street of Millham, so the garden was looking lovely.

As she picked a bunch of sweet peas to take to her mother, Rebecca looked forward to the time when she could simply get out a deckchair and sit there amongst the flowers and relax.

At the moment, though, there was so much to do it was out of the question. Finding the right wedding dress was far too important.

Once again they went to Salisbury, because none of the shops in the small neighbouring towns had anything suitable.

'We could order from a catalogue,' Rebecca suggested.

'We can't do that!' her mother exclaimed indignantly. 'You want a dress that fits you perfectly. It's your big day, remember!'

When Rebecca suggested they should go to the shop where Cindy had bought hers, her mother shook her head.

'I don't think so. We want something different. You don't want to look like two peas from the same pod.'

'Have you seen Cindy's dress? I haven't.'

'No, of course I haven't But I'm pretty sure that what suits

Cindy won't be right for you. Your colouring is so different and she's much plumper than you these days. Must be all that good living up on the farm after what she had to endure.'

The wedding dress they eventually chose was very simple but very lovely and it fitted perfectly, so no additional fittings or alterations were necessary. The soft white-silk material seemed to flow over Rebecca's figure, revealing every curve. The heart-shaped neckline was trimmed with lace and tiny pearl beads, which added to its femininity.

'I think the only things left to do now are the invitations and the ordering of the wedding cake. Perhaps the two of you should leave the cake to Mavis and me?'

'That's fine as far as I'm concerned,' Rebecca agreed. 'You might let Cindy have a say in the matter, though.'

'What about the invitations? Is there anyone special that you would like to add to the list of family and friends?'

'No, I don't think so. I'm not sure about Nick, though. He might have someone to add.'

'His parents are both dead and he has no brothers or sisters. I've already asked him and there's no one extra he wants to invite.'

'Only another six weeks and then it's the end of term, thank goodness,' Rebecca commented as Nick drove her back to Blissford. 'I'm beginning to feel exhausted by all the preparations.'

'We've still got the wedding celebrations to get through. Do you think you will be able to stand up to all that?' Nick asked, with a sympathetic smile.

'I'll try. I want to move into our cottage. I wish we could do so right now!'

'We wouldn't be very comfortable there at the moment. We haven't any furniture. Remember?'

'True, but it is all ordered. You will come and get me so I can see it as soon as it's delivered, won't you?'

'Wouldn't you sooner wait and see it for the first time after we're married?'

Rebecca thought for a moment. 'Is that what you want me to do?'

Nick nodded but kept his eyes on the road. 'Much more romantic,' he murmured.

'Very well. It will be your fault, though, if we've made the wrong choice and it doesn't look right.'

Nick gave an elaborate sigh.

'What is far more important,' Rebecca went on, 'is that we find a name for our cottage.'

'Name? It's got a number on the gate and on the front door. Didn't you notice?'

'Yes, I did. But I want it to have a name. Something outstanding.'

'Well, I'll leave that to you. I've already done most of the work on the cottage, so now it's your turn to take some responsibility.'

'Very well. I'll phone and let you know when I've decided on something appropriate.'

Fifty

The last days of August were hot and sunny, the perfect weather for a wedding. The arrangements, which seemed to have been going on for such a long time, had at long last come to fulfilment.

The two bridegrooms stood waiting outside Saint Peter's church in Shelston. Both of them looked resplendent in morning dress with a white carnation in the buttonhole, but there the similarity ended. Danny, tall with a shock of red hair, looked even broader across the shoulders than he did in his policeman's uniform. Nick, equally tall, his dark head almost on a level with Danny's, was very much slimmer.

Standing nearby was a crowd of villagers, gathered there waiting for the arrival of the two brides.

Both men quickly disappeared inside the church as the crowd drew apart to allow the first bridal car, carrying Rebecca and her father, to pull up by the church door.

There were gasps of admiration as Bill helped Rebecca out

of the car and Sandra hurried forward to make sure Rebecca's dress was uncreased and hanging correctly.

Then the second ribbon-bedecked car, carrying Tom Mason and Cindy, drew up and the crowd gasped again as another vision in white stepped out.

For a moment the two girls, so alike and yet so different in colouring and looks, stood there smiling encouragingly at each other. Then as each of them took their father's arm, ready to walk into the church, the two bridesmaids, Grace Flowers and Cindy's daughter, Poppy, joined them.

Grace was wearing a long oyster-satin dress, and little Poppy looked quite lovely in a pale-pink organza dress trimmed with lace.

As they took their place and walked down the aisle in time to the music supplied by the village organist, there were murmurs of admiration from the crowd, many of whom had followed them into the church for the service.

When the two couples emerged an hour or so later, they posed in front of the church for photographs. As well as an official photographer taking pictures, a great many of the villagers insisted on using their own cameras.

Finally, they left for the reception in the village hall, which had been specially decorated for the occasion, both inside and outside.

Professional caterers had been hired, so there was no need for Sandra or Mavis to do anything except take part in the babble of chatter and laughter that filled the hall. Soon the sound of voices died down and was replaced by the chinking of glasses and cutlery as everyone settled down to enjoy the meal.

Afterwards there were speeches that seemed to delight in recalling anecdotes relating to the two couples in their younger days and providing forecasts for their futures.

Rebecca began to think the festivities would never end. All she wanted to do was to be alone with Nick in their cottage. She knew, though, that it would be several hours before that could happen. After the reception there was to be a buffet supper and dancing. All the villagers had been invited to join in the celebration, and judging by the size of the crowd that had been outside the church she knew it would be well attended.

She also knew that along with Nick, Cindy and Danny, she would be expected to stay on for most of the evening.

Three hours later, when she thought she wasn't going to be able to stand another minute of noise and chatter, of congratulations and good advice, Nick drew her aside.

'Ready to leave?' he whispered.

'I certainly am. My head aches, my feet are burning, and I want to go home.'

As they circled the room saying their goodbyes to family and friends, Cindy murmured, 'We'll be leaving as soon as you've gone. I've been expecting Poppy to collapse at any moment. I really don't know where she gets the energy from.'

Rebecca smiled and turned to watch Poppy as she twisted and twirled in time to the music, holding the hem of her pretty dress in one hand as she did so.

'She's certainly enjoyed herself today, hasn't she? She's won everybody's heart.'

'Come on! You said over an hour ago that you wanted to leave,' Nick reminded her, taking her firmly by the arm. 'Where shall I take you? To *The Flower Patch*?'

She looked up at him and laughed. 'Yes, to *The Flower Patch*. Do you like the name?'

He didn't answer, but bent his head and kissed her lightly on the lips.

'Well, do you?' she persisted.

'It will do,' he told her, chuckling.

Half an hour later, when they drew up outside the cottage the first thing that met her eyes was a newly painted sign on a polished wooden board hung above the garden gate with *The Flower Patch* embossed on it in gold lettering.

The name was repeated on a small plaque fastened to the wall inside the porch, a porch that was covered by sweet-smelling pink and yellow roses.

Rebecca paused for a moment to turn round and view the garden, now ablaze with summer flowers against the velvety green lawns, and sighed happily.

Nick swept her up into his arms and she relaxed against him as he carried her over the threshold and into the living room.

It was the first glimpse she'd had of it since the furniture they chose together had been delivered and as she looked round she gave a long sigh of pleasure. The room looked beautiful, they had certainly chosen well.

'Well, does everything come up to your expectations, Mrs Blakemore?' Nick asked as their lips met in a long tender kiss.

'Yes, it does indeed, Mr Blakemore,' she whispered as once again their lips touched. 'And so do you.'

Rebecca sighed happily as he finally put her down. This really was married bliss, she told herself, and the beginning of a new way of life.